The Mak

Nicola put her hands on my shoulders. "I hate to tell you this, princess, but it's time."

If what she was talking about was what I *thought* she was talking about, I was in big trouble. "Do you mean—?"

She nodded. "Yup. The makeover part of the movie of your life. Complete with some nauseating up-tempo song sung by a pop star with a nose ring."

I cringed. I *hated* those things. The makeover montage was so corny.

"You know, you might actually end up having fun," Nicola said.

Nicola took out a piece of notebook paper and pen. "Operation Falcon," she announced as she wrote.

"What's Operation Falcon?" I asked.

"It's what we're going to call the makeover. It makes it sound all top secret. Number one," she announced, "glasses."

"Okay, don't they normally go the other way—girl with glasses gets contacts? I'm already not liking this Operation Eagle thing."

"It's Operation *Falcon*."

"Same thing."

As she went back to making her list, I sighed. I didn't have to be psychic to know this was going to be a very big makeover.

BOOKS BY ROBIN PALMER

Cindy Ella

Geek Charming

Little Miss Red

Wicked Jealous

FOR YOUNGER READERS

Yours Truly, Lucy B. Parker 1: Girl vs. Superstar

Yours Truly, Lucy B. Parker 2: Sealed with a Kiss

Yours Truly, Lucy B. Parker 3: Vote for Me!

Yours Truly, Lucy B. Parker 4: Take My Advice!

Yours Truly, Lucy B. Parker 5: For Better or For Worse

Wicked Jealous

ROBIN PALMER

speak
An Imprint of Penguin Group (USA) Inc.

SPEAK
Published by the Penguin Group
Penguin Group (USA) Inc., 345 Hudson Street, New York, New York 10014, U.S.A.
Penguin Group (Canada), 90 Eglinton Avenue East, Suite 700, Toronto,
Ontario, Canada M4P 2Y3 (a division of Pearson Penguin Canada Inc.)
Penguin Books Ltd, 80 Strand, London WC2R 0RL, England
Penguin Ireland, 25 St Stephen's Green, Dublin 2, Ireland
(a division of Penguin Books Ltd)
Penguin Group (Australia), 250 Camberwell Road, Camberwell, Victoria 3124, Australia
(a division of Pearson Australia Group Pty Ltd)
Penguin Books India Pvt Ltd, 11 Community Centre,
Panchsheel Park, New Delhi - 110 017, India
Penguin Group (NZ), 67 Apollo Drive, Rosedale, Auckland 0632, New Zealand
(a division of Pearson New Zealand Ltd.)
Penguin Books (South Africa) (Pty) Ltd, 24 Sturdee Avenue,
Rosebank, Johannesburg 2196, South Africa

Penguin Books Ltd, Registered Offices: 80 Strand, London WC2R 0RL, England

First published in the United States of America by Speak,
a division of Penguin Young Readers Group, 2012

1 3 5 7 9 10 8 6 4 2

LIBRARY OF CONGRESS CATALOGING-IN-PUBLICATION DATA IS AVAILABLE.

Speak ISBN 978-0-14-241894-9

Printed in the United States of America

For Lusia Strus,

a beautiful example of what perfectly imperfect

looks like

prologue

In movies, you pretty much know when a Life-Changing Moment aka LCM is happening. Not only does the characters' hair just happen to look perfect—like they just got it professionally blown out with some special gloss thing added in—but they light them just the right way so that any oil slicks on their face aren't visible. And then there's the Song—sappy, but just indie enough to get away with it à la Regina Spektor or Ingrid Michaelson. The one that you download from iTunes as soon as you get home and then play over and over as the sound track to your own imagined LCM until you get sick of it.

But in real life? Not so easy to know when one is happening. Especially if it occurs in a noisy Chinese restaurant in L.A. on a Sunday night in March of your junior year, while fluorescent lighting beams down on a group of waiters as they sing a Chinese-accented "Happy Birthday" to an old grandpa-looking guy at the table next to you.

Nothing about the night was out of the ordinary. Like usual, my dad, his girlfriend, my brother, and I were having our weekly bonding dinner over moo shoo pork and spare ribs. And also like usual, there was absolutely no bonding going on. My workaholic father was pacing in the parking lot with his iPhone glued to his ear, arguing yet again with the head of the network that aired *Ruh-Roh*—the sitcom he wrote and produced about a man in a dog's body—about why making the show animated when it had always been live action was a really bad idea.

And so, in an attempt to fill the uncomfortable silence at our fatherless table, my "the glass is always half-full" older brother Max went through his list of crazy conversation starters—things like "If you were a vegetable, what kind would you want to be?"—while Dad's girlfriend Hillary kept trying to fill my plate with fried dumplings and egg rolls. Like always, I kept moving the plate from side to side to dodge her, which resulted in more than one egg roll rolling off the table onto the floor.

"Hey, Hillary, I'll take some of that lo mein," Max said, shoving his plate under the spoonful that Hillary was trying to dump on mine.

I gave him a grateful smile. As annoying as he could be with his always-sunny personality and the fact that he was totally a morning person, I had totally missed him the last two years he had been away at college at CalArts, especially after Hillary had moved in with us that previous fall.

"Simone, are you *sure* you don't want it?" Hillary asked.

"I'm sure," I replied.

She sighed. "Fine," she said as she dumped it on his plate. She turned to me with a hopeful look. "How about some Kung Pao chicken?"

"I'm good," I said. I pointed to the nearly empty chicken and broccoli dish. "I ate almost that whole thing."

"Yes, but it's so . . . *healthy*," she said, sounding disappointed.

Luckily, before I was forced to come up with an argument as to why healthy was a *good* thing—especially for someone like me, who, not so long ago, would have considered a carton of Kung Pao chicken an appetizer—Dad came back, wearing his bonding-is-fun grin. "Kids, we have some news," he announced.

Max and I exchanged a worried look. The last time Dad had said that was this past summer when he told us that he'd started dating Hillary. Hillary, who then convinced him to let her stay over for a few weeks while they redid the floors in her condo. Which, to no one's surprise but his, resulted in her never moving back out and dropping hints about what she wanted her engagement ring to look like.

"What is it?" I asked warily.

"I've rented us a house in Tuscany for a month this summer!"

"Tuscany, as in . . . Italy?" I asked.

He nodded.

"But why?" asked Max.

"Because Dr. Melman says that extended family vacations really step up the bonding process," Dad replied. "Especially if I promise to limit my writing time to an hour a day." Dr. Melman was Dad's therapist. Dad had been going to him twice a week for the last ten years to help him with his workaholism. Clearly, it hadn't done much good. "Doesn't that sound *fun*?"

Uh, no. The whole thing sounded about as fun to me as getting weighed during my annual checkup. "But we're not officially a family yet," I said.

Hillary looked up from one of the many mirror compacts in her collection—this one was silver with the etching of a snake ("It's a very, very old antique from Egypt," she had told me when I had asked about it, despite the fact that it had MADE IN CHINA stamped on the back of it). "Maybe not in the eyes of the courts, because your father is still struggling with his commitment issues and hasn't asked me to marry him yet, but we're getting closer."

I rolled my eyes. Some women, when they were trying to snag a guy, liked to play it cool. Hillary? Not so much. She preferred the direct whatever-means-possible-and-I-will-stomp-on-whoever-is-in-my-way-with-my-pointy-Christian-Louboutins route, which may have explained why she had recently been named one of the *Hollywood Reporter*'s "30 Under 30 Rising Film Execs to Watch"—a fact she liked to remind people of about every fifteen minutes.

"Wow. You know, that sounds like an awesome idea, but I can't," Max said. "I got a job today at a photo gallery in Culver City." Max was a photography major. He said it was because he had an overwhelming urge to express himself through the medium of images, but sometimes I was pretty sure it was more because it was a good way to pick up girls.

"Oh, yay for you, pooh for us," cooed Hillary, while my dad tried to get away with checking his e-mail on his lap in a way that made it look like that wasn't what he was doing. "You'll be missed." She turned to me and smiled. "And seeing that Simone wouldn't have anyone to hang around with other than us two adults, I'm sure she has no interest in coming now."

Actually, she was right—I didn't. But it wasn't like she had the right to kick me off the family vacation!

Hillary turned to my dad. "I have a great idea—we can send her to camp."

Camp?! I was so not a camp girl. First, I was too old—how many sixteen-year-old campers were there? The only time I had ever gone to camp was when I was eleven and managed to shoot myself in the leg with an archery arrow. And the only friend I made was Florence, the woman who worked in the dining hall, who smuggled me out extra bug juice and oatmeal raisin cookies.

Hillary turned to me. "I'm thinking . . . theater camp. There's one in upstate New York called Stage Door Manor that's *very* famous—"

Not just camp, but *theater* camp?! I may have been a lot of things but theater geek was not one of them. I looked over at Dad for help, but he was still e-mailing. He was so good at it that he could type one-thumbed while shoveling food into his mouth with the other hand.

I turned to Max and gave him a get-me-out-of-this-or-I'll-tell-everyone-about-that-folder-of-photos-of-Kristen-Stewart-on-your-laptop look.

"I have an idea," he announced.

I smiled. Of course he did. He was my big brother. It was in his job description to save the day. Right after tormenting me by putting fake rodents under my comforter.

"Simone can come stay at my place while you're away!"

Okay, that was *not* saving the day. Max lived in Valencia—miles from Lost Angeles and home to Six Flags Magic Mountain and not much else. The last time I had been to his dust-bunny-filled apartment, his roommate Nick, a music major, had asked if he could tape the sound of my stomach rumbling to use in one of his songs.

"Uh, thanks, Max, but I don't know. Valencia is sort of . . . far . . . from, you know, civilization."

"Oh, not there. We just found out the place in Valencia is going to be condemned," he said happily, "so a few guys and I from school found this awesome Craftsman to rent in Venice for the summer."

Huh. Venice was cool. My best friend Nicola and I hung out there a lot, especially because my favorite vintage store, One Person's Garbage Is Another's Treasure, was there. But still—me plus a house of guys equaled awkward. "How many guys?" I asked warily.

"Six."

Me in a house with *seven* guys equaled off-the-chart awkward.

"I don't know—" Dad started to say.

"Oh, I do!" said Hillary. "I know that's a *fabulous* idea!"

Max turned to me and smiled. "Living together would be fun. Like old times!"

"Yeah. If our parents had had six other kids," I replied.

"Think of all that wonderful quality time you'd be able to share!" said Hillary.

Personally, I would have enjoyed some quality time with Dad, but ever since his TV show had become a hit a few years ago, he spent less time doing things like trolling the Rose Bowl flea market on Sundays with me (he collected old record albums while I hunted around for stuff from Paris and vintage concert T-shirts) and more time in his office coming up with wacky-but-believable scenarios if dogs in men's bodies really existed. Nowadays, forget it. Our bonding time took place when we passed each other on the stairs as I was leaving for school and he was going to sleep after all-night writing sessions.

I turned to him. Sure, ever since Hillary had come into the picture, he had pretty much let her run the show, but this time he wouldn't. We weren't talking about leaving me behind for a weekend while they went to that fancy Two Bunch Palms spa in Palm Springs, where Hillary walked around in a bikini covered with mud and Dad broke his promise to Dr. Melman and wrote an entire script in four hours. This was an entire *month* of my summer vacation. Which, for someone like me—whose high school experience was definitely not filled with parties and dates and pompoms—was the only two months of the year to look forward to. Before I could open my mouth to tell him that, Hillary beat me to the punch.

"Sweeettiiie," she purred, as she snuggled up to him, "did I tell you how great I think it is that you've raised two kids who are so generous and loving and self-sufficient?"

Dad smiled. "Really? You think so?"

She snuggled in closer. "Nope—I *know* so."

I couldn't believe it. My father—a guy who was in charge of a staff of fifteen comedy writers and made millions of dollars a year off talking-dog bobble heads—was *blushing*.

"And not that it's any of my business or anything, but because you're such a wonderful father, I think you'd be doing them a real disservice if you didn't give them the opportunity to spend the month together," she went on. "Think of all the great memories they'll get out of it."

Which ones? Me wading through empty pizza boxes and athletic supporters? Or triple-locking bathroom doors so no one would walk in on me?

"As much as I'll miss having Simone with us, I really think you owe her this opportunity. If not, she may hold it against you and end up spending three weeks of therapy sessions on it when she's in her thirties."

Okay, this was enough. Hillary may have had a killer body because she went to the gym six days a week and didn't eat carbs and read magazines with articles like "How to Drive Your Man Wild with Just a Wink," but my dad wasn't *that* stupid. He had to see through her, right?

He turned to her. "Hillary, I have to say—"

You're a total suck-up whose main goal in life is to snag a rich husband like me so you don't have to work anymore and can afford to have your Pilates teacher make house calls. C'mon, Dad, you can say it.

"I'm always so impressed by your ability to take the future into consideration like that." He turned to me. "Simone, I agree with Hillary. I think staying with your brother for the month is a great idea."

Okay. Apparently, he did not see through her.

Hillary clapped her hands. "*Fan*tastic! Not that we have to worry about money or anything, but now we can upgrade to the extra deluxe villa instead of just the plain old deluxe one!" She reached over and grabbed my arm with her perfectly pink manicured hand. "Simone, I'm so excited for you. This could turn out to be the best summer of your entire life!

Sure. Or it could also be the worst.

I wish I could say that being shoved off on my brother and his six roommates for a month because my normally meek and boring workaholic father had fallen under the spell of a blonde-haired, blue-eyed Hollywood executive with zero body fat was the beginning of the end for me. But to be honest, things hadn't been going all that swimmingly for me for a while. Like, say, since birth, when my mother had literally died while popping me out. ("You do realize you so win the Most Dramatic Way to Lose a Parent for that one, right?" Nicola liked to say. "That's even worse than Staci Simon's mother's face literally exploding from all the cosmetic filler she had injected.")

Despite all my wishing and hoping that my junior year of high school would be different, the fact that it was going to suck just as much as the two years that had come before it had been obvious, even way back in the fall when school started.

"Look at it this way," Nicola had said one Tuesday afternoon back in October as we went through the racks at One Person's Garbage Is Another's Treasure. Owned by a beer-bellied guy named Brad with long hair who spent his weekends poking around garage and estate (read: fancy garage) sales, One Person's Garbage (not a great name, but less of a mouthful) specialized in stuff that had been "pre-owned by major celebrities." Although in this case, "major celebrities" were people who had one-line speaking roles as bus drivers or waitresses. "Studies have shown that people whose high school years suck are ninety-nine percent more likely to have wildly exciting adulthoods filled with fame and fortune and travel to exotic locales with superhot boyfriends."

Because Nicola's parents were English, she had this Madonna-esque Continental accent. Which, when she was trying to make a point—like now—got more English because she knew it made her sound smarter.

I looked up from the vintage robin's-egg-blue satin dress I had been stalking since the end of August. According to the handwritten tag, it had belonged to an actress who had played a teacher in an Academy Award-nominated musical from the 1960s before she had a religious vision while drinking a martini at Musso and Frank's restaurant and gave up her Hollywood career to become a nun. At fifty bucks, it was a total steal, especially with the 15 percent discount that I would get because of my

"Inside Outsider" status (granted to me after I sat there one afternoon nodding sympathetically as Brad updated me on the saga between him and Luca, his on again/off again boyfriend who owned the lighting store down the street). "What study?" I asked suspiciously.

Nicola held a neon-pink spandex dress circa 1980s to her stick-straight, so-flat-chested-she-kind-of-resembled-a-twelve-year-old-boy body and checked herself out in the mirror. The dress was pretty hideous, but something about the purple-tinted cornrows she was rocking that day made it work. ("I'm an Aquarian. We're expressive," she was always telling her mother.) "Let's see . . . you know, I can't remember where I read it. I read so many of them."

Nicola was very big on throwing out facts and figures from studies, none of which actually existed once you started drilling down. That being said, the fact that she was such an optimist (even though she hated being called that) was one of the reasons I was drawn to her as a friend. Well, that and the fact that when your nickname is That Weird Fat Girl, like mine was, you don't tend to find yourself neck-deep in Facebook friend requests. But even if I had looked like Dylan Schoenfield, who was the most popular girl in our grade, Nicola would have been my best friend. She just got me, and I got her. Although if I had been Dylan Schoenfield, Nicola would've hated me.

"Nice try," I replied.

"Yeah, well, what about all those John Hughes movies? The misfits always win in *those*."

"Yeah, because they're *movies*—not real life," I said as I picked up a black velvet shrug and placed it over the dress. I smiled. With that small addition, it looked like something that the actress Jeanne Moreau would have worn in a 1960s French film directed by François Truffaut. While other kids my age lined up at the multiplexes for the *Twilight* movies, I spent my Fridays at the Nuart and New Beverly watching black-and-white foreign films with subtitles—hence, the "Weird" in "Weird Fat Girl."

I loved the French vintage look. And from the photos of my mom that I kept on my nightstand, she had, too. In fact, my name—Simone Colette Walker—was in honor of the famous French feminist philosopher Simone de Beauvoir and the novelist Colette.

Nicola took off the orange cowboy hat that had swallowed up her head ("That belonged to an actress who had a bit part on the TV show *Dallas* in the seventies before she became a political activist with migrant workers in northern California," Brad explained) and glanced over at me. "Will you just buy that dress already?"

I glanced at the tag at the neck, ridiculously hoping that somehow the "size 8" had miraculously changed into a "size 16." It hadn't. Putting it back on the rack, I grabbed an extra-large vintage Doobie Brothers T-shirt and held it up. "What do you think of this?"

"I think it's yet another T-shirt that smells like moth balls and makes you look schlumpy," Nicola replied. She turned to Brad. "No offense about the moth-ball thing."

"None taken," he said, not even looking up from his computer, where, from the way his brow was all furrowed, I could tell he was either scouring eBay or Etsy for vintage dresses or trolling OkCupid for a new boyfriend.

I shrugged. "So I like to be comfortable and not buy into the lies we're sold by the advertising and fashion industries about how tight clothes somehow make you more attractive to the opposite sex, which ultimately results in growth in world population and an even more troubled education system."

Nicola shook her head. "Okay, that's way too many syllables for me to deal with when I haven't had my four P.M. mochachino yet," she said before she dropped the whole thing and went back to hunting through a box of old scarves.

Although I was grateful that women had the right to vote, the fact that my wardrobe was made up of baggy cargo pants from Old Navy and vintage concert T-shirts (my all-time favorite? a baseball-style Fleetwood Mac *Rumours* T-shirt from 1977 that Brad had been sweet enough to keep on hold for me even though a two-time Grammy winner offered Brad like five hundred dollars for it) wasn't because I was a member of the Young

Feminists of the New Millennium Club. It was because there was nothing more uncomfortable than the feeling of elastic cutting into your skin or having to go through an entire day of school barely breathing because you were sucking in your gut the whole time.

Brad looked up from his computer. "Hey, Simone—some new purses came in."

I shook my head. "Thanks, but I think I'm good on that front."

Because of the weight, I had also become a girl with a purse collection. Not even regular leather bags that I could use every day, but these itty-bitty evening bags that could fit only a lipstick (something I didn't even wear) and *maybe* a pack of gum. Seeing that my evenings were spent at home in my room or in movie theaters, they didn't come in real handy and instead lived on the top shelf of my closet.

I once overheard my dad on the phone with my grandmother trying to insist to her that I actually wasn't fat; it was that all my baby fat had just redistributed in such a way that made it so that I *looked* fat. That was just him using the skills he had learned back when he was pre-law in college so he could get off the phone with her as soon as possible.

Although before high school, I never would've been accused of being skinny, my discovery January of freshman year of Tastykake Butterscotch Krimpets and the fact that you could order them by the case online at tastykake.com made it so that by the time summer rolled around, I had graduated from being someone you'd consider "normal" to officially fat.

According to Dr. Gellert—the shrink whom Dr. Melman suggested to Dad I go see after Lupe, our housekeeper, presented him with two cases of Krimpets wrappers she had found stashed in the way back of my closet—the Tastykake thing was a way for me to "eat my feelings." Apparently, the loneliness I was experiencing now that Max was away at college and my dad was at the studio until late at night had triggered the loss I had never let myself feel over the fact that I had never had a mom, and so sugar became a way for me to check out and self-medicate.

Seeing that he was the one with all the diplomas on the wall from places like Yale and Columbia, I'm not going to say he was completely off the mark, but I do think that at first the stuffing-my-face thing was less about loneliness and grief and more about the fact that Tastykakes have a really interesting texture. Kind of like if you ripped off a piece of a Nerf football and put it in your mouth.

Even pre-Tastykakes, I had never been one of those kids who got comments on her report cards like "Simone needs to do a little less socializing with her neighbors and a little more paying attention in class." But it's not like I was some weird kid who sat in the corner muttering to herself, either. I always had a decent number of friends and invitations to sleepovers and bar and bat mitzvahs—not Dylan Schoenfield league, but decent.

But once high school started, the four or five other girls Nicola and I had been hanging out with since middle school got all boy-crazy and started spending entire lunch periods discussing the merits of OPI's Bubble Bath nail polish versus Essie's Ballet Slippers. It quickly became just the two of us—especially when Dylan Schoenfield anointed me with the nickname Ghost Girl, because I happen to have very dark hair and very pale skin. The name stuck.

Max had suggested I go play a sport or join a club, but with limited coordination and lung capacity, I had no interest in after-school sports teams. Although I wouldn't have admitted it on Twitter or anything, I much rather would have watched a rerun of *One Tree Hill* after school than take part in a sit-in staged by SAAMP (Students Against All Mean People).

Nicola held up a black cocktail dress covered with feathers. "When did you say Max is coming home again?" she asked. "'Cause I think I'll wear this the next time I see him."

For some reason that I had yet to figure out, Nicola had had a crush on my brother for years. "So you can see him and not say a word to him?" Even though she normally couldn't keep her mouth shut, whenever she was around Max, she totally clammed up. Which meant that other than things like "Hi" and "Whoops—I didn't know this was the door to your bedroom, I was looking for the bathroom" she barely ever spoke to him.

"That was in the past. I've changed," she said before she sneezed.

I did miss my brother. Especially at dinnertime. But even before *Ruh-Roh* went on, my freshman year at Castle Heights, Dad had been on staff of another sitcom. Which meant that he rarely got home before nine. Which meant that Max and I had been on our own food-wise. Not that I was complaining—very few of my friends got to eat pancakes with caramel sauce for dinner.

Although we definitely bickered like all siblings do, there was something about dinnertime where, no matter how much we had been screaming at each other a few hours earlier, a cease-fire was always called and I'd spend an hour cracking him up with different voices (if there was an after-school club for *that*, I might have joined it, but there wasn't) or listening carefully as he told me every fact he knew about our mom, even though I had committed them to memory long ago.

I may not have been super pretty, or five-minutes-in-the-future cool, or crazy smart, but it didn't matter. My older brother just *got* me. He laughed at my jokes that other people considered a little weird. He didn't give me a hard time for bursting into tears whenever the Sarah McLachlan ASPCA commercial came on TV. He didn't tell anyone that I was addicted to the TLC show *Strange*

Addictions, about people who couldn't stop eating sofa cushions or toilet paper. I didn't advertise it or anything, but I actually *liked* hanging out with my brother.

I picked up a T-shirt that said NEIL DIAMOND—LIVE AT THE GREEK. "My dad likes this guy," I said. "I remember he bought the album when we were at the Rose Bowl one Sunday."

Brad looked up from his computer. "Your dad has great taste. Neil is *awesome*."

My dad hadn't been in danger of winning any sort of Touchy-Feely Dad of the Year award, but pre-*Ruh-Roh,* he was still pretty on top of what was going on in my life. Most of which I downloaded during our Sunday outings at the Rose Bowl or Santa Monica flea markets. Not like an eighth grader had all that much going on, but he knew about what I was working on in school; and the drama of the week in my circle of friends (none of the Real Housewives have anything on a group of eighth-grade girls).

But once the show took off, our flea market outings became rarer and rarer, and the time Dad got home from the production office was later and later. Andrew Chomsky, the star of *Ruh-Roh,* was a Method actor and therefore liked to come from a dog's point of view in terms of the dialogue. The problem being, dogs don't talk. Around then, Lupe, our housekeeper, started dating a guy she met on Match.com, so she wasn't around all that much, either, which left me all alone in a very big house.

At first the Tastykake thing was totally under control.

One package every week or so, which I bought after walking to 7-Eleven. (I figured that, in a preemptive strike, I was working off the calories on the walk there and back.) But as freshman year went on, and my IM list began to shrink, my Tastykake consumption expanded. As did my purchases of sheet cakes from Ralph's supermarket, Uncle Eddie's vegan chocolate chip cookies (you'd think because they were vegan they'd be healthier, but not so much), and peanut-butter-covered pretzels.

When that happened, I got a new nickname: That Weird Fat Girl. Which also stuck. As did my thighs, on really hot days. Although I'd start each morning saying that that day was going to be different—I was done with the eating and that afternoon, instead of bingeing, I was going to . . . go for a bike ride. Or take a yoga class. But something would happen throughout the course of the day that would stress me out and make me feel that what I really needed to do was come home and relax and take the edge off with a snack. Not a *huge* one. Just a little sweetness to make up for the lemon of a high school experience I had been given.

So I'd come home from school, bring some food up to my room, lock the door (weird, seeing that I was the only one in the house, I know), and eat. While I was pretty disciplined when it came to things like school, with food I was missing an Off button. One Butterscotch Krimpet turned into three turned into six, and before I knew it I was sitting on the floor with an empty snack cake box feeling sick to my stomach, wondering how I'd ended up here, yet again, on a day I had sworn up and down to myself and whatever it is that runs the universe that I wasn't going to binge.

Most people, if they heard that story, would see how crazy it was, to eat until I made myself sick to my stomach. But for a little while I forgot that I was That Weird Fat Girl. I forgot that I didn't have a mother. I forgot that my father spent more time living in a make-believe world run by a talking dog than with me. For however long it took for me to eat my way into numbness, I forgot myself.

And I'd forget that I was never going to be able to fit into the robin's-egg-blue satin dress, which I had found myself holding again.

"Okay, well, if you're not going to buy that dress, can I buy it for you?" Nicola asked. "It'll be your birthday gift."

"My birthday was last month. There's a whole year before September rolls around again," I replied.

"Exactly."

I knew what she really meant by that: that it would give me the time to lose the weight so I could fit into it. If only it were that easy. Nicola was my best friend, but even she didn't know about the stash of snack-cake wrappers and cake boxes in the back of my closet that I threw out every few weeks. Maybe because of the English thing, Nicola wasn't so into talking about things head-on. Instead, she did it in roundabout ways, with bribes.

"I'll even throw in the shrug for being such a good friend for letting me copy your trig homework all the time."

And more bribes.

I shook my head. "That's really nice, but no thanks." As much as I loved the dress and knew that, had I lost a bunch of weight and removed a few of my ribs and then taken the time to blow dry my straight dark hair instead of just jamming it up on top of my head with a clip, I kind-of-sort-of-maybe would have looked a little bit like Jeanne Moreau's shorter, squatter, less-pretty second cousin, it felt wrong to take it off the market. This was a dress that deserved to go places. To parties. On dates. For walks on the beach at sunset. (Although because the dress was so cool, it might find that activity a little corny.)

It deserved to be worn by someone who had an actual life—not to hide out in a dark movie theater and end up with petrified pieces of popcorn on the butt. I put the dress back and picked up the Doobie Brothers T-shirt instead. Maybe one day that dress would be me, but for now it was concert T-shirts and cargos.

You'd think that someone with the nickname That Weird Fat Girl would totally stand out at Castle Heights, but not so much. In fact, the weight had the opposite effect: as time went on, it was as if I was slowly being erased, to the point where I was invisible. Letting my long dark hair fall in front of my face and being given the nickname Cousin Itt after the character in *The Addams Family* didn't help this.

How else to explain the fact that, as I sat in study hall in the auditorium the next day, flipping through a book of the French photographer Brassai's photos I had found at one of the few used-book stores on Abbot Kinney that hadn't closed down when I really should have been working on my English paper about *The Scarlet Letter* (and why I thought the movie *Easy A,* starring Emma Stone—my favorite actress next to Jeanne Moreau—did such an awesome job retelling it), I kept getting boinked in the back of the head by kids walking by.

"Ow," I cried when it happened the fourth time as one of Josh Rosen's many video cameras made contact with the back of my skull so hard it almost knocked my contact lenses out.

"Oh. Sorry about that, Simone," Josh said as he almost took out my eye with the end of a tripod. "I didn't see you there." Because they were so low on the social food chain, film geeks were generally very nice people, but apparently, I barely existed even in their eyes. Which, seeing that artists are supposed to be such keen observers of life, was a little alarming.

"It's okay," I sighed as I rubbed my head. Maybe if I was lucky I'd have a concussion and I'd be able to miss the chemistry pop quiz that was scheduled for tomorrow. Apparently, Mr. Weiner, our teacher, never got the memo that announcing pop quizzes ahead of time kind of defeated the whole "pop" of it all. I liked to think that chemistry was a waste of time, since in 245 days—which is when I would be graduating, not that I was keeping track or anything—the odds of my having to call on my knowledge from the periodic table of elements were about as great as coming across a rhombus or isosceles trapezoid.

After Josh walked away, I went back to my book, happy to see that Parisian women from the 1920s hadn't been stick thin, either. Even more evidence to support my argument that I had totally been born in the wrong country.

"You know, if you start feeling dizzy or start having sensitivity to light or noise, you might want to go to the nurse and get that checked out," a voice from behind me said in my ear. "Those are two of the main symptoms of a concussion."

Startled, I slammed the book shut. Mostly because the photo I had just flipped to happened to be of a woman who, when my eyes adjusted, I realized was totally naked. I whipped my head around, butting my forehead right up against Jason Frank's.

Great. Of all the people to smack foreheads with, I had to choose one of the most popular guys in the grade and the leader of what Nicola liked to call the Testosterone Twits. Jason had been on the varsity squad of like seventeen different sports teams since kindergarten. The TTs were so popular that even though they were only juniors like me, they got to sit up on the Ramp in the cafeteria, which literally put the popular kids above the rest of us mere mortals. Jason grimaced as he rubbed his forehead. "And maybe I'll go with you." As he smiled, I saw that one of his top front teeth was a little bit chipped. It was nice to know that someone so perfect wasn't so perfect. Although the way his curly dark hair framed his blue eyes? That was a little on the perfect side. "You ever think about trying out for the football team?" I glanced down. The minute the question hit the air, I could see he felt bad. "Not, you know, because . . ." He made some weird gesture with his hands, which I assumed was shorthand for "that gut's not from 100 calorie snack paks, is it?" "I meant because your head is so hard you wouldn't even need a helmet." He cringed as he realized that didn't sound so good, either. "You know, I think—"

"You're going to stop talking while you're ahead?" I suggested.

He nodded. "Exactly." He stood up. "Well, see you in history," he said as he started to walk away. He stopped and turned. "By the way, nausea is another symptom," he went on. "And sleepiness."

I nodded. "Okay. Thanks. I'll keep that in mind."

He nodded back. "You should."

As I watched him walk away, I had to admit I did feel a little nauseous. It wasn't every day a popular person talked to me.

Let alone a Testosterone Twit.

two

"Obviously Jason Frank is completely smitten with you," Nicola said for what had to be the tenth time as we drove to my house in Brentwood after school. Although her mom had wanted Nicola to get an after-school job so she could learn the value of money and buy her own car, like she had been forced to do back in England when she was growing up, Nicola's dad's guilt over leaving them for his acupuncturist, selling his software company for millions of dollars, and moving to Sedona, Arizona, where he now made sand paintings, had resulted in a nice wad of cash for a car.

Unlike most kids at Castle Heights who drove BMWs or Priuses or—in this hippy-dippy girl India's case—an old VW bus, Nicola put her money toward a candy-apple-red 1976 Cadillac, which, according to my dad, was the exact car that my grandfather and every other old Jewish guy in Florida had driven about twenty years earlier. Although it smelled like one of those Christmas tree air fresheners, even though there wasn't one in it, it was such a brave choice and so totally Nicola that I couldn't help but love it. Especially since my car—a used blue Saab—was in the shop even more than hers. "This is all so *Pretty in Pink* I can't *stand* it!" she squealed.

I turned to her. "Okay, (a) you're insane, and (b) why is it *Pink*ish?"

"Because Jason is sort of like Blaine. You know, preppy; maybe not whip smart, but cute. . . . He even looks a little like Andrew McCarthy if you were to put a hand over one eye. . . . And you're funky-with-a-love-of-cool-vintage-clothes Andi!"

I rolled my eyes. "I think you've been huffing Magic Markers. There is nothing *Pretty in Pink* about this. Especially because last time I watched the movie, Molly Ringwald was a size zero."

"It so is!" she cried. "The way he crossed the room—not to mention all social boundaries—to approach you . . ."

I shook my head. "He was sitting in the row behind me and he saw Josh Rosen whack me in the head. Because he's not a complete sociopath, he wanted to make sure I didn't die right in front of him."

She cocked her head. "What do you think of dyeing your hair red like Molly's? I totally think you could pull it off."

"Okay, that's enough. There will be no hair dyeing and no more insane talk about some popular guy liking me," I said firmly. "We have much more important things to discuss." As we pulled into the driveway, my stomach sank at the sight of a powder-blue BMW convertible. "Like the fact that Hillary is at my house in the middle of the afternoon."

There were a lot of things you could say about my father's girlfriend Hillary—like, say, she wouldn't eat or shop anywhere that wasn't *Elle*- or *In Style*-approved—but because she was incredibly ambitious, she did work her butt off. Like just as hard as my dad, which meant that her leaving the office before eight o'clock on a weekday was almost unheard of—unless it was for a screening or work-related drinks or dinner. Her official title was Senior VP, Production, at LOL Films. ("That stands for Laugh Out Loud," she had explained to me, "but as a Millennial, you're probably aware of that.") But really, Hillary was what was known in the film and TV business as a D-girl. D-girl was short for "development girl," which meant that she spent her time having meals with agents and managers trying to find the next script or idea that would become a hit movie that was so successful that McDonald's ended up making Happy Meal toys based on it.

She and Dad had met when his agent had forced him to unchain himself from his computer and go to her office to pitch her some ideas that might be right for movies. While she didn't like any of the ideas (a cat in a girl's body who goes through sorority rush, an elephant in a cop's body who is forced to spend twenty-four hours with a turtle in a prisoner's body, and other animal-in-human-body combinations) she did like Dad.

In the six months they'd been dating, I'd only seen her about five times, and every time she talked about her job and managed to work in the "30 Under 30" thing over and over. Other than grilling me about what kind of movies I liked ("You know, Simone, as a Millennial, your demographic is *so* important!"), she didn't ask me anything about myself other than asking my dad—*right in front of me*—if he had ever looked into any of the fat camps that were advertised in the back section of the *New York Times Magazine*. Nicola was convinced that underneath her big job, flat stomach, and killer wardrobe, Hillary was probably deeply unhappy, but I wasn't sure about that.

As we got out of the car, a U-Haul arrived. "And a moving truck just pulled up," I said nervously.

As the front door opened, Hillary came *click-clack*ing out in her Gucci snakeskin stilettos, holding her sterling silver snake compact. Despite that fact that it was one of the few humid days in Los Angeles, her shoulder-length blonde hair was stick straight and curled under, and there wasn't one wrinkle or stain on her black pencil skirt or starched white blouse. Plus, even though I wasn't close to her, I already could tell she smelled good. Not in a gross perfumey way, but in a just-got-out-of-the-shower way, because that's the way she always smelled, even right after spinning class. I, on the other hand, had just spent the entire car ride multitasking as I dabbed at the Coke Zero stain on my left boob while picking churro crumbs out of my bra.

"Hello, hello!" she trilled as she finished applying dark red lipstick. Hillary was a big triller. She was also a big tweeter, both in the literal sense of the word and the Twitter one. ("I feel it's very important to be an example for young women as to what's possible if they work hard and pledge the right sorority.")

I put on the biggest fake smile I could muster, which, since I was not a big fan of anything fake, probably wasn't all that convincing. Hillary, on the other hand, while picky about certain things, was okay with certain things being fake. Like, say, her boobs. "Hey, Hillary," I said. "Look at this—you're here. At my house. In the middle of the afternoon."

After rubbing her lips together, she examined them closely in the mirror before nodding approvingly. "You know, I think I may have finally found the perfect shade!" she announced. I had no idea why so many women were obsessed with red lipstick. It was as if they thought that if they got the color just right, it would somehow solve all their problems. As she looked over at me, a flash of annoyance crackled across her face before she resumed her usual smug expression. "Although your color is better. What is it?"

"It's called Au Naturel," I replied.

"Au Naturel. I like that. It sounds very Chanel-ish."

"I was trying to make a joke," I replied. "These are my real lips. I don't have anything on them." My lips always looked as though they were perpetually stained by a cherry Popsicle.

The smile evaporated. "You're joking."

I shook my head.

"Talk about unfair," she said. "I'd kill for lips like that," she sighed.

"Why does that not surprise me?" Nicola muttered next to me.

As two big guys began to get out of the U-Haul, I turned to Hillary. "So, uh, what's going on?"

Without answering me, Hillary began to *click-clack* over to the truck, stopping to yank out one lone weed that Joaquim, our gardener, had missed. "Someone's been slacking," she muttered to herself. "Don't think *that's* not going to change."

Just then my dad walked out of the house. He was home, too? What was going on? As always, he was typing on his iPhone as he walked, which meant that, as usual, he tripped on the last step and almost went flying. "Um, Dad? What's going on?"

"Just a sec, honey. Let me just finish this e-mail to the president of the network about why doing a Very Special Episode about cutting would be a real downer for a half-hour sitcom," he said.

"Dad, watch the—"

He tripped on the indentation where the lamppost used to be before he knocked into it because he was texting while driving.

As he tried to brace himself by grabbing onto a rosebush, I cringed. "—rosebush," I finished.

After he righted himself and began to pick the thorns out of his hand, Nicola shook her head. "Don't take this the wrong way, Simone, but I feel like all the stuff that happens to your dad is a lot funnier than that talking dog."

"Tell me about it," I agreed. As the doors to the U-Haul opened, I saw that it was filled with suitcases, garment bags, and an elliptical exercise machine. "Okay, I'm going to ask again. Can someone please tell me what's going on?"

Hillary looked over at me and flashed me a smile. "Didn't your dad tell you? I'm moving in!"

I didn't have to look in a mirror to know that my face had become even paler than usual. Talk about a nightmare scenario. This was worse than that time the curtain outside the changing room in the girls' locker room had come crashing down when I was in the middle of pulling up my underwear. Dad finally looked up from his iPhone. "Hillary, we talked about this—you're not moving in," he said nervously. "You're staying here for a few weeks while they redo the floors in your condo."

She shrugged. "A few weeks, moving in—same thing."

"A few *weeks*, Hillary," Dad corrected.

She ruffled his hair. "Right. That's what I said, babe."

"Actually, Dad, no, you didn't tell me," I said.

Dad looked confused. "I didn't?"

I shook my head.

His brow got all wrinkled, which, because his hairline was starting to recede, made him look like a shar-pei. "Oh wait—I wrote a scene for next week's episode about it. *That's* what happened. Sorry about that."

I wondered if other kids of TV and movie writers had to deal with parents who were constantly mixing up real life and their make-believe worlds. It was too bad there wasn't some sort of support group for us, like that Alateen thing that Nicola went to sometimes because of the fact that her mother—although she wasn't drinking anymore—sometimes still acted totally nuts.

"*Anyways*, I am so looking forward to this, Simone!" Hillary cried. "It'll really allow us to get to know each other so that when your dad and I *do* get married, it won't be like we barely know each other!"

As the movers began to heft the elliptical into the house, I could see Dad's left eye was starting to twitch. Maybe he was beginning to question what he had gotten us into.

"It'll be like we're *sisters*!" she went on. "You know, because we're so close in age."

That part was true. I was sixteen and she was twenty-eight. We were closer in age than she and Dad were—he was fifty-one.

As Hillary walked over to the movers and began to chastise them about how they were holding the machine, Dad joined me. "It's not forever, Simone," he whispered. "It's just a few weeks. Hillary's in a bit of a jam."

Getting new floors was a jam? It wasn't like her house had burned down.

Hillary *click-clack*ed over to us and put her arm around me. "To quote one of my favorite movies and a true Hollywood classic, *Sunset Boulevard*, 'I think this is the beginning of a beautiful friendship.'"

It was a quick one, but I saw Dad cringe. He may have been writing bad sitcoms about talking dogs now, but Dad had been a film studies major at Harvard with a minor in experimental German expressionism. "Actually, honey, that's from *Casablanca*."

"Oh right. With Lauren Bacall and Spencer Tracy. Another one of my favorites." She turned to me. "I minored in film at Pinewood Community College."

He cringed again. "Actually, it was Ingrid Bergman and Humphrey Bogart."

Even I knew that. Not because I had seen the movie, but from *Jeopardy!*

Hillary shrugged. "Well, they're both black and white.

The important thing is that Simone and I are going to have *such* a great time getting to know each other!".

I'm glad someone was such a positive thinker.

"For someone who's only going be here for a few weeks, she sure has a lot of stuff," Nicola whispered later as she finished painting her nails yellow while we watched my dad struggle with Hillary's last big suitcase.

"Tell me about it," I said with my mouth full of some of the pretzel-topped fudge that my grandmother had mistakenly sent me the month before with a gift tag that said *Dear Olive, Happy 14th!* (Olive was my cousin in New Jersey. I didn't send it back.) Some people, when they're stressed, lose their appetite and stop eating. I eat more.

"Babe, try not to let it touch the floor," Hillary ordered. "You know how I feel about scuff marks." As she walked by us, she stopped and smiled. "Nigella! So nice to see you again!"

"It's Nicola," she corrected.

"Right," Hillary replied as she whipped out her snake compact and began to apply some more red lipstick. After she was done she looked at me. "Are my lips as red as yours now?"

"Mm, I'm not sure," I replied as I wiped my face. I turned to Nicola. "What do you think?"

I could see the impatience flicker on Hillary's face as Nicola took her time looking first at her mouth before turning her gaze to mine and then back again. Finally, Nicola nodded. "Actually, I think they're pretty close."

Hillary smiled.

"Oh, wait—nope. Sorry about that, Hillary. I think it was just the way the light was hitting them. Simone's are still a lot darker."

The smile turned to a scowl before she recovered it again. "*Anyway*, I think it's just great how you use so much color to express yourself, Nicolette," she said, pointing at her nails. "All the research about you Millennials says after tattoos and piercings, color is your third biggest mode of self-expression." Hillary may have had no clue about how to relate to kids my age, but that sure didn't stop her from spouting research about us whenever she could. She pointed to Nicola's feet. "But could you be a dear and take your feet off my coffee table?"

Nicola and I looked at each other. *Her* coffee table? I thought she was only going to be here for a few weeks.

She reached down and put my Coke can on a coaster. "Coasters, coasters, coasters!" she trilled. "Don't want any rings now, do we?"

"Except for ones with diamonds," Nicola said.

Hillary laughed. "That's *good*. I *like* that!"

Hillary may not have known her movie trivia, but she got an A for going after what she wanted. The coffee table comment was a warning for what was to come. From the minute she crossed the threshold, the house went from being ours to *hers*. I could have used some company on the family front, although I would have never admitted it in public because it was kind of uncool. But hers was not the company I wanted. Within days, I went from my house being the only place I felt comfortable and safe to feeling like a total stranger. Within weeks, our comfy Spanish hacienda-style house, with its overstuffed couches and chairs and colorful antique rugs from Morocco that my parents had gotten on their honeymoon, had been moved out to make room for all this stiff, uncomfortable modern furniture that Hillary said was on every What-You-Need-to-Buy-in-Order-to-Look-Cool-So-It'll-Take-People-That-Much-Longer-to-Realize-You're-an-Idiot list in every magazine.

To make matters even worse, my dad was even more MIA than usual since Andrew was refusing to shoot the episode where he fell in love with a cat in the body of a tall blonde yoga instructor because—not like he was judging other dogs who went that way—he personally didn't feel that his character would do that.

The kicker was the day Nicola dropped me off after our latest One Person's Garbage outing, where I had scored a mint-condition 1982 The Who farewell concert T-shirt and I went upstairs to find that my red-walled bedroom, with its iron sleigh bed and flea-market knickknacks that I hoped made it look like it was on the Left Bank of Paris rather than north of Montana Avenue in Brentwood, had been dismantled and turned into this blechy boring beigy *thing*.

"Oh good—you're home!" Hillary tweeted as she *click-clack*ed onto my now-bare-wood floor because my awesome Indian dhurrie rug was gone. "So what do you think? Isn't it great?"

I doubted that even a forklift could've picked my jaw up off the floor so that I could answer her.

"I know how fond you were of all those . . . *used* things that you bought at the flea markets back when your dad and you used to go on your little bonding outings, but according to Mercury—she's the psychic-slash-feng-shui-expert-slash-interior-designer I found through an article in last month's *Vogue*—they really stop the flow of new and creative energy, which is going to be important once I start trying to get pregnant."

Not only was I not going to be able to pick my jaw up off the ground, but I was afraid my eyes had just opened so wide they were going to be permanently stuck like that.

"That's still two years out in the ten-year plan, but still, you can never start taking care of yourself too early." She *click-clack*ed over to my closet. "Speaking of which, I cleaned out your closet and replaced it with some healthier snacks."

My closet—my snacks. She sounded so nonchalant about it—as if it was completely normal for a person to keep boxes of snack cakes hidden in their closet with a paper bag full of wrappers next to it. This was even more humiliating than the locker room thing.

As she threw open the door, I saw that all my Krimpets were gone. In their place were boxes of Hostess Apple Pies, an apple tart, and an apple cobbler.

"How are those healthy?" I managed to get out.

She ruffled my hair. "Because of the *fruit* aspect, silly!" She laughed. "Did you know that apples are an excellent source of fiber?" She picked up a lock of my long dark hair and examined it. "This is really your natural color?" she asked doubtfully.

I nodded.

She sighed. "Wow. Women pay a lot of money for something so rich-looking." She flashed a smile. "So what do you think?"

What did I think? I thought the woman was completely insane. I walked over to the closet and began to drag the boxes out.

"What are you doing?!"

"Hillary, I'm allergic to apples. Remember?" I replied. Just thinking about apples made my arms start itching, my eyes start to water, and my throat start to get all tickly and begin to close up.

She squinted. "Huh. Oh, riiiiiiiiiight—now it's coming back to me. Yes, I vaguely remember you and your father mentioning that at one point."

Mentioned. More like a half-hour oral history of the severe allergic reactions I'd had over the years after inadvertently eaten something with apple, as told by my father during the Sunday drive the three of us had taken up the Pacific Coast Highway a few days after she moved in. From anyone else, that would've come off as an odd remark, but seeing that Hillary was so self-centered and totally disinterested in what people said, unless it directly had some bearing on her life, it was kind of par for the course.

"Well, lucky for you, because all the books talk about the importance of being extra sensitive to a stepchild's needs during those critical first months of blending, I had my assistant purchase some non-apple snacks as well," she went on, reaching for a brown paper bag on the floor next to her. "Although because there isn't a fruit component, they're not very healthy."

She handed it to me. Inside were Ho Hos, Devil Dogs, Big Wheels, and Sno Balls. Jeez. It would've been nice if Hillary had given me a *little* credit. Those things tasted like cardboard and Styrofoam mixed with dishwashing liquid and Windex.

"Hillary, what'd you do with my stuff?" I demanded. It was taking everything in me not to scream, but I didn't want to give her the benefit of seeing how much she was getting to me.

A perfectly formed pout appeared on her (not-as-red-as-mine) lips. "That's fine. I won't take your passive-aggressive comment as yet another rejection of all the effort I've been putting into developing a relationship with you for your father's sake. I had it put in one of those storage places," she replied. "You know, the ones you hear about on the news where murderers store bodies and stuff?"

"I want it back. Now." The sooner I had my room back to normal, the sooner I could breathe again.

She shrugged. "Suit yourself. I'll have my assistant take care of it." She flashed a smile as she smoothed her unwrinkled red dress and fluffed her already fluffy mane of hair. "Now if you'll excuse me, I'm going to go call the decorator about replacing all those horrible old mirrors around here. I mean, what's the point of a mirror if it's so old that you can't actually *see* yourself in it?"

As soon as she moved in, I discovered that Hillary's obsession with mirrors wasn't just limited to her collection of compacts. It was wherever she could glean a reflection of herself. In a window, in our stainless steel refrigerator . . . I once even caught her crouching down, looking at herself in the sliver of chrome that surrounded the dishwasher. As for me, I tried everything I could do *not* to look in a mirror—which, when you're attempting to tweeze between your eyebrows because your best friend has told you in the most gentle way possible that you're starting to resemble a monkey, isn't easy.

But those "old" mirrors she was referring to were actually expensive antiques. BH (Before Hillary) the whole house had been filled with antiques. In fact, that was one of the things people had always liked best about our house—the fact that everything in it, while old and eclectic, ended up mixing together perfectly and, in a world of CCRPH (Nicola's abbreviation for Cookie Cutter Rich People's Houses) made it feel warm and inviting.

But Hillary wasn't into antiques. According to her, they were depressing. And Dad just let her get rid of them. So now, with its new furniture that looked like a collection of geometric shapes, our house was just as cold and soulless and uncomfortable on your butt as every other house in L.A. Not exactly the kind of place that screamed "Come hang out here!"

I walked over to my desk. She'd even taken the bulletin board with all the photos of Nicola and me. Who took away someone's *pictures*? I looked under my bed. Mowki! Where was Mowki, the stuffed donkey that I had had since I was four?! There was definitely a circle in hell for people who took other people's stuffed animals. I stood up and looked at the closet.

If she touched my shoe box, I was going to have to kill her.

I walked over to the closet, relieved to find a beat-up shoe box still tucked away in the top left-hand corner. As I took it down and opened it, I took out a photo of a woman who looked a lot like me, minus the snack cake weight.

"I'm not sure where you are right now," I whispered to my mom, "but if you could help me out here, I'd really appreciate it."

"I know—you can get a hobby," Nicola suggested a week later at One Person's Garbage as she tied a paisley silk scarf around her head, making her look like a boho hippy circa 1975. If boho hippies had had lavender streaks in their hair.

"I guess so," I replied unenthusiastically. Due to my distaste for exercise and my Weird Fat Girl status, I wasn't exactly a hobby kinda girl. But I couldn't go home—not with Hillary taking over. "Aren't they expensive?" Seeing that the only hobby I had was hanging out at the Nuart watching old French films, I hadn't ever been exactly breaking the bank with my activities. But because of the redecorating at the house, and the fact that the Nuart was closed for renovations, I had been spending less and less time at home and more and more time at One Person's Garbage. Even though I considered Brad a friend, I still felt guilty when I didn't buy anything, which is why I was quickly going broke—vintage concert T-shirts are a lot more expensive than movie tickets.

She shrugged. "They can be, if you choose something like . . . collecting tribal artifacts from lost civilizations, like my grandfather does." Nicola's grandfather was this very bizarre guy who had made boatloads of money when he invented this screw that every airplane in the world used. He also dressed up in a different costume before dinner every night. Which, when you're that rich, you can afford to do.

Brad looked up from his computer where, from the way he had been super focused and taking notes, I knew it had been an OkCupid versus an eBay kind of day. "You could try the AFCC over on San Vicente," he suggested. "They've got lots of classes. That's where I took that Find Your Soul Mate While Learning How to Make Jewelry! one." AFCC stood for All Faiths Community Center. It used to just be a JCC—Jewish Community Center—but then the Christians and Muslims got all mad, so they changed it.

"I remember that!" Nicola exclaimed. "You came back with that beaded Native American breastplate thingie and the phone number of that actor-slash-life-coach guy."

"I don't know," I said doubtfully as I petted the blue satin dress again. Now that I couldn't spend my afternoons in the house visiting with Tastykakes, my pants were loosening up a little (well, at least they weren't cutting into my skin and leaving marks), but I still wasn't anywhere near fitting into a size 8. "I'm not sure I'm interested in something so . . . social. I'm kind of into hobbies you can do by yourself."

Brad clicked away on the computer. "What about pottery making? That's a solitary kind of hobby. Especially if you sit off to the side and don't talk to anyone in the class."

Pottery sounded kind of cool. Maybe I would become so good at it I could open up a little online store on Etsy. Or at least make one mug that wasn't so crooked that all the liquid sloshed out of it whenever I tried to take a sip. "It *is* close to my house," I said.

"Yeah. You could even ride your bike there," Nicola said. "Might get you into that blue satin dress faster."

I shot her a look. That was pushing it. Physical exercise *and* spending my afternoons around strangers? No thanks. I'd be like every other person in Los Angeles and contribute to the pollution problem by driving there.

Well, I *would've* driven there if my Saab had started. But it didn't. Again. And because L.A. is not a real city—like, say, Manhattan or Paris—I couldn't just walk out my door and get a cab. And because I'm one of those people who, if I miss the first five minutes of a movie I can't watch it, I didn't even want to think about how uncomfortable it would be to miss the beginning of a pottery class. Which is why I was forced to wade through old lawn mowers, a moth-eaten volleyball net, a Big Wheel, a Slip 'N Slide, and a few empty propane tanks in the garage to get to my very dusty bike. It had been years since I'd ridden it, and although they (whoever "they" are) say that you never forget how to ride one, from the way I wobbled down the driveway before finally getting my balance, I was pretty close to proving them wrong. Luckily, by the time I got to the end of my street my memory had come back and I felt safe enough to brave my way to the AFCC.

When your physical activity for the last few years has been limited to chewing and channel-changing, heavy aerobic activity like biking is somewhat of a shock to your system. Not to mention your clothing. By the time I arrived, my Psychedelic Furs T-shirt had sweat stains in places that I hadn't known were possible. And my long hair looked like I had just washed it. In body oil.

As I walked in, an older woman with frosted blonde hair wearing a pink Juicy Couture velour tracksuit looked up from the desk and gave me a big smile. "Hello. I'm Cookie. And look at you—a workout before the workout!" she said before cringing at the drop of sweat that plopped off my forehead onto the counter. "Aren't you the little overachiever!"

"I'm here for—" I gasped.

"Zumba, I know," she said as she slid a clipboard across the desk with what looked to be a novella's length stack of forms. "Just fill these out. And don't forget the section about whether you're a convicted criminal with a previous record," she said. "People think just because we're in Brentwood that would never be the case and they can skip over it, but I'm here to tell you, you would not *believe* the number of middle-aged housewives in this town who have been arrested for shoplifting. . . . It's actually quite shocking. But you need to hurry." She looked at her blinged-out watch. "Class started five minutes ago."

"Actually. I'm. Here. For. The. Pottery. Class," I panted before mopping my forehead with the edge of my T-shirt.

"Oh, honey, I'm sorry—we canceled that."

"What?!" I had gotten my heart rate up for nothing?

She nodded. "Yeah. No one enrolled." She shook her head. "I keep telling Waheel—he's the programmer here—that if you want to draw a crowd, it's got to be something that helps them either slim down or meet their soul mate." She sighed. "But I've only worked here for five years, so what do *I* know?" She flashed a smile. "But lucky for you, our ten-week Zumba Your Way into Health and Happiness starts today—which I know you're just going to *love*. And it's just in time for the holidays! Now will that be cash or charge?"

It was a little obnoxious for this woman to think that I automatically wanted to lose weight. I mean, maybe I didn't. Maybe I liked being fat. I sighed. Okay, fine. Maybe I didn't. Maybe I had just gotten used to it and felt like even if I wanted to do something about it, I didn't know how. Plus, I could tell that "No, thank you" was not an answer that computed in her world. I'd give it a try. One class. And if I hated it—which I obviously would—I'd never come back again.

She peered over the counter at my beige cargo pants, which, thanks to my bike, were now streaked with grease stains, before standing up and waddling over to the boutique area, which was filled with bedazzled yoga pants and bedazzled tank tops. There were even bedazzled water bottles. "Now, while you can get away with wearing the T-shirt, you're going to need something a little more appropriate pants-wise." She held up a pair of orange-camouflage yoga pants. "And I think these would just look *fabulous* on you!" She looked at the tag. "They're an extra large, so I think they'll fit, but I'm telling you—five sessions into this course and I bet my bottom dollar you'll be *swimming* in them." She waddled back to the counter. "And because you're a new member of the AFCC family, you get a fifteen percent discount on them, which means"—she clicked on a calculator with her pink nails with little flowers painted on them—"they're only going to set you back ninety-two shekels! You're just gonna *love* Zumba, honey!" Cookie said. "It's completely off the doorknob!"

"Huh?"

"You know . . . amazing!" she explained. "My eight-year-old granddaughter taught me that phrase. Isn't it so catchy?"

"I think what you mean is that it's 'off the hook.'"

"Huh?

"It's not 'off the doorknob' . . . it's . . ." From the look on her face, I could tell she was very confused. "You know what? Never mind. So are we talking *Zumba* Zumba?" I asked. "That dance thing that they made fun of on *Saturday Night Live* last weekend?"

"Yes, but maybe if those *Saturday Night Live* people actually tried it, they would realize the wonderful benefits to it and wouldn't make fun of it," she replied, all huffily. "Now cash or credit?"

I sighed. I wasn't psychic or anything, but I intuitively knew that the chances of my convincing a woman named Cookie with nail art that Zumba wasn't really for me were slim to none. And seeing that the reason I was here was because I was kind of like one of those displaced persons from World War II whom we studied about in history class, I figured my dad could pay for it. "Credit," I said, handing over the American Express card I carried around in case of emergencies. Which—if this Zumba thing was going to require any sort of coordination—this could end up being.

After I had filled out the application to the best of my ability (who walked around with their passport in their bag at all times? Or their vaccination records?), I went into the locker room. As I started to undress, I told myself that if the yoga pants didn't fit, I could leave. Unluckily for me, while definitely tight, the Lycra made it so that there was enough give that I could get by.

"OMG—orange is *so* your color!" Cookie exclaimed when I walked out. "BTW, OMG is short for 'oh my gosh.'

Or is it 'God'? Oh, and BTW is 'by the way,'" she said as she pulled me toward the gym and opened the door. Inside, about twenty middle-aged women with muffin tops hanging over their waistbands were shaking their booties as Latin music blared out of an old-school CD player.

"See Rona over there?" she asked, pointing at an equally frosted blonde woman wearing a neon-pink yoga top with lemon-yellow yoga pants. I could see that the charm bouncing up on and down on her chest as she shook and shimmied said WORLD'S #1 GRANDMA. "When she first started coming, all she wore were these awful caftans from International Woman over on Sawtelle. Now she's into *jeggings*."

I wasn't sure how I felt about the world's number one grandma wearing jeggings, but still, the idea that you could lose weight from Zumba-ing rather than just die from laughter because it looked so ridiculous was pretty impressive.

"Ay carrrrrrramba!" yelled a twentysomething guy in lime-green short shorts and a purple I'M THE REALEST BITCH YOU KNOW *Mob Wives* tank top. Even from far away I could see that underneath his yellow bandana, his curly dark hair was smothered in hair gel. "Shake those *tuchuses, guapas*!"

"That's Jorge. Isn't he the bomb shelter?"

"I think it's just 'the bomb.'"

"Huh?"

"It's not bomb shelter . . . it's just 'bomb.'"

More confusion.

"Never mind."

"I just love that he's able to mix Yiddish and Spanish in the same sentence," Cookie went on. "It's so creative."

I shook my head. "I don't know if I can shake my *tuchus*—"

"Of course you can. Now go! Go!" she cried, shoving me toward the group of women. "You don't want to miss one more calorie-burning moment!"

I landed between Rona and a tiny woman with close-cropped dark hair and huge red-framed glasses that made her look like an owl, I tried to shake my *tuchus* but instead ended up shaking my right arm. So hard that my bracelets kept flying off, once even getting caught in a blonde woman's bun.

"Oy vey. *Mami*, what are you doing?" Jorge demanded after he pressed Pause on the CD player and took a giant swig of his Gatorade, even though there was no reason he should've been exhausted, seeing that he was just yelling at us rather than shaking his own *tuchus*.

"Zumba-ing?" I replied meekly as I pulled my hair back from my face to swipe at the sweat. If I kept this up, I was going to have to invest in some ponytail holders. And some Stridex pads.

"That is not Zumba-ing!" he bellowed. "That's . . . I don't *know* what that is, but it's not Zumba!"

I could feel myself turning red. You would have thought that Zumba teachers would be nicer than gym teachers, but apparently not.

"Don't mind him," Rona whispered. "It's the hot-blooded Latin thing. He doesn't mean it. You'll see—at the end of class he'll kiss you on both cheeks and everything."

But by the end of the class, I had stopped shaking my arm and started shaking my *tuchus,* even if it wasn't exactly in time with the music. Which not only made my T-shirt even more sweaty but also reminded me for the first time in a long time that my hips did more than just take up space in my pants—that they actually *moved.* And Rona was right—Jorge did kiss me on both cheeks. Right after he shook his head and sighed and told me that lucky for me, coordination-challenged white girls were his specialty.

"So what'd you think?" Cookie asked excitedly as I limped behind my fellow Zumba-ers into the lobby, realizing that my rubbery legs were going to *kill* in the morning. "Was it totally red?"

"Huh?"

"You know—*red.* Awesome. Hard core."

"Do you mean . . . *rad*?" I asked.

Cookie thought about it. "You might be right." She reached into her studded orange leather handbag and dug out a little notebook whose pages were covered with writing. After looking at it, she nodded. "Yes, you're right. I made this little cheat sheet to keep all the slang straight, but sometimes I can't read my own writing. So was it?"

A bunch of the women had stopped, waiting for my response.

"It was . . . an experience."

"That's the *exact* same reaction I had!" exclaimed the owl lady. "That it was a life-changing experience that opened a portal to a new era of my life!"

The woman with the bun, whose heavy makeup made me think she was probably a rock-and-roll groupie at some point, gasped, "Cheryl, I can't believe you just said that. That was my experience as well. How did we never talk about this before? I was actually thinking of writing something for Oprah's magazine about it. You know, the whole 'aha moment' of it all." She smiled at me. "I'm Marcia. You're coming with us to Coffee Bean, right?"

"After class, we go to Coffee Bean and Tea Leaf," explained a preppy-looking Brentwood-mom type. The kind who didn't say sorry as she wheeled her double stroller down San Vicente Boulevard and over your feet.

"Oh. That's really nice of you to invite me, but I can't," I said nervously. "I . . . have to get home and do homework." Actually, what I had to do was get my butt to 7-Eleven and purchase a smorgasboard of snack cakes, because the stress of trying to get my butt to shake instead of my arm and being surrounded by a group of middle-aged women inviting me to be social over coffee when I was not really a social kinda girl was freaking me out.

"You heard her, Beth—she's got homework," chastised Cheryl. "Well, we'll see you in class on Thursday."

"Oh. Um. Well, see—" Sure, I had forked over (or, rather, my father had) a decent amount of money for ten classes—not to mention a very bright pair of yoga pants—but it's not like I was planning on actually coming *back*. I didn't know these women, and had spent only forty minutes sweating next to them, and yet, as I looked out at the sea of made-up faces smiling back at me, I did know one thing—that they were the kind of women who would badger and nag you to death until you said yes.

"—that sounds just great," I said weakly. "I'll see you then."

You would think that after what I had just been through, the universe would cut me a break. Whoever ran it would just let me make my way peacefully to 7-Eleven, and when I arrived, not only would there be some Butterscotch Krimpets waiting patiently for me to claim them, but there'd be an ice-cold fuschia-colored Tab can smiling at me from the refrigerator section.

Instead, I got my yoga pants leg stuck in my bike chain so that when I tried to get it out, the semi-cool oil-based design it had left got smeared and turned into one big blob. And when I got there, not only were there no Tabs, but due to an earlier power outage, all the sodas were warm. Warm soda made me nauseous, and so that left me having to drink plain old boring water. With my luck (or lack thereof) so far, I had given up on the hope of Butterscotch Krimpets, but when the gum-snapping Goth girl behind the counter looked up from her *Fangoria* magazine to tell me that because of a pit stop by a troop of runway models on their way downtown to a fashion show for L.A. Fashion Week, pretty much the only snacks left were salt and vinegar potato chips ("Salt is to models what garlic is to vampires," she informed me), I was about to lose it. *This* was exactly why I didn't like to leave the house—because when you did, you lost any kind of control over what happened to you. My life may have been on the small side because of it, but that just gave me that much more time to think about what it would look like when it was actually *big* in Paris or New York.

"I love those," a voice said as I gazed woefully at a box of Nilla Wafers, thinking about what a pathetic excuse for a cookie they were.

I turned around to see Jason Frank. Of course it was him. I was sweaty, wearing orange yoga pants with an oil stain, and about to cry. The way my afternoon was going, who *else* would it have been?

"Don't you?" he asked.

"Actually, I don't. On the cookie scale I'd have to rate them . . . a negative seven," I replied.

His face fell. "How come?"

I shrugged. "Lots of reasons. First there's the whole consistency issue," I replied. "They're a little sandpaper-like."

He thought about it. "I guess they are."

"And then the taste thing," I went on. "Meaning there isn't any. They're supposed to be vanilla, but they fail miserably. Which is probably why they call themselves 'nilla.' You know, so they don't get sued for false advertising."

He shrugged. "Personally—"

"But then again, vanilla *is* a synonym for bland, so maybe what that's what they're going for," I added.

He looked a little offended.

"I'm not saying you're bland or anything," I quickly corrected. "It's just that I can get passionate on the cookie front."

He nodded. "I see."

As my eyebrow went up, his face turned red. "I didn't mean 'I see' like that," he quickly said. "I meant it as in just from the tone of your voice, I can see. You see?"

Wow. So popular kids babbled sometimes, too. Who knew?

He motioned to my outfit. "So, uh, just finish a workout?"

I looked down. Oh God. I had almost forgotten that I looked like something that had gone through the spin cycle using Crisco oil instead of water. "Yeah, I guess."

"Yoga?" Jason asked.

I totally could have lied right then and it wouldn't have been a big deal. I mean, it's not like Jason Frank was going to take time out of his very busy life and trail me like some detective in one of the *Law & Order* shows to see if I was telling the truth. That being said, I was one of the people who, no matter how much time I took to make up a lie, and how foolproof it sounded when I practiced it in front of my mirror, somehow I always got busted. Which is why I decided to tell the truth.

"Umm . . . something . . . *kind of* like yoga but . . . not exactly," I replied. Okay, maybe not exactly the truth. Maybe something that *resembled* the truth. A little. If you closed one eye and turned the lights down really low.

"Pilates?"

"Nope."

"Ballet?"

Ballet? Was he was taking me for someone with *grace*? "Uh-uh."

"Tae kwon do?" Jeez. Talk about nosy.

"Oh! I know—is it that thing where—"

"It was Zumba, okay?" I blurted out. Whoa. Did I really need to be that honest?

"Zumba."

"Yeah, it's this thing—"

"I know what Zumba is. My mom does it."

Oh great. With my luck, she was probably one of the

women in my class. "Well then, if your mom does it, you probably know that it's an excellent form of exercise," I said defensively. I was defending Zumba? How'd that happen?

He nodded. "Yeah. She's looking good. She even stopped wearing mom jeans."

I winced. Could he make it all sound any *less* cool?

Suddenly, he started bobbing his head. "Oh man—I *love* this song!

I listened, but didn't recognize it. Probably because it was poppy and Top 40–ish, which was so not a world I lived in. I didn't even like to go there for weekend get-aways. "Who is it?" I asked.

He laughed. "That's a good one."

As the daughter of a sitcom writer, I knew how to joke around at times, but this wasn't one of them. "You're being serious."

I nodded.

"It's *Bieber.*"

"As in . . . Justin?" I asked, confused.

"Well, yeah," he said. "What other Biebers are there?" I kept waiting for the "just kidding" part, but it didn't come. I even looked over my shoulder to see if I was being Punk'd.

"I'm not sure," I admitted. Maybe one who sang songs that were more appropriate for a sixteen-year-old varsity-soccer-playing boy to listen to rather than a thirteen-year-old girl.

"So if you don't listen to the Biebs, what *do* you listen to?"

I shrugged. "Lots of different stuff. Jazz . . ."

"Jazz?" he said, surprised. "Like *jazz* jazz?"

I nodded. "Yeah. Miles Davis? John Coltrane?"

He squinted. "I think my dad has some CDs by those guys." Jason's dad was this famous Academy Award–winning director named Stan Frank who made Films-with-a-capital-*F* versus movies-with-a-little-*m*. A lot of the parents at my school worked in the business, but the whole Academy Award thing was as close to royalty as it got in Hollywood, which therefore made Jason Frank sort of a prince. Although his dad's movies weren't my kind of thing (films set in the 1950s about the Mafia, Vietnam things, biographies about famous boxers), I had once read an article in the *Los Angeles Times* about how François Truffaut was his biggest inspiration, which therefore made him okay in my book. "But it's not really my thing."

I nodded. It was understandable that he didn't like jazz. As Nicola was always reminding me, not many teenagers listened to it. ("Maybe the kind who wear sunglasses indoors and then grow up to write angsty memoirs do, but not, you know, *normal* ones.") But if that was the case, I wasn't even going to bring up how I liked French music by Edith Piaf and Serge Gainsbourg, because if he barely knew who Miles Davis was, he probably wasn't going to be familiar with two dead French people.

We stood there, both staring at the Nilla Wafers as if they somehow contained the secrets of the universe.

"Well, I guess I should get going," he finally said.

I nodded. "Yeah, me, too."

"I gotta get to SAT tutoring."

"And I have to . . ." He really didn't need to know that I had to get home and jump in the shower so that the sweat that had now dried on my skin wouldn't turn into some disgusting rash. "Anyways, nice talking to you."

He grabbed a box of Nilla Wafers. "All this talk about cookies made me hungry. See you around," he said as he walked away.

Hungry? He had no idea what I was planning on inhaling once I was back in the safety of my own room.

three

It made sense that after gorging on frozen yogurt from Red Mango, peanut-butter-covered pretzels from Whole Foods, and iced sugar cookies from Ralph's, I'd feel nauseous. However, I was pretty sure the queasiness came from replaying the image of Jason bobbing his head to the Biebs.

"So he doesn't have great taste in music," Nicola said the next afternoon as I helped Brad go through garbage bags full of stuff that he had gotten at a garage sale of some sitcom actress from the eighties. I got really excited when I saw a fake leopard A-line coat. Not only was it something you could totally have seen Jeanne Moreau wearing in a Truffaut film, but it was large enough to fit me. I was all set to buy it . . . until I saw the cigarette burns in the left sleeve. ("I think I remember reading something in *People* about how she had a little problem with the bottle and would pass out with lit cigarettes in her hand,"

Brad said when I pointed it out.) "It's not like it makes him a bad person," Nicola added.

I looked up from a colorful-looking caftan with long flowy sleeves ("I think that was from her *Eat, Pray, Love* stage," Brad said, "when she took the money she made when the show went into syndication and went to India for a year to find herself.")

"Nicola. We're talking the *Biebs.*"

Brad stopped his Etsy surfing. (Because he and Luca were back on—at least for that week—he had turned off his OkCupid profile.) "This Testosterone Tweet guy listens to Justin Bieber?" he asked.

"It's Twit, not Tweet," I corrected. "And, yes, not only does he listen to him, but he *admits* it," I said. "Like without any irony whatsoever."

Brad wrinkled his nose. "Oh, that's not good," he said. "Even my people don't admit to that. In fact, I don't think my people even *listen* to him." Brad's "people" were gay men. I don't know if any official studies had been done, but I was pretty sure that if they had been, research would have shown that they were the ones responsible for keeping all the CAPS (Cheesy Awesome Pop Stars) such as Cher and Britney neck-high in feathers and belly rings.

I looked at Nicola, who was checking out a high-necked, long-sleeved blouse. ("I think I remember reading that when she was done in India, she became born again-Amish and moved to Pennsylvania," Brad said.)

"That, from a guy who has not one but *two* box sets of Barry Manilow's greatest hits," I said. I turned to Brad. "I hope you don't take that the wrong way. I'm just making a point."

"No offense taken," he replied. "And I still say that 'Copacabana' is the single greatest song ever written."

Nicola shook her head. "I can't believe *you* of all people are judging someone based on something so superficial. So he's got awful taste in music. That's exactly what a girlfriend is for!" she cried.

"I'll say it again—the idea that you think Jason Frank is interested in me is insane."

"To teach guys right from wrong and *mold* them," she continued. Her eyes narrowed. "So then, after you do that, they can break up with you and hook up with the Madison Stovers of the world, who then get to reap the benefits of all *your* hard work."

Brad and I looked at each other nervously. If Nicola got going on one of her rants about Nate Buckner, her one and only boyfriend whom she met last June because they both "liked" Apu from *The Simpsons* on Facebook, only to break up with her six months later after he met this skank Madison on the "I Hate Farmville" page, we'd be here for hours. "Don't worry—I'm not going to go there," she promised.

"Thanks. And you know where else we're not going to go? To any more conversation about Jason Frank," I said as I marched over to the rack where the blue satin dress lived. Except it wasn't there. "Brad. Where's my dress?" I asked, panicked. "I mean, *the* dress. The blue one."

"I moved it over to the Dresses for Winter Even Though L.A. Doesn't Really Have Seasons display," Brad replied. Brad was always coming up with displays that he hoped would sell more stuff.

I relaxed. Not like I was ever going to buy it, but I couldn't imagine letting anyone else own it, either.

"Look, Simone, I feel like I can say this because you're my best friend," Nicola said. "You've spent your life having people judge you and make cracks based on how you look, right?"

I nodded.

"But if they took the time to get to know you, like I did, they'd learn that you're totally cool, right?" she asked.

"We were seventh-grade lab partners," I reminded her. "It was me or that weird kid who was into furry animal costumes, so you *had* to get to know me. And by the way—it's not just the Bieber thing that's weird. There's also the fact that he likes Nilla Wafers."

"Nilla Wafers? Those are so . . . not exciting," Brad said, disappointed.

"Thank you," I said.

Nicola shook her head. "I can't believe I'm best friends with someone who is so judgmental. You should be ashamed of yourself."

Maybe Nicola was right—maybe I wasn't being fair.

But it didn't really matter what Jason Frank listened to or snacked on, because even though we may have lived in the same zip code literally, figuratively we lived on different planets.

Although I had told the Zumba-ers I'd be back on Thursday, I wasn't planning on actually showing up. Instead, I was going to come up with a totally viable excuse so that if the group hunted me down or saw me on the street or something, they wouldn't burn me at the stake. But then I got home from school that afternoon to find that Hillary had hired these two women named Summer and Rain she had read about in some The-People-You-Must-Know-If-You-Want-to-Be-Thought-of-as-a-Hip-Angeleno list to go through each room of our house and clear it of all negative energy by burning sage and incense. I had to get out of there. Especially when they launched into some weird modern dance that was supposed to call in health, wealth, and prosperity ("And," Summer said, glancing at her notes, "a four-carat diamond engagement ring").

With Nicola at therapy ("I'm thinking today's the day I tell him that sometimes I hear voices," she mentioned during our drive home, "just to shake things up a bit."); One Person's Garbage closed for the weekend because of "remodeling" (Brad's code for "Because Luca just told me that he can no longer deal with the way I pull back whenever he tries to get close because I'm terrified of intimacy, I'm going to lie on my couch all day with my cat LiLo and watch *The Way We Were* over and over and try not to sob so hard that I break a rib when Babs says 'Your girl is lovely, Hubbell' at the end"); and nothing playing at the Nuart Theater that I hadn't already seen five times, I didn't have anywhere to go. Which is why, after I changed into my Tom Petty and The Heartbreakers T-shirt and a pair of my brother's old Castle High sweats he had left behind (I didn't care how expensive those orange yoga pants were—they were never going on my body again), I jumped on my bike and pedaled over to the AFCC.

"Simone! You're back!" exclaimed Cookie excitedly as I walked in.

"Well, yeah," I replied, a little less winded than last time. "I said I would be, remember?"

"Oh, that's just *wonderful*. You know, a lot of the girls didn't think you'd actually return because they didn't think you had that Zumba spirit, but I said, 'Hey—just cool out. She'll be back.'"

"It's '*chill* out,'" I corrected.

"Huh?"

"It's not *cool* out—it's *chill* out."

Her brow wrinkled. "Are you sure?"

I nodded.

She took out her little notebook and made a note. It was like she had her own Urban Dictionary going there.

"Thanks. But I'm going to double-check that with my granddaughter when I see her."

"That's probably a good idea," I agreed. I could hear the techno-Latin-fusion music start up in the gym. "Well, I'm going to go in," I said. "I don't want to miss a second of fun."

Cookie smiled. "You don't know how happy this makes me, to see a young person like yourself embrace the Zumba lifestyle. Most kids your age just make fun of it."

"Oh, I wouldn't do that," I said.

At least not out loud.

Maybe it was karma, because I *did* make fun of it in my mind, but the first fifteen minutes of class Zumba kicked my butt. Big-time. Which I guess is what it was supposed to do. But to my surprise, after that, the strangest thing happened. Not only did I get my limbs to work in the order in which they were supposed to, but I actually started . . . *enjoying* it. Like I was *having fun.* To the point where, at the end, when Jorge said, "And that's a wrap!" I added my own semi-disappointed "Ohhh" to the chorus in the room.

I still wasn't willing to go to Coffee Bean and Tea Leaf with the group ("I have a feeling she's very introverted," I heard Marcia—a therapist—whisper to the women after I sputtered the very lame excuse that I had to get to the vet, because even though I didn't have a cat, I liked to visit the sick ones there), but this time when I left, I didn't go straight to 7-Eleven in search of Tastykakes. I was going to, but for some reason, the idea of scarfing that much sugar made my stomach do flip-flops. So I went to Whole Foods and after standing in front of the gluten-free, fruit-juice-sweetened cookies for a long time (at least they were *healthy* cookies), I found myself drifting over to an area of the supermarket where I had rarely ever set foot, unless it happened to be on the way to the snack aisle.

The produce department.

It was actually a beautiful sight—the dark lush green of the spinach and kale. The sunny, happy yellow squash. And the shiny bright red peppers that were the exact color of the walls in a Paris living room in this *Paris in the Sixties* photo book I had picked up at the Santa Monica flea market the weekend before.

I had actually had plans to go to the flea market with my dad, like we used to. He'd even scheduled it in his iPhone, laptop, BlackBerry, *and* iPad—but right as we were walking out the door, Hillary told him they were booked for brunch with her mother and her new husband, and now that he was out of the hospital and was allowed to go out as long as he brought his oxygen tank she really wanted them to meet before the guy died. Although I had held my breath and said, "Pleasedotherightthingpleasedotherightthing," silently to myself, the minute Hillary started swinging her hips as she *clicked-clack*ed over to convince Dad, I saw his eyes glaze over, and I knew I'd be going alone, again.

I sighed, and looked over the vegetables. For someone who tended to stick to the four major food groups of flour, salt, sugar, and artificial flavorings, facing the wall of colorful produce was also really overwhelming—especially when all the misters clicked on at the same time and hissing filled the air. That's when I walked over to the deli section and bought myself a pound of prepared vegetables. They were smothered in oil and feta cheese and other things that probably made them a little less than healthy, but it was better than my usual dinner of pizza and pasta. I wasn't sure if it was the exercise or the veggies or what, but that night I slept better than I had in ages.

Much to my surprise, the veggie thing wasn't a one-shot deal. A few days later, the craving for red peppers hit me like a shot. I wasn't sure if it was the color reminding me of France, or that first pound of prepared veggies. In health class the year before we saw this DVD about the dangers of "gateway" drugs—things that led to more serious ones. Like, say, pot leading to cocaine, which then led to crack. In my case, veggies in butter and oil and cheese were a gateway food to other harder, healthier vegetables. Like red peppers with the teensiest bit of olive oil and garlic powder. And baked yams. And roasted brussels sprouts.

The following Thursday when I got home from Zumba I did something that only weeks ago would have been unthinkable: I unbookmarked the Tastykakes page. I had no idea why my cravings for Butterscotch Krimpets were replaced with a desire for cinnamon-roasted butternut squash, but they were. I even started cruising the Web for veggie recipes and using the oven to cook things. A few weeks into the veggies and eating better, I realized my cargos were loose—really loose. The weight was coming off.

During the holiday break, I added in another Zumba class on Tuesdays to escape Hillary. And when I finally caved in to the Zumba ladies' pressure in January, and added a Saturday morning Zumba class into the mix on top of my Tuesday and Thursday ones (there was no way I was staying in the house while Hillary hosted a six-week How to Become a Modern-Day Goddess workshop in our living room), it *really* started to drop off. Soon I was trading my size 16 Old Navy cargos for 12s. If Nicola had her way, I would have traded them in for something all together different—like some of the vintage dresses at Brad's—but a girl could handle only so much change at once.

The thing about showing up at Zumba three times a week was that it wasn't very long before I ran out of semi-viable excuses as to why I couldn't join the ZB (Zumba Brigade) for coffee afterward. There were only so many made-up doctor and dentist visits a sixteen-year-old girl could go on before a bunch of mothers got worried and wanted to get involved by giving referrals for second opinions and stuff.

Which is how, one Thursday afternoon in March after Jorge had me demonstrate one of the more complicated steps during class (recently, Cookie had confided in me that Jorge's name was actually George, that he had graduated from Yale with a degree in theater, and that he had about as much Latino blood in him as I did, which was zero), I found myself sitting around a table with five middle-aged women at the Coffee Bean and Tea Leaf on San Vicente in Brentwood sipping an iced coffee and feeling like a suspect from a *CSI* episode.

"So where do you live, honey?" Cheryl asked as she sipped her half-caf-no-whip-two-Splenda mochachino and peered over her glasses.

"Off of Montana," I replied.

"North or south?" Marcia demanded.

"North."

"Ahh . . . very nice," said the group in perfect harmony. Because Brentwood was one of the nicer parts of L.A., there wasn't really a wrong-side-of-the-tracks situation, but north of Montana was considered the very nice part of town instead of just the nice part of town.

"And what does your father do?" asked Gwen, an African American woman who had gone as far as to change into a different matching yoga outfit post-Zumba.

"He's a TV writer. He created that show *Ruh-Roh*?"

The collective gasp was so loud you would've thought I had said, "He came up with the cure for cancer?"

Cookie gasped. "Oh my God—I *love* that show! It's an acute case of excelitis!"

The women looked at one another, confused. "Huh?" Cheryl said.

"You know, like extremely excellent," Cookie explained.

"Actually, the 'excel' in excelitis has to do with looking at Microsoft Excel spreadsheets online for too long," I replied.

"It does?"

I nodded.

She took out her notebook. "Duly noted."

"But the show *is* marvelous," Gwen said as the rest of the group nodded in agreement. Apparently, I was one of the few people on the planet who didn't get why a talking dog was so funny.

"And your mother? Does she work?" Beth asked.

Oh no. The dreaded Mom moment. You'd think with sixteen and a half years worth of them, they would have gotten easier, but not so much.

"Actually, my mom's . . . not around," I admitted.

"Rehab?" Cheryl asked.

"Up and moved to an ashram in Oregon?" Gwen suggested.

"Left your dad for another woman?" Marcia guessed.

Wow. Maybe my situation wasn't as bad as I thought. "No. She died."

Cheryl patted my hand. "Oh, honey. I'm sorry. Cancer?" she asked with a cringe.

I shook my head. "No. She, uh, died while she was giving birth to me."

The gasp at that was so loud that the old man and his much younger girlfriend at the next table looked over.

"Oh, how *awful*!" Beth cried.

"You poor thing!" Gwen exclaimed.

I sipped at the last of my almost-empty iced coffee in order to avoid their eyes. I know I should have appreciated the fact that people felt bad for me, but I would rather have skipped the whole subject all together. When I had been seeing Dr. Gellert, he had tried to tell me that all my eating was an attempt to numb out from the unexpressed grief I had over my mom's death and keep it from coming to the surface. And then he offered me a crystal bowl of M&M's when I started to cry.

"But your dad, he remarried, right?" asked Beth. "I mean, with his success, I'm sure women are lined up around the block."

I shook my head. "He's had girlfriends over the years, but no one that serious until now. Hillary—this woman he's been dating—moved in a few months ago. It was only supposed to be while they redid her floors, but—"

Gwen held up her hand. "You don't even have to continue. We all know exactly where this is going."

"You do?"

"The floors are finished, and she's still there," Cookie said.

"Right."

Marcia sighed. "That's *exactly* the MO my ex-husband's third wife used," she said. "She was an executive at Paramount until she finally roped him into giving her a ring, and now she's pregnant with their second child and is planning on having a water birth and wants me to be the midwife." She looked at the group. "Just so you know, I said no."

The women nodded and clucked in approval.

My stomach got all wonky. I had a feeling that if anyone knew the way evil gold-digging D-girls like Hillary worked, it was this group.

Cheryl reached over and pulled me to her, surprising me with her strength. For someone so tiny, she was like a well-dressed barnacle. "Oh you poor, poor girl!" she *tsk*ed. "And you don't even have a mother to commiserate with! I don't even want to *think* about what it would be like for my son without me here."

I smiled. Her son was lucky. Out of all the women, I liked Cheryl the best. Although I got the sense that because she was so overprotective, he was probably the nerdy type—like a Russian Club member who tried to scrape together a goatee with very limited facial hair. Or a tie-dyed, faux dreadlocked MAKE PEACE, NOT NUCLEAR ARMS T-shirt-wearing type.

"Oh look—here he is!"

I managed to wrestle my head out of the death grip Cheryl had me in, and I saw that I was way off. Because her son was Jason Frank. Who, at that moment, was giving me a very strange look. Probably because his mom was holding me against her boobs while I sat around drinking coffee with a bunch of middle-aged Zumba-ers.

"Jason, honey, this is—"

"We know each other," we mumbled in unison.

"She goes to Castle Heights," Jason said.

"Really?! What a coincidence!" Cheryl said. "Honey, did you know that Simone doesn't have a mother? She died *giving birth to her.* Isn't that just *awful*?"

Okay, really? Suddenly, I was wondering whether I needed to rethink my positive opinion about Cheryl.

"I have a question, though," she said. She turned to me. "Honey, what did you do when it came to things like menstruation? Did your dad explain it to you, or did you—"

Okay—*really* really?! This seemingly sweet little woman was making it so that I was now going to have to transfer schools?!

The good news was that with all the sweat that came pouring out of my forehead at that moment, I probably lost another three pounds. The bad news was that Jason looked like he was going to hurl right then and there. *"Mom,"* he said. "Stop."

"Okay, okay," she said. "I was just curious." She stood

up. "Ladies, I'll see you next class. I have to take Jason to the doctor. He's got a bit of a rash that starts—"

"Mom!" he barked.

It was good to know that Cheryl was an equal-opportunity embarrasser. As much as it had sucked to grow up without a mom, I did have to say I didn't miss that kind of thing.

"I'm willing to pretend the last five minutes never happened if you are," I mumbled as Cheryl said her good-byes.

"Deal," he mumbled back.

Almost being embarrassed to death by the ZB was bad enough, but dinner with my family? Even worse.

Per Dad's shrink Dr. Melman, he wanted us to start having family dinners together on a regular basis. It was bad enough having to pass Hillary in the upstairs hall at home (I tried to time it so that didn't happen often), so having to spend a Sunday night at Twin Dragon—especially when there was a special on IFC about *Best Moments in French Cinema*—was not high on my list of Things I Look Forward to Doing Now, Or at Any Time in my Life. I was, however, super excited to see Max, who was driving down from CalArts for the dinner.

"Whoa!" he exclaimed when he walked up to the table as Dad e-mailed with his iPhone on his lap and Hillary stared into her snake compact, reapplying some of the latest red lipstick she had bought in her quest to get her lips the same color as mine. While I had inherited our mother's jet-black hair, Max looked more like our dad, with brown hair that in the summer turned a little red, and big brown puppy-dog eyes. ("Doesn't it all just scream, 'Adopt me before they euthanize me?'" Nicola liked to say.) "Simone, you've lost even more weight since I saw you last month!"

Hillary snapped her compact shut. "I keep telling her that she needs to make sure she doesn't get *too* thin," she warned. "Too thin is really not becoming. Believe me, I've been there. I know. Plus, the research about the Millennials—"

"Yeah, well, I don't think that's going to be a problem," I cut her off.

"Remind me again how you're doing this," she asked. "Fat Flush? South Beach? Weight Watchers? The Flat Belly Diet—"

"Zumba."

Hillary squinted before remembering that squinting gives you crow's feet and makes you look old. "I'm not familiar with that," she said. "Is it more protein or fruits and vegetables?"

"It's not a diet. It's like a dance-exercise thing. To Latin music. You probably don't know it because I don't think it's big with the Millennials," I replied. "It's mostly middle-aged housewives who do it. But it really works. Oh, and I stopped eating Butterscotch Krimpets after you went into my closet without asking and completely cleaned it out and replaced it with subpar chocolate." I glanced toward my dad, but there was nothing other than more one-handed e-mailing.

"Well, that's great," Hillary said, "but as your soon-to-be stepmother, I worry about you." She shoved a plate of egg rolls toward me. "Which is why I think you should have an egg roll." She plucked the one that my dad had in his non-e-mailing hand out of it and put it on my plate. "Or two."

I glanced over at Max and gave him a quick see-that?! look. He may have been one of those annoying give-someone-the-benefit-of-the-doubt-and-look-on-the-bright-side types, but even he had gotten with the program and realized that no matter how good Hillary may have looked in a bikini, she was *nuts* and had our father under some sort of weird spell and couldn't be trusted. Especially after I called to tell him that I had overheard her telling the interior decorator that it was okay for her to move everything out of his bedroom so that they could start to talk about possible nursery designs.

Luckily, I was saved by Sol, our waiter. Although everyone who worked there was Asian, they all had old Jewish men names like Sol and Murray and Hymie.

"I'll have the shrimp and vegetables," Hillary said after my dad and brother had ordered. "With a few changes. No vegetables, and only three shrimp."

It was hard to tell for certain, but I was pretty sure he mumbled something about how high maintenance rich white women were. He turned to me. "And you?"

"She'll have the Kung Pao chicken, the lo mein, some sweet and sour pork, and an extra side of rice. Brown, not white." She smiled at me. "Brown is *much* healthier than white."

It was like she *wanted* me to stay fat. I turned to Sol. "I'll have the chicken and broccoli. No changes."

He nodded approvingly.

After he walked away, my dad went outside to make a phone call. When he came back, they dumped the Italy news on us. Disinviting me from a family vacation. Sending me off to live with my brother and six random guys for the summer.

"I'd like some time to think about it, if that's okay," I said. I turned to my father. "That *is* okay, right?"

"Of course it is, honey," he replied. I rolled my eyes as I watched him glance toward Hillary to make sure that it was, indeed, okay. I couldn't believe it. *My* father—a guy who had been in charge of rooms full of *Harvard Lampoon*-trained writers and stand-up comedians, two of the most difficult personalities known to man—melted into a puddle whenever he was around her. It really was like she had him under some kind of spell.

"But try and think fast because those extra-deluxe villas go very quickly," Hillary said.

I could only hope that my dad's reverse lobotomy would happen quicker.

"I can't believe I have to wait sixty-seven days until you move in," Nicola moaned at lunch the day after Dad's Italy announcement as we sat at our table in the way, way, way corner of the cafeteria. During the early fall and spring months, we liked to sit outside, but because it was March we were forced to sit inside. The good news about being considered weird is that you're not just invisible to your classmates, but also to your teachers, which is why Nicola was able to have her feet up on the table and paint her toenails turquoise without Mr. Machowksy, our gym teacher, commenting on it as he walked by.

I looked up from my photography book about Paris in the sixties. I loved all the photographs of the French women in their sundresses and pumps and "How could you break my heart into a million pieces when I gave you my soul?" pouts. Nicola kept telling me that with all the weight I had lost and my newfound muscle tone ("*That's* what that line on my calf is?!" I exclaimed when she pointed it out to me), it was time for me to ditch my cargos and T-shirts for sundresses, too, but I still wasn't ready.

"I didn't say I was definitely doing it," I said for like the seventeenth time that day.

"Oh, you're doing it," she replied, for the eighteenth.

She began to bounce up and down in her chair. "And I'm going to be over there every single night!" she squealed.

"Okay, who are you, and what have you done with my best friend?" I demanded.

"What do you mean?"

"Squealing? Bouncing in your chair?"

She settled down. "Sorry about that." She began to bounce again. "But it's just so exciting!"

I rolled my eyes. I should have known that, unlike me, who considered living with my brother and his friends some sort of karmic payback for something hideous I must have done in a past life, Nicola would think this was the best news ever. "You know, it would be one thing if you tried to do something about your crush and actually *spoke* to my brother once in a while," I said. "Then I could understand why you were so excited."

"But that's the thing," she replied. "I *am* ready to do something about it. I'm ready to have him fall madly in love with me and give him the gift of becoming his girlfriend. Plus, I think the experience will really help socialize you," she said, pulling at the extensions that she had finally convinced her mother to let her get. Which she immediately had braided into cornrows by a woman on the Venice boardwalk and then dyed pink.

I looked at her. "That makes me sound like I'm a rescue dog or something."

"Hmm. It does, doesn't it? Let me think of another way

to put it." She thought for a second. "Okay, got it. How about . . . if you're lucky, maybe you'll run into one of the guys coming out of the shower, and there'll be a breeze from the ocean and it'll blow his towel right off."

I shook my head. "Not helping."

She sighed. "Do you realize most girls would kill to have the opportunity to live with seven guys for a summer?! I bet after this you could get a book deal with all the secrets you learn about guys and the way they think!"

"Okay, 'most girls' sit over there," I said, pointing across the room at a clique of giggling girls. "*We*," I said, pointing at Nicola's multicolored toes and my French photo book, "are not most girls."

"Amen to that. But we're still girls. And this is still an awesome opportunity to practice being around guys, so that when we finally get away from all these pod people and go to college, we know what we're doing." She looked at me. "Wait a minute—are you *scared*?"

"No."

Her right eyebrow went up.

"Yes," I admitted.

"Why?"

"Because! I don't know how to talk to guys! Let alone live with them!"

"But you have a brother." She sighed. "A totally dreamy one."

"Yeah, but a brother is not a *guy*."

"This is why this is good! You'll get one month's worth of practice!" she cried. "And I'm telling you, you really should start a blog about it, because if you don't, I will—"

"But what about the whole farting/burping thing?" I demanded.

She shrugged. "So? You'll teach them to stop that. Like some sort of *My Fair Dude* thing."

"No—I meant *me*. It's one thing to accidentally fart or burp in front of a boy you used to take baths with when you were little because you have the same DNA," I explained. "It's a whole other thing when there's the risk that some guy not related to you hears you do it. Plus, while the whole veggie thing might be healthy, there *are* some . . . loud side effects."

"Hmm. That's a good point," she admitted. She shrugged. "So maybe they'll teach *you*. You know, turn *you* into a lady."

I sighed. If I wanted to get anywhere with this, it was probably better if I just had a real heart-to-heart conversation with my brother. We were close. I could tell him how I was feeling, and he'd understand.

"Okay, not to sound stupid or anything, Simmy, but you keep losing me," Max said that night as we FaceTimed.

"Oh. Sorry." I held my iPad up to my face really close. "IS THIS BETTER?" I yelled.

I saw him jump back. "No, I can *hear* you just fine. I meant, I don't *understand* what you're saying."

"What part don't you understand?" I asked for the fourth time.

"The part where you keep saying that you think you'll feel weird around a bunch of strangers," he said for the fifth. "Because, you know, they're really not strangers."

"Do I know the guys? I didn't recognize any of their names when you told me about them," I said, confused.

"That's because you technically haven't met them . . . yet. But that's the thing—strangers are just friends you haven't met yet!" he said all glass-three-quarters-full-like. "I saw that on a bumper sticker last week. It's great, right?"

I shook my head. Really? He and I came from the same gene pool?

"Look, they're all awesome guys," he said. "I mean, we're *artists*—we're all sensitive and stuff. Plus, I really meant it when I said it would be like old times." He gave me a sweet smile, the one that showed the slight gap between his two front teeth and had the power to make me forgive him no matter what sort of jerky thing he had done to me. Like the time he had erased this totally obscure François Truffaut movie I had DVR'd off IFC before I had a chance to watch it. "You know, back when the biggest problem we had with Dad was whether he was going to drop dead from a heart attack from working so hard rather than whether he was going to marry Hillary." The smile got sweeter. "I miss you, Simmy."

I looked away. "Please don't call me that." He *knew* I had a soft spot for that nickname.

"But I do! And I know you'll like these guys. I wouldn't have suggested it if you wouldn't. Plus, do you really want to spend a month cooped up in a house with Hillary and have to watch her order people around in broken Italian?" He shook his head. "That woman is *evil*."

I had to say, I was glad that he finally came around and saw that when it came to her, the glass was pretty much empty.

"Why don't you talk to Dad," he went on. "See what he says. Maybe if you get him alone, he'll tell you that he really wants you to go on the trip."

As close as my brother and I were, I didn't tell him that that's exactly what I was hoping. Not that I wanted to be trapped in a house where I wasn't even sure there'd be English programming on the cable channels, but just the idea that my dad wanted me there would make it bearable.

To most people, having to have your dad's assistant pencil you into his schedule doesn't exactly scream "I want you!" but it was either that, or hope to run into him at home at some point. Which had been happening less and less over the last few months. Dad spent more and more time at the studio rewriting scripts after the star of *Ruh-Roh,* Andrew, married his twenty-years-older-than-him acting coach, who had lots of ideas of how his character should evolve and therefore wouldn't sign off on the scripts.

"Sorry I'm late," he said as he rushed into his home office the next night, which, thanks to the feng shui expert Hillary had hired, had been moved out to the garage. The room that had originally been his office was now a walk-in closet for Hillary's things.

"That's okay. Thanks for making the time to see me," I replied. I felt a little nervous, like I was meeting with the guidance counselor or something.

He pecked out an e-mail. "Okay. Done. And now for some time with my favorite daughter," he said. He powered off his iPhone. "I'm even going to turn this off." He flashed me a smile. "So! How are you?"

"Fine."

"You know, not that you didn't look good before, honey, but the weight loss really suits you."

"Yeah?"

A sad smile came over his face as he nodded. "You're looking more and more like your mom every day."

I felt a golf ball grow in my throat. "Thanks." I tried not to think too much about how things would have been different if I had a mom. Because when I did, this is what happened.

"But I will say that Hillary's a little worried about you. She thinks you're getting too skinny." He glanced over at his iPhone but, to his credit, didn't reach for it.

Yes, I had definitely lost weight, but there was no way anyone could accuse me of being too skinny. Brad and Nicola had decided that I was more like the women on that TV show *Mad Men*. ("Not fat, but definitely hauling a caboose," said Brad.)

"I'll keep that in mind," I replied. Whenever Hillary said something—that I was getting too skinny, that I should think about wearing pink lipstick to lighten up my lips—that was the stock answer I gave her. I wasn't agreeing with her, but it was enough to shut her up. "So Dad, listen. What I wanted to talk to you about—"

"I have to say, it really warms my heart to see Hillary take such an interest in you kids." This time as he looked at the iPhone, I saw his hand twitch.

I waited for the "KIDDING!" that should have followed that phrase, but all I got was the goofy smile that appeared whenever he talked about her. "Yeah, anyway. So what I wanted to ask you—"

"Don't you love what she's done with the house?" he asked. "At first I was worried that she was going a bit overboard, but I've really come to appreciate how driven she is. She knows exactly what she wants."

She sure did. Like, say, disinviting me from the family

vacation, when she wasn't even part of the family. "I guess that's one way of putting it. So listen—"

"And I think that was very sensitive of her to take your feelings into account with the vacation."

"How so?"

"Well, about how you'd probably be bored hanging out with two old people like us."

"Dad, Hillary's not even *thirty*."

"You know what I mean," he said.

"So what you're saying is that you think it's a good idea that I don't come."

He looked uncomfortable. "I didn't say *that*. I just meant . . ."

I didn't need to know what he meant. I had my answer. At that moment, my veggie cravings flew out the window. I wanted nothing more than to get in the car and drive to Ralph's and buy the biggest sheet cake they had. Maybe even an Entenmann's Louisiana Crunch Cake to go with it. Perhaps even a box of doughnut holes as a chaser.

If I did that, it might help soften the blow that he was pretty much choosing Hillary over me. At least it would soften it for a little while—as long as it took for the sugar to wear off or for me to feel completely sick to my stomach. But there were two huge problems with that particular solution—(a) my Saab was in the shop *again,* and (b) I knew it was only a temporary fix. Plus, the last few times I had had a sugary baked good, I had broken out in this weird rash on my chest because my body wasn't used to it anymore.

"Don't worry about it," I said, trying to keep my voice steady, although what I really wanted to do was cry. "Because what I wanted to tell you is that I'm really glad you're letting me stay with Max while you're gone. I'm really looking forward to it."

"You are?" Did he have to look so *relieved*?

I nodded. Because Nicola said I had one of those faces where everything showed, I tried extra hard to look convincing, but seeing as how by that time my father was in the process of turning his iPhone back on, it didn't matter anyway.

"I'm glad you came to your senses," Nicola said the next day at lunch, yelling over Castle Height's resident treehugger, rally organizer, and all-around protester Wally Twersky's daily rendition of "We Shall Overcome" on his guitar a few tables away. "And not just because that means I'll get to see your brother a lot more." She cringed as Wally got louder. "What's he trying to overcome this week?"

"I think I heard him tell Ajara Monihan that it's the unethical treatment of bunnies for cosmetic testing."

"They do cosmetic testing at Castle Heights?! Where? In the chemistry lab?"

I shook my head. "No. Just, you know, unethical treatment of using them for testing in general."

"Oh. Anyways, speaking of unethical treatment . . . now that we have a deadline on our hands, we really need to address *your* unethical treatment of that totally smoking bod you've got growing in that veggie/Zumba petri dish. Because BFFs don't let BFFs show up at a houseful of college guys with a suitcase full of ratty old cargo pants being held up with safety pins and T-shirts that are way too big."

As I looked down at my cargos, I had to admit she had a point. Even using the last hole of the belt I had to wear to keep them up, they were still big.

She grabbed my arm and turned me toward her and gave me an After-School Special look. "Simone, listen to me—you're not the fat girl anymore, okay?"

I began to examine my left cuticle as if it contained all the secrets of the universe. I knew where she was going with this. She wasn't talking about my weight—she was talking about how I still wanted to keep hiding from the world behind the invisible pane of glass that I felt kept me apart from people. Sometimes the glass was Windexed and was so clear I almost forgot it was there—like in gym class the week before, when Ananda Desai told me she liked my Olivia Newton John T-shirt. But sometimes it was dirty and covered with fingerprints and hard to see through, like when Marc Rabel said, "Here comes Cousin Itt," under his breath as I passed him on my way to the board in trig class. It had been there for so long it was as if it had grown roots.

"Obviously, I already know how awesome you are," Nicola went on. "But now it's time that other people get to see that, too. And more importantly, that *you* do. And this is the perfect opportunity."

I felt like I was in therapy again. And there wasn't even a bowl of M&M's around. I knew that there was some truth to what she was saying. Being That Weird Fat Girl meant I could hide out and not have to deal with people. The nickname hurt for a while, and yeah maybe at first I had been lying when I told myself I didn't care. But the longer it went on, the more I got used to it—I really did stop caring, I think; it was easier to hide. Any whispers or mean comments just stopped touching me. My size became this armor—to protect me from people getting too close. Because they'd always end up disappointing or hurting you if you let them.

But as the weight started melting away, I didn't feel happy or relieved or anything. I felt naked. Who was I if I wasn't That Weird Fat Girl? I didn't want to be invisible anymore, but the idea of actually being out there, in the world, with no protection, instead of hiding in dark movie theaters or in my room, was terrifying. My baggy clothes were the last bit of protection I had—wearing them I could at least *pretend* that I still had some armor against whatever was out there.

But still, Nicola was right. There was a difference between learning to swim in the shallow end while wearing water wings with the Zumba ladies and being thrown into a choppy, college boy–infested ocean.

Nicola put her hands on my shoulders. "I hate to tell you this, princess, but it's time."

If what she was talking about was what I *thought* she was talking about, I was in big trouble. "Do you mean—?"

She nodded. "Yup. The makeover part of the movie of your life. Complete with some nauseating up-tempo song sung by a pop star with a nose ring."

I cringed. I *hated* those things. The makeover montage was so corny. It was one of the reasons why I preferred indie and foreign films.

"You know, you might actually end up having fun," Nicola said.

I gave her a look.

"I mean, obviously it could be a total disaster, too," she went on.

That was better.

"But you have a fifty-fifty chance."

I sighed. "I guess you're right."

It was hard to think positively, though. I wasn't exactly a happy-ending kinda girl.

Nicola took out a piece of notebook paper and pen. "Operation Falcon," she announced as she wrote.

"What's Operation Falcon?" I asked.

"It's what we're going to call the makeover. It makes it sound all top secret. Like some government thing. Plus, in case I lose this piece of paper, no one will be able to link you with it." She looked up from the page to find me reaching into my left eye and taking out my contact. Gross to do at a lunch table, I know, but Nicola was used to it. Even after three years, I could never get them in right.

"That is disgusting. Number one," she announced as she picked up the pen, "glasses."

"Okay, don't they normally go the other way—girl with glasses gets contacts? I'm already not liking this Operation Eagle thing."

"It's Operation *Falcon*."

"Same thing."

As she went back to making her list, I sighed. I didn't have to be psychic to know this was going to be a very big makeover.

four

"Hey, Simone," Brad said when we walked into One Person's Garbage the next afternoon. "I got some great old evening bags this weekend from this estate sale in the Palisades of this woman who was an extra in a Bruce Willis movie."

"Nope," Nicola said. "No purses. No band tees. Today, Bradley, we are on a mission."

I so did not like the sound of that. And I especially did not like it when she marched me over to the dresses.

"Okay, nowhere on that Operation Cardinal list did it say anything about *dresses*," I said.

"Operation *Falcon*. And it said 'new wardrobe.' Dresses are considered wardrobe." Flipping through the racks, she began to grab things. A black sundress with white polka dots. A blue Chinese silk one with a slit up the leg. A red one with little bows on shoulders. "Ooh—this is *fun*!" she squealed. "It's like playing Barbies!"

"But you hate Barbies," I said as she loaded up my arms with the stuff. "You did your oral presentation last year on why the Glamorista Barbie was responsible for setting the feminist movement back twenty years."

"Yes, but you can be the *cool* Barbie—the one with a brain and killer taste in music."

She walked toward the rack—the one that held the dress on it. "No! Not the blue dress!" I yelled.

"How come?"

"I can't. Not yet. Let's start with some other ones first." If I tried on that blue dress and it didn't fit, I'd feel awful. Unworthy. It was better just to stay away from it. If you didn't have any expectations, you couldn't get hurt.

"Okay, okay," she grumbled.

When my arms were so full I could barely see over the top, she pushed me into a dressing room. Well, into the closet with the tacked-up sheet that made it so that the people on Abbot Kinney Boulevard couldn't see you in your underwear. I never tried things on when I was shopping. I didn't need to see how shlubby I looked. I turned toward the window and tried to gauge whether I could haul myself up and out to escape.

"And don't think about climbing out that window," she called out. "Because I will hunt you down using my brand-new Stalker GPS app on my iPhone."

I sighed as I started to take off my cargo pants and New Order T-shirt. When the moment of truth came—the one with a lot of pasty naked skin staring back at me—I looked down at the ground. I was somewhat of an expert at that. In fact, I could even not look at myself in the mirror as I was putting on mascara (for the most part I was anti-makeup, but when you were as pale as I was, it was wear mascara or have your face completely melt away).

Although with Hillary in the house, it was next to impossible to escape the mirrors. They were all over the place now. But as I pulled the polka-dot sundress on, my eyes landed on the small mirror by accident. Weirdly enough, when I saw myself I didn't cringe. Instead of focusing on everything about myself I didn't like, I saw things I *did.* Like my nose, and the way it was a little crooked from when I was ten and it got broken when I mistakenly crossed Tim Klasky's path as he swung a baseball bat, even though I had *said,* "Tim, don't swing yet, okay?"

And my neck, which was on the long side but not so long that I looked like a giraffe. And my arms, which, ever since I had started Zumba-ing, had gone from these blobby sausage things to where you could see I had a shoulder, and then a tricep, and then a forearm. It wasn't like I was going to sit there all day and admire myself. While I wouldn't go as far as to say I was pretty, I had to admit I was kind of . . . interesting looking. Especially now that I had cheekbones.

But while I may have been interesting looking, from

the amount of time it took me to zip the zipper (and only halfway up at that), one thing I wasn't was a size 8.

"Let's see," Nicola called out.

Holding my breath, I walked out and stood in front of the full-length mirror while she and Brad checked me out.

Me. In a polka-dot sundress. With a poufy skirt. Who knew I could look so . . .

"Okay, you look like a dancer in one of those Disneyland shows," Nicola said as she pushed me back toward the dressing room.

"Thank you. That's exactly what I was going to say," I said as I exhaled.

"Well, it *did* belong to a woman who played a teacher in that Shia LeBeouf Disney show," Brad said.

"You know, I really think I should just stick to pants. In fact, I've decided I'm ready to move to jeans," I said. "And I found this great Echo and The Bunnymen T-shirt on eBay the other day. It's very colorful, so that will help with my look—"

She shook her head. "Nope. We're not leaving here without something that shows your legs."

"I hope you don't take this the wrong way and sue me for sexual harassment, but you do have lovely calves," Brad said.

I smiled. "Thanks, Brad." Coming from a gay man that meant a lot.

Nicola reached for a flowery shift and shoved it toward me. "Try this one."

As I looked at the tag, I wrinkled my nose. "This Lilly Pulitzer person sure likes pastels."

"It belonged to Betty White's stand-in back in her *Golden Girls* days," Brad said.

I put it back and reached for a simple black sleeveless dress with a flared skirt. "What about this one?"

"That's one of our more famous pieces," Brad said proudly. "It belonged to an actress who played a villain in an episode of the original *Charlie's Angels*."

"I dunno. Looks a little boring," Nicola replied. "Or like you're going to a funeral."

I shrugged and looked at the tag. "Yeah, but it's a size ten, so maybe I'll be able to actually breathe," I said as I shut the dressing room curtain.

Not only could I breathe, but I could zip the sucker up myself.

As I walked out, they both stared at me.

"It looks that dumb, huh?"

"No. You look amazing!" Nicola gasped.

"I think you look like you should be sitting in a café on the Left Bank of Paris," Brad said.

I brightened. "Paris? Really?"

He nodded. "Yes. Drinking an espresso while some painter professes his undying love to you and apologizes for the time you walked in on him making out with the nude model he was sketching."

As I turned toward the mirror, I couldn't help but

smile. It was the perfect dress for me. Simple, but elegant. Sophisticated, but not snobbily so. And the contrast between the dress and my pale skin and my lips was pretty cool.

"So what do you think?" asked Brad.

I slowly turned around so I could get the full effect. "I think I look like . . . such a *girl*."

"And that would be . . . ?"

I shrugged. "Not so bad, I don't think."

I felt so girly that I half expected myself to start giggling. Which, if that happened, I'd have to give Nicola permission to shoot me.

Right then, the Edith Piaf song *La Vie en Rose* came through the iPod speakers.

"Is that a sign or is that a sign?!" squealed Nicola. "Wait—that *is* French she's singing in, right?"

We nodded.

She walked over to the jewelry section. "It just needs a little something," she said as she rummaged in a tray. She held up a giant gold snake bracelet. "How about this?"

"A *little* something? That's the size of my entire forearm." I wrinkled my nose. "Plus Hillary has something like that."

"Forget it then." She held up a long strand of pearls. "Can't go wrong with pearls."

"Yeah, if you're going to some fancy cocktail party," I replied. "Not to eleventh grade."

She sighed. "I knew you were going to be difficult."

I reached up and took out my contact. "I am not. But I'll tell you what *is* difficult. These stupid contacts." I sighed.

"Good thing 'new glasses' is part of Operation Falcon," she replied.

Brad took out the tray of vintage eyeglass frames and placed them on the counter. He held out a pair of black-rimmed nerdish ones. "Try these."

"Brad, we're supposed to make her look hot," Nicola said. "Not like a librarian."

"Hey, I have some pictures of my mom wearing glasses like these," I said as I put them on.

"Whoa. Color me wrong," she said. "I think we just found the perfect accessory. Simone, you're so . . . *you*!" she cried. "I mean, you were you before, but now it's like you're *you* you!"

With only one contact in, it was difficult to get the full effect, but I could vaguely make out that the glasses did indeed look good. Who knew the thing that made me *me* was a pair of nerd glasses? "But do I still look French?" I asked nervously. The French part really sold it for me.

"Yes," Brad said, "but instead of a girl crying over her dumb painter boyfriend, now you look like an intellectual discussing philosophy at Café de Flore." He smiled. "Like your namesake Simone de Beauvoir."

I smiled. I liked that.

"You know, I don't even think you need any jewelry

now," Nicola said. "The glasses are the perfect accessory. But shoes! We need shoes! I'm thinking. . . . red pumps," she announced as Brad walked over to the shoe section.

"I'm thinking I'm way ahead of you," he said, holding up a pair that, thankfully for me, weren't too high. "These belonged to the actress who played Jaclyn Smith's mother in a highly rated NBC miniseries back in the eighties," he said proudly.

"Really?!" I asked excitedly.

"Who's Jaclyn Smith?" Nicola asked.

I turned to her. "Um, Kelly Garrett, original *Charlie's Angel*?" People may have considered me a bit of a snob because I liked French movies, but I also had a real thing for the original *Charlie's Angels,* which was on TV back in the seventies. Especially Jaclyn Smith, who was the prettiest and nicest angel of them all.

"And they're a—"

"Seven and a half? Yup," said Brad as he handed them to me. I wondered if all gay men could tell a girl's shoe size just by looking at them, or if Brad had a special gift.

"So what do you think?" Nicola asked as I slowly twirled around.

"I think . . . I might be able to get used to this," I replied. Right before my left ankle gave out and I took down a mannequin that was wearing an outfit that had belonged to a woman who had played Cameron Diaz's best friend in one of her dumber comedies.

****

By the time we left, I had bought (or, rather, my dad had bought me with his Amex) the black dress, the glasses, a red A-line swing dress, and a pair of black sandals with a tiny bit of a heel. ("They're called kitten heels," Brad explained, "but don't ask me why. I'm gay, but it's not like I have a PhD in fashion history.") Out of guilt, I bought the glasses with cash and received a two-dollar Chinese paper fan in return.

"Why do I need a fan?" I asked Brad.

"Because I don't have any singles in the register to give you as change," he replied.

"Got it," I nodded. Those types of things happened all the time in Venice.

Wearing my new dress and shoes ("Because you don't have any experience wearing this kind of stuff, it's going to take a lot of getting used to," Nicola said), we made our way to an eyeglass store on Abbot Kinney so they could call my eye doctor and get the right lenses put in the vintage frames.

I turned to Nicola and smiled. "Do I have something in my teeth?" I whispered as the guy made the call.

"No. Why?"

"Because I feel like the guy keeps staring at me."

"Um, maybe because you're looking *hot*," she hissed.

"Oh please. The only thing that's hot is my face," I said

as I felt it turn red again. If they gave out grades for taking compliments, I'd get a D. It was definitely not one of my strong points.

The guy hung up the phone and walked back to us. "These are terrific frames," he said with a very white smile.

"Thanks."

"They're vintage, right?"

I nodded.

"They don't make them like this anymore." Another smile. I wondered how often he bleached his teeth.

He was starting to creep me out. "Uh-huh. So, um, when will they be ready?"

"Three hours?"

"Thanks," I replied, dragging Nicola to the door. "What was his problem?" I asked when we got outside.

"Dude, he was flirting with you!"

"He was?"

She rolled her eyes. "Yes."

Okay, maybe getting used to it was going to take longer than I thought. "Can we have lunch now?" I asked hopefully. I was starving. I had no idea shopping could be such a cardio workout.

"Soon. But there's one more thing we need to do first."

"What?"

She pointed across the street at a hair place called Shear Genius.

I shook my long hair. "Uh-uh. No way."

"But it's part of the operation!" she cried.

I kept shaking it, to the point where the split ends whacked her in the eye. *"Ow."*

"Sorry."

"Why do you have to be so *stubborn*?"

"Do you know how long it took me to grow it to this point?!" I asked, holding it as far away from her as possible.

"Yeah, and do you know how long you've been hiding behind it?!"

I rolled my eyes. "I don't *hide* behind it," I replied. "I just . . . pull it over my face for warmth. You know I get cold easily."

She rolled her eyes. "Maybe I'd buy that if we lived in Vermont, but we're in L.A. You know, I bet that's five extra pounds right there." She reached over and poked my head.

"*Ow*. What are you doing?"

"Feeling for birds."

I sighed. It was either keep arguing with her and still end up losing while getting more and more hungry, or just give in. "Okay. A *trim*. Not a cut. Not something all style-y that I'll need to put tons of goop in every morning. Not even something that needs to be blow-dried."

She touched her own hair, which on that particular day was red and styled into some poufy French twist-looking thing and had real chopsticks sticking out of it.

"So you're saying you want something a little less fancy than mine."

"A *lot* less fancy."

"We'll just let a hair-care professional decide," she said as she hauled me across the street.

After walking around the chair and examining me from every angle, Kimmy, my "hair-care goddess" ("My life coach told me I'd attract more abundance to me if I called myself that rather than a plain old hair-care professional") nodded. Although with hair bleached so blonde that it looked like it was about to break off and crumble, she didn't exactly seem to be a walking example for healthy hair. "I'm thinking . . . Clara Bow. I'm thinking . . . Nicole Richie. I'm thinking . . . Katie Holmes when she went short, I'm thinking—"

And I was thinking . . . *crazy.* What part of "trim" did this goddess not understand? "Excuse me, not to be rude or anything, but all those people you mentioned—well, at least Nicole and Katie because I don't know who that Clara person is," I said as politely as possible, "have *bobs.*"

She nodded. "That would be correct."

"But see, I just told you that all I wanted was a trim—even though, to be honest, I don't think it's all that necessary, and the only reason I'm doing it is to make my friend here happy so we can go eat," I went on, "and bobs are . . . *short.* Like inches and inches shorter than my hair now."

Kimmy looked over at Nicola and raised her eyebrow.

"Believe me. I feel your pain. I have to deal with this on a daily basis," Nicola said.

"It's just that if you cut it all off, I'm afraid I'm going to get really cold," I rambled. "And because my blood sugar is on the low side, that's already an issue for me, so the hair is actually necessary for *warmth.* Not to, you know, *hide* behind, like Nicola keeps trying to say, and that's why—"

Kimmy put her hand over my mouth. "Enough. Here's the thing, Amber—"

"It's Simone."

"Right. Anyways, as I was saying before you interrupted me, the thing is, I'm an *artist.*"

"Oh really? What medium?" I asked. "Painting or photography or—" Maybe if I could change the subject, we wouldn't have to deal with the hair issue anymore.

"What I mean is that *hair* is my art," she replied. "Although I have been told that my Hipstamatic photos are so good that I could probably get a gallery to give me a show. But that's neither here nor there. What *is* here is you. Sitting in my chair. When I graduated from cosmetology school in Jersey, I made a solemn oath to myself that I would go to any length to make my clients look as . . . *them* as possible."

I was tempted to tell her I didn't think that was grammatically correct, but somehow I didn't think she'd appreciate it. And to get back at me, she'd just start snipping away.

"And when I look at you, Taylor—"

"Simone."

"Right. What I see is . . . a bob."

"I appreciate the fact that you've put so much time into thinking about this," I said, "but what I see is a trim."

"And the thing of it is," she went on, "when I look at a client and I see who they really are and that the Universe has guided them to me to help them get there, like a hair . . . midwife, I just can't go against that. Not good on the karma front."

"But what if I wrote a note saying that it was my decision?" I asked.

She shook her head. "Sorry. Can't do it. When it comes to hair, I have a gift—on the psychic side—"

Now the woman was psychic? Sure, this was Venice, where the boardwalk was filled with fortune-tellers willing to read your tarot cards for ten bucks, but still. I looked over at Nicola. Even she was starting to look a little less sure of her brilliant idea.

"—and what I'm seeing and hearing when I look at you, Ashley—"

"Simone."

"—is that you're a *bob* girl. Not a trim girl. So what's it gonna be?"

It was one thing to get glasses. Or a dress that showed

off my legs. Especially because it meant I was going to have to shave them on a regular basis. But to cut all my hair off? I'd just feel so . . . *seen.* "Do you know how long it took me to grow it this long?!" I cried. "My entire life!"

She shrugged. "So if you don't like it, it'll grow back."

"Yeah—in sixteen years!"

She looked at her watch. "Listen, I have a drag queen coming in an hour, so if we're gonna do this, we need to start now."

I looked over at Nicola.

"Haven't I been right so far?" she asked.

I sighed. It was true. Plus, I had gone this far, why stop now? Hopefully, I'd be so unrecognizable that no one would know it was me and would think I had moved away or something. I plopped down in the chair and squeezed my eyes tight. "I guess we're gonna do this."

I didn't open my eyes once the entire time Kimmy was washing and rinsing and combing and snipping and drying. Not even when Nicola oohed and ahhed and said things like, "Wow. I've been best friends with the girl for six years, and I never knew she had a neck!" before she went over to the eyeglass place to pick up my glasses, which were now ready.

I guessed if I looked beyond horrible, I could always get a wig. A wig could be fun. Maybe something in a platinum blonde, like Kimmy. Although I was looking for a low-key approach, and that would probably make me stand out. I could always transfer to another school. That was an option. As I mulled over my future, or the lack thereof, if my hair ended up looking ridiculous, the stench of very strong perfume hit my nostrils.

"Girl, I am on a *schedule* here," snapped a very deep voice, "so you best get *her* out of that chair and *me* in it."

"I'm assuming that's the drag queen," I whispered to Nicola, now back with my glasses. My eyes were still closed.

"That would be correct," she said. "And if I were you, I wouldn't want to make him angry because she's *really* large."

I opened one eye. Standing in front of me, with his arms crossed and a high royal-blue heel impatiently clicking on the floor, stood a very large African American man who—had he not decided he liked to wear women's clothes and makeup and fake nails—probably would have made a great football player. Or possibly an entire football *team*.

"But that is one fabulous bob, child," he said as he looked at me. "Kimmy, you did *good*."

The idea that a drag queen liked my new haircut was either really good . . . or really bad. Unfortunately, I was still too chicken to open the other eye and take a look in the mirror.

"Thanks, Lady GaGantuan," Kimmy replied. "That means a lot coming from you."

"What was the before picture?"

She put up a hand. "Let's not go there."

He turned to me and smiled. When he did, it made him very pretty. "Child?"

"Yes?" I said meekly.

"Out of my chair," he ordered.

"Okay," I said as I scrambled out, still not looking in the mirror.

Kimmy walked around me, examining her handiwork. "I'm thinking you look very . . . French."

At that I perked up. "How so?"

"Mm . . . kind of like . . . as if you should be sitting across from a man telling him that even though he's your soul mate, you're not going to be able to be with him because you think it's better for your art," she said.

"Ooh—I like that one."

"Wait—before you open both your eyes and check yourself out, you need to put these on first," Nicola said, placing the glasses on the bridge of my nose. I opened my eyes. After she was done, she smiled. "Okay—*now* look."

"I'm not going to have to end our friendship over this, am I?" I asked anxiously. "Because it would really suck to have to go find a new best friend."

"*Au contraire*, my BFF," she replied. "If anything, you're going to spend the next twenty years coming up with creative ways to repay me with gratitude. By the way, they announced this morning that Arcade Fire is coming to town this summer, so you can start with tickets to that." She turned me toward the mirror. "Okay, now open them."

I did. And sucked in my breath so fast I began to choke, until Lady GaGantuan handed me his purple Hello Kitty water bottle.

"Whoa," I said as I stared myself. I had a bob, but it wasn't bowl-like, or all poufy like a TV news anchor. It was on the longish side, with wispy bangs, and it curled under gently with the corners of it pointing it toward my mouth. "I look . . ."

"Completely babelicious?" Nicola suggested.

"Like Christina Ricci, but less alien like because she's too skinny?" Kimmy asked.

". . . even more like . . . *me*," I finished.

This being L.A., judging people by how they looked wasn't only acceptable, but expected. But when you walk around being called That Weird Fat Girl, you tend not to do that. I liked to think of myself as being able to see beyond how people looked. If I hadn't, my becoming best friends with a girl who had ever-changing hair color and piercings, and who occasionally wore combat boots, probably wouldn't have happened.

But that moment, as I looked at myself in the mirror and saw a girl who looked both sophisticated and French, I finally had a sense of what it felt like to be in the world and not want to disappear. Or to have the courage to look people in the eye instead of looking just to the right of them. And to not have your back ache because, instead of slumping, you were standing up straight with your shoulders back because you felt like you had just as much of a right to be on the planet as everyone else.

Part of it was finally seeing the weight loss, part of it was the dress, the haircut, and the glasses. But I knew it was more than that. It was as if some switch had been flicked and the pane of glass had just shattered, so there wasn't anything stopping me from joining the world, rather than sitting on the sidelines.

As corny as it sounded, and as much as I found fairy tales to be really offensive because they portrayed girls as helpless beings who needed to be saved by dumb princes, I felt like a character who was about to go on some big adventure.

five

"I don't know if this is a good idea," I said as I stumbled on my heels as Nicola dragged me across the Coffee Bean and Tea Leaf parking lot.

"You'd never hear the end of it if these guys found out they weren't the first ones to gaze upon my handiwork," she replied. She stopped and turned toward me, taking me in. "Correction—my *genius* handiwork." She removed my hand from the back of my neck, which I kept swiping at in hopes of finding my hair.

"Stop futzing," she ordered.

"Is it possible to miss your hair?" I asked.

"I thought you liked it!"

"I do," I replied. "But still, I think I'm having separation anxiety."

My hope that the ladies of the Zumba Brigade wouldn't embarrass me by making a big deal about my look was squashed the minute I walked (okay, tripped) through the door.

Even with her oversized glasses, it took Cheryl a moment to realize it was me. "OH MY GOD, I CAN'T BELIEVE IT!" she screamed when it registered.

As the rest of the crew turned, they shrieked. It was like I was Godzilla, only the five-foot-five version.

"Okay, maybe this wasn't the best idea," Nicola murmured.

"Sweetie, I hope this doesn't offend you," Cookie said a few minutes later as I tried to sip my iced coffee while they pushed and prodded and pulled at me, "but you're looking like a real Baberaham Washington."

"Who's Baberaham Washington?" Nicola asked, confused.

"I think she means Baberaham *Lincoln*," I replied.

Cookie thought about it. "You might be right. History was never my strong suit."

Cheryl grabbed my hand. "Simone, I think I speak for all of us when I say that while we're old enough to know that it's inner beauty that counts, you look like you could be in a magazine."

"I don't know—" I said doubtfully.

"Hey—we practiced this in the car, remember?" Nicola asked. "When someone gives you a compliment. you say *thank you*."

"Right." I cringed. "Thank you," I said, trying to make it sound as honest as possible. But boy, was that hard.

"What a beautiful dress," Marcia said. "Where'd you get it?"

"One Person's Garbage Is Another One's Treasure."

From the looks on their faces they were not impressed. In fact, it was more like they were frightened.

"It's a thrift store in Venice," I explained.

"Pre-owned stuff from minor celebrities," Nicola added.

"That sounds . . . lovely," Cookie said.

"Just do me a favor and make sure you get it dry cleaned," Cheryl said. "So I'm not up half the night worrying that your house is being infested by bedbugs. Those things are a nightmare to get rid of."

"I have an idea—now that you're open to wearing things that actually fit, we should do a little shopping!" Marcia cried.

Cookie clapped her hands. "A field trip!"

Uh-oh. As much as I loved the ZB, with the amount of bedazzlement that could be found on their exercise wear, there was no way I was going to put myself into their hands and let them dress me.

"We should definitely hit T.J. Maxx," Marcia said. "I saw this *magnificent* fuchsia velour tracksuit, which would look just darling on you. Rhinestones all along the collar. To die for."

"Um, I don't think—" I started to say, nervously.

"And of course there's always Loehmann's," Cheryl added. "I'll let you use my fifteen-percent-off birthday-month discount that comes with my Insider Club status."

I had been in Loehmann's once, to use the rest room, and the amount of large Russian women wearing way too much perfume was enough to stop me from ever going back. "That's so sweet of you, but—"

"It's a little far, but the Kohl's over the hill is to die for," Rona interrupted. "And the sales they have! Last time I was there, they had these Keds with little hearts made out of sequins."

Okay, it was time to put a stop to this. "You know, I really appreciate the fact that you guys would take time out of your busy days to help me shop, but I'm sort of tapped out on the finance front at the moment."

"Plus, I think Simone wants to stay with the vintage look," Nicola added. She looked at her Disney Princess watch. ("Irony is the new black.") "Wow—look at the time! We've got to get home and study. Or go admire all her new loot. One or the other."

"Okay, but before you go, let me give you a little something," Marcia said, digging in her wallet and handing me a twenty.

"What's this for?"

"It's an early birthday gift. Put it toward another dress."

"I can't take this!" I said pushing it back toward her. "Plus, my birthday's not until September."

The others started reaching into their wallets as well. As much as I tried to stop them, they wouldn't take no for an answer. Before I knew it, the Help-Simone-Show-the-World-She's-Got-Curves fund was 120 dollars richer.

"You guys, I can't," I said as I swiped at my eyes. Over

my glasses at first, which I quickly realized didn't help. I couldn't believe I was crying. Although now that I wasn't stuffing myself with sugar, I did find that it happened more than it used to. Back when I was numbing out with Krimpets, I practically never cried.

"Of course you can, honey," Cheryl said as she patted my cheek gently. "It's what mothers do. Even the ones who didn't give birth to you."

"And because you're family now, that means you can't say no," added Cookie.

After years of being bumped into, whacked in the head, and ignored, suddenly being seen was a lot to get used to. For the first few weeks after Operation Whatever Bird It Was Called, everyone at Castle Heights began to call me the New Girl because they thought I had just transferred there. Once word got around that, actually, I had gone to school with most of them since middle school, the buzz became even louder. How had I done it? Liposuction? Fat camp? Some sort of spell that I had gotten from the in-store witch at the Psychic Eye Bookshop? After being invisible for so long, the stares and whispers kind of freaked me out, especially when Nicola told me that the ones from guys were because they thought I looked good—not stupid. The hardest part was learning to trust it. Every time someone said, "I like your dress" or "Your hair looks good," I kept waiting for that to be followed by something like, "But really . . . who do you think you're kidding?" I used to go through my days holding my breath in an attempt to hold my stomach in—now I was holding my breath because I was waiting for the entire school to line up and point and laugh at me. Nicola told me to get used to it, and that the more time that went by, the more normal it would feel. But it was still hard.

One night, after a pseudo family dinner (takeout from the Whole Foods because Hillary felt that learning how to cook made her less of a feminist), I holed up in my room to do my homework. Right after I allowed myself a quick glance at Jason Frank's Facebook page. Even though we weren't officially friends, he was one of those people who didn't change his privacy settings, which meant the entire world could see everything on his page. I didn't look often—just *occasionally*, in case those find-out-who's-been-viewing-your-Facebook-page apps really did work, even though Nicola said they didn't. She better hope they didn't, because if they did, then Nate Buckner—her ex, who was dating That Skank, aka Madison—would have some serious grounds for having her arrested for stalking.

I wasn't sure why I was wasting my time. Sure, Jason grunted hello to me if and when we crossed paths in the hall, but that didn't mean he liked me—even if Nicola kept insisting she had recently seen him staring at me a few times during lunch from the Ramp post-makeover. And I didn't like him because . . . well, because that would be a total waste of time and energy. Maybe now the idea of my someday having a boyfriend wasn't completely out of the realm of possibility, but someone as popular as Jason? Forget it. If I were going to let myself crush on someone, it would have been someone more appropriate for my social standing. Which I guess meant either (a) someone in one of the unsexy language clubs, like the Ukrainian or Korean, or (b) a total burnout. Seeing that (c) I only had an interest in learning French and (d) I considered drugs really stupid, neither of those was going to happen, which meant that I was going to stay crush-less. And just sneak peeks at Jason's page every once in a while. In case, you know, he had posted a photo of Cheryl of something.

I was in the process of trying to figure out where his latest friend Sunshine Ray from Topanga (hippy central) went to school (it was probably Crossroads, but I wasn't sure) when there was a knock on the door. Before I could say, "Come in," it opened. "Hello, hello," Hillary bubbled. She held out a plate of cookies. "You barely touched your food at dinner," she said. "So I figured you might be hungry."

I barely touched dinner because it had been macaroni and cheese and German potato salad drowning in mayonnaise. Ironically, Hillary was the one person who barely showed any reaction to my new look, even though she was the one most into appearances. The first time she saw me post-makeover, I saw the surprise on her face, but instead of saying something like, "Wow—look at your haircut!" or "I had no idea you actually had legs!" all she said was, "Simone, you haven't seen my box of Frownies, have you?" which were these little patches you put on your face while you slept in order to prevent wrinkles.

"Thanks, but I had a big lunch," I replied, looking around for something heavier than a pillow to hit her over the head with in case she tried to force-feed me. It was like the woman was trying to kill me with carbs.

She shrugged as she dusted off the seat of my desk chair before sitting down. "So Simone—now that you're finally starting to show an interest in fashion, even if it's, you know, used things that might be infested with bed-bugs—"

What was up with the bedbug thing? "I prefer the term vintage, pre-owned, or gently used."

She shrugged. "Vintage, covered with bedbugs—same thing. By the way, are bedbugs fatal?"

"I don't think so."

"Too bad," she replied. "I mean, *good*. Anyway, I thought maybe we could have a whole girls' day and go shopping this weekend!" she said. "It's such a mother/daughter thing to do."

"But you're not my mother."

"Well, no, but I'm your father's soon-to-be wife," she said.

"You're not engaged," I clarified.

"Well, not *officially*, with a ring or anything," she admitted. "But obviously, that's the plan."

Sure, it was her plan, but what about my dad's? The few times I had tried to ask him, he had changed the subject.

She stopped looking in the mirror and glanced at the walls I had recovered with old French movie posters. Luckily, Nicola and I had been able to get all my stuff back from the storage space, so it was now my room again. "I keep meaning to tell you, if you want, I can have my assistant get you some posters of some current movies. The one for the new animated musical about the cow who wants to be a Broadway dancer is *so* cute."

"Thanks, but I'm good," I replied. Maybe I was being too mean. Obviously, Hillary and I would never end up with a Hallmark commercial-type relationship, but she *was* trying . . . in her own twisted, warped way. "So this shopping thing . . . that sounds fun. I'd love to."

"Fabulous! We'll make a whole day of it on Saturday, complete with lunch. Maybe somewhere with Italian food or milk shakes. We're going to give your dad's credit card a *serious* workout." As she walked out, she stopped at the smoke detector above the door. "You don't really need this, do you?"

"Well, if there were ever a fire, it would be kind of helpful, don't you think?"

"Mm, I guess. It just ruins the whole . . . look of the room, though." She shrugged. "It's okay. We'll keep it up. For now."

I was a bit surprised when, instead of turning right on Camden Drive into the Barneys New York parking lot on Saturday, Hillary kept going down Wilshire toward Hollywood. And I was even more confused when she made a left onto Fairfax and then a right into the parking lot where Ross Dress for Less and Kmart were.

"What are we doing?" I asked as Hillary pulled into a parking space next to a beaten-up gold Chevy Impala. "Do you need socks or something?" For people who actually cared about clothes like she did, Kmart and Ross were solely socks-and-underwear destinations.

"No. This is *your* day, Simone!" she said as got out of the car and walked toward the Ross entrance. "But I've been dying to check this place out. It's supposed to be *very* cool."

The only thing that would make Ross Dress for Less cool to someone like Hillary is if Justin Bieber tweeted about it. Which would probably make Jason Frank shop there.

As soon as we walked in, Hillary made a beeline over to the misses section and held up a very large sweatshirt that said MY HEART BELONGS TO MY CAT over a picture of a kitten playing with a ball of yarn. "Ooh, look!" She held it up to me. "This would look so cute on you!"

I pushed it away. "I'm allergic to cats." I looked at the tag. "Plus, it's a size XXL."

She went through the racks and held up one that said PROPERTY OF A SPOILED ROTTEN CHIHUAHUA. "How about this one?"

Cute animal sweatshirts? Really? "If I had a chihuahua—or even a dog—that might work," I replied, "but I don't."

"Wow. I never would have guessed from your wardrobe that you were so picky," she replied. Once I managed to get myself disentagled from the reindeer Christmas cardigan that Hillary was trying to wrap me in ("You can never stock up on holiday wear too early!" she cried as I started sneezing from the acrylic) and made my way over to the juniors section, I was in business. I'm not sure where I had picked up the idea that the bordering-on-too-much-cuteness of a pink-and-white seersucker sundress could be fixed by putting a black mohair cardigan with little pearl buttons over it, but when I tried the outfit on, it totally worked. And the same sweater with a white tank top, denim pedal pushers, and black ballet flats was also a great look. Still, every time I tried something on, I was half waiting for someone to come in and arrest me for impersonating a girl with style.

"Simone, look what I found," I heard Hillary say as I tried on a stretchy denim jacket with a blue-and-white-pinstriped sundress.

I turned around to see her holding an orange and brown caftan. "Oh wow. That's . . . *interesting*," I said. "If I were, I don't know, going on a cruise or something. With a bunch of senior citizens."

"Did you put that outfit together yourself?"

I nodded. "Yeah. And the whole thing together only costs thirty-two dollars." Not only did I have a flair for putting together French-looking ensembles, but I also seemed to have a nose for bargains. "What do you think?"

She shrugged. "Oh, I don't know. I mean, it looks like what the model on the cover of last month's *Elle* was wearing, which I guess *some* people might think is cool and all, but . . . do you really think it's your style?"

"Well, seeing that I've never had a style before, I'm not sure," I replied. "But it's so cheap, I figure why not give it a try, right?"

She sighed. "I guess." She held up a green rayon dress with an autumn leaf print that was so wrinkled it looked like it had been run over by a car, which then had backed up over it again. "You sure this isn't more your speed?"

I shook my head. "I think I'm good. Thanks."

Just then some crazy lady a few doors down, who had been muttering about how she used to be someone before the recession, lumbered over to us. She leaned in and squinted. "What color lipstick is that?" she shouted.

I leaned back. Wow. Someone sure liked onions. "I'm not wearing any," I replied. "This is their natural color."

Now that my hair was short, it seemed to make them look even more red.

Hillary tapped her on the back. "Excuse me, ma'am, but if you're interested, I'm wearing M.A.C. Ruby Woo," she announced as she pursed her lips.

The woman squinted at Hillary. "Nah. Too much of a bluish tint. But this one over here," she said, pointing at me, "she's got the perfect red." She patted me on the cheek. "I hope you put those smackers to good use, honey." She turned to Hillary. "She's a real beauty, isn't she?"

Hillary forced a smile. "She sure is."

I saw a red corduroy newsboy cap sitting on a bench and picked it up and added it to my outfit. I wasn't usually a hat person, but it worked really well with my bob and glasses. I looked at Hillary and smiled. "You know, I think I might actually be able to get into this whole shopping thing."

The thing about shopping at places like Ross and Kmart (While I am so not a Selena Gomez fan, her cork-wedge sandals? Super cute.) is that you get a lot for your money. Which is why, after we had paid for it (well, after my dad had paid for it), I ended up bogged down with bags as we made our way back to the car. None of which Hillary even offered to help me carry, even though she hadn't bought anything ("Wear stuff from *here*? I don't think so," she sniffed, after I held up a cute little lavender Jaclyn Smith tank top in Kmart that I thought might look good on her). And because I was bogged down with bags, I couldn't walk very fast. Which meant that when I saw Jason Frank coming out of Whole Foods, all sweaty in shorts and a tank top, chugging some sort of Gatorade thing, I couldn't just take off.

"Simone!" a voice called. A voice that, unfortunately, sounded very similar to Jason's. "Wait up!"

I didn't wait up. I kept walking. Faster.

Hillary, though, did not. She stopped and turned around. "Is he talking to you?" she asked.

"Probably not," I said, walking faster. "There are a lot of Simones in L.A.," I lied. "Almost as many as there are Madisons."

"Hey! Simone Walker!" Jason called.

"He *is* talking to you," Hillary said. "But he's so . . . *cute*."

Realizing my options were to either make a run for it and get mowed down by the white Cadillac that was weaving its way through the parking lot, driven by what looked to be a very old, very short woman peering over the steering wheel, or just stop walking and attempt to be a normal human being who had some experience talking to human beings who happened to have penises, I went with the latter. Although the thought did cross my mind that if the Cadillac swerved and hit me, it wouldn't suck.

"Hey Jason," I said as nonnervously as possible when he got to us. Why was I nervous? I hadn't been that way the last few times we had talked. Was it because I had a lot less skin covered?

"Hey," he said.

Usually, I found sweatiness really gross, but I had to say it was a good look for him.

"You, uh, cut your hair," he said.

I nodded. "A few weeks ago."

"It looks good. You can see your face now."

I nodded again. Maybe I could get away with convincing him I had laryngitis. The last thing I needed was to embarrass myself in front of Hillary by saying something dumb.

"It *is* cute, isn't it?" Hillary asked. "Although if my eyes aren't playing tricks on me, I'd swear that the right side is just a *little* longer than the left. And not on purpose. But I guess that's what you get when you go to one of those walk-in places!"

Luckily, Hillary was going to do it for me.

She flashed a smile at Jason and held out her hand. "I'm Hillary Stone, senior VP of development and production at LOL Films and Simone's soon-to-be stepmother." I wondered if people in other cities introduced themselves with their job title or if it was only here in L.A. "And you are?"

"Jason."

"Nice to meet you, Jason. I'm assuming you're a classmate of Simone's rather than a boyfriend, since the time I peeked on her Facebook page when she was in the bathroom, her relationship status said 'single.'"

I looked at her, horrified. Soon my location would say "in jail," because I was going to kill her. Luckily, before she could do any more damage, her cell rang.

She looked at it. "It's my shrink. I have to schedule an emergency session to process my frustration that your father is having so much trouble moving through his commitment issues. Excuse me," she said as she walked away.

At least she didn't have any problem embarrassing herself, either.

"So that's your stepmother, huh?" Jason asked.

"Not yet," I replied. "Hopefully, not ever."

He nodded.

As we stood there in silence, I was glad to see that he seemed to be no better than I was in terms of the whole conversation-making thing. Instead he looked at the ground, where he seemed to be fascinated with an empty Rockstar can that was rolling around.

He pointed at my bags. "So you did some shopping?"

I nodded as I tried to juggle my bags. "Yeah. Just a few things for summer." As I juggled, I dropped one of the bags, and it spilled open. Unfortunately, it happened to be the bag with the bra and underwear portion of my purchases. "And, some, uh, other things," I said as I quickly shoved them back in the bag. I may have never kissed a boy before, but I could go to my grave saying that Jason Frank had seen my underwear.

"Okay, well, I should probably get going," he said, sounding a little freaked.

"Yeah. I think that would be a good idea," I replied.

"See you around."

"Uh-huh," I mumbled.

As I watched him walk away, Hillary drove up. "You ready?" she called out the window.

I nodded and started to walk toward the car.

"Simone, before you get in, can you do me a favor and take a look at the trunk and make sure it's closed? I feel like I hear it rattling."

As I walked behind, the car moved back, right toward me.

"Hillary?" I called out. "What are you doing?"

Instead of stopping, it continued. Faster.

"Hey, what are you doing?!" I yelled. "You're going to hit me!" Just as I was about to get mowed down, I jumped out of the way.

She stuck her head out the window. "Whoops. Sorry about that. Sometimes the gear gets caught in reverse instead of drive," she said with a smile. "You okay?"

I nodded and, wobbly-kneed, made my way over to the passenger side. Hadn't she ever heard of brakes?

At least if I had gotten flattened into a pancake I wouldn't have to worry about having another awkward conversation with Jason Frank.

"She sounds like a real Shelly Stewart," Naomi said a few days later when I told the Zumba Brigade about my outing with Hillary, leaving out the part about my run-in with Jason because I didn't need his mom, Cheryl, knowing about it and embarrassing either of us. Naomi was a new member of the ZB and my latest Facebook friend. You would have thought that as women with husbands and kids and jobs, they'd be too busy for quizzes and Farmville and YouTube videos of dogs nursing a litter of motherless kittens, but that wasn't the case. While I appreciated being considered one of the five special women in Marcia's life on those post-this-on-the-walls-of-five-special-women-in-your-life-and-let-them-know-how-much-you-care-(or-else-risk-a-lifetime-of-bad-luck) messages, and Cookie's all-caps "U R DA BOMB, SIMONE!!!!! (DID I SAY THAT RIGHT?) XOXOXO" messages, it was starting to get a little embarrassing. Especially because it made it look as if my only real friends other than Nicola were middle-aged moms. Which was pretty much the truth, but Facebook didn't need to know that.

"Who's Shelly Stewart?" I asked. She wasn't part of our group. "Is she that woman who was in class last week wearing the I BRAKE FOR LOEHMANN'S T-shirt?"

"No. Shelly was Morty Cushman's girlfriend," explained Cheryl.

"Who's Morty Cushman? Is he that chiropractor you threatened to sue?" Nicola asked. People in L.A. loved to sue other people.

"No. Morty was Brenda's ex-husband," Gwen replied.

Nicola and I looked at each other, confused. Although

I hadn't been able to convince her to Zumba with me ("Simone, you know you're my best friend in the whole world, but even quality time with you can't cure my allergy to exercise"), she had begun to join us post-workout for coffee. Unlike Hillary, the Zumba ladies hadn't gotten the memo that Nicola's ever-changing hair color was a very popular form of self-expression, which meant that every time she showed up with a different look, there was some major cringing going on. At least on the lesser-Botoxed faces in the group.

"They're from *The First Wives Club*," Rona explained.

"What's *The First Wives Club*?" Nicola asked. "Is that over on Wilshire Boulevard near Whole Foods?"

A row of lipsticked O's faced us. "It's only one of the greatest movies ever made," Cheryl said. "Bette Midler? Diane Keaton? GOLDIE HAWN?"

Nicola shook her head. "Never heard of it. I tend to stick to Monty Python," she said. She pointed to me. "As for her, if it's not a depressing French film where people sit in cafés debating the meaning of life while puffing on cigarettes, she's not interested."

"That's not entirely true," I said. "It doesn't *have* to be depressing. It just has to be French."

Cheryl sighed as she patted me on my arm. "My husband would love you." I wondered how Jason's dad—a man with such great taste—felt about the fact that his son listened to Justin Bieber.

"Shouldn't you girls be watching movies with that Austin Katcher boy? Or Tyler Laufer?" Cookie asked. "They're both such warmies."

" 'Hotties,' " I corrected.

She took out her notebook and made a note.

"Who?" asked Nicola.

"I think she means Ashton Kutcher and Taylor Lautner."

Nicola wrinkled her nose. "But they're such . . . *boys*. Simone and I, we like . . . *real* men. Like . . . loggers. Or ranchers."

I looked at her. "What are you talking about? We hate being outside."

She shrugged. "Well, *we* wouldn't actually go outside. *They* would. We'd stay by the fire and . . . I don't know . . . *knit*."

I rolled my eyes. "Speak for yourself. I have no idea what my type is." Although after my run-in in the parking lot with Jason, I was thinking maybe I could hold off on that whole interaction-with-the-opposite-sex thing for a while longer.

"Anyway," Cheryl went on, "in the movie, Shelly Stewart was this very mean young woman, played by Sarah Jessica Parker, who started dating Morty—I can't remember who played him—when he divorced Bette Midler—"

"Sarah Jessica Parker played someone mean?" Nicola asked. "But she's always so nice. Probably because she made all that money off of *Sex and the City*."

"I know," Cheryl agreed. "This was before that show. Oh, and I should add that she was *a lot* younger than Bette."

"Well, Hillary *is* a lot younger than my dad," I said. "And I think it would be fair to say that she's a little . . . *challenged* on the nice front."

Cheryl rolled her eyes. "Oh please, honey," she said. "You're with friends here. From everything you've said, the woman sounds like an overwaxed, overstraightened, unwrinkled nightmare."

Wow. Who knew middle-aged women could be so harsh? It sounded like something you'd hear coming from one of the tables on the Ramp, except these girls had poochy stomachs.

"I guess that's one way of describing Hillary," I agreed.

"She's probably just jealous of you," Cookie said.

"Jealous of *me*?" I asked. "For what?" As far as I could see, the only thing I had going for me that Hillary didn't was the fact that, because I was double-jointed, I could touch my wrist with my thumb. And although I was pretty proud of it, the one time I showed her, not only did she not seem impressed, but she told me to please stop right away because we were in the middle of dinner and it was making her nauseous.

"Because you're smart . . ." Gwen said.

". . . even if you've never seen *The First Wives Club*," Marcia said.

Okay, so I was a little bit smart. Like fourth-in-my-grade smart, even though I didn't advertise it, because I didn't need to be called That Weird Fat Smart Girl.

". . . and witty," Brenda added.

Fine. Maybe I was a little bit witty. But when your social life is kind of nonexistent, you've got a lot of time on your hands to work on that stuff.

". . . and not afraid to be your own person," Rona said. She shook her head. "I'm telling you, what I would've given for my Marci to have been more of her own person when she was your age, instead of trying to be like all the other girls at her school," she sighed. "Do you have any idea how much we ended up spending on therapy for her when she graduated from college and wouldn't get out of bed for the next three months after she decided she had no identity?"

"Ladies, not to sound superficial or anything," Cheryl said, "even though, because it *is* L.A. that would obviously be forgiven, but there's a giant elephant in the room that everyone seems to be avoiding."

Maybe it was because of the brain cells she had wasted back when she was younger and had followed this band called the Grateful Dead around the country, but I wasn't too surprised to see Marcia nervously glance around the Coffee Bean as if she were on the lookout for an actual elephant.

"What?" I asked.

"The elephant is the fact that you happen to be *gorgeous*!" she trilled. "Especially with your new look."

"Riiiiiiight," the rest of the women said in unison as they nodded their heads.

I looked over at Nicola for some help, but all she did was shrug. "Maybe no one's called you gorgeous before," Nicola said, "but when I was in line in the cafeteria the other day, I did hear Matt Durkin tell Charlie Rackoff that you had a nice butt."

I looked at her, surprised. "You didn't tell me that."

She rolled her eyes. "We're talking *Matt Durkin* here," she said. "The kid who has yet to outgrow his paste-eating habit. Would that really have been of interest to you?"

"Good point," I agreed.

"It will be good for you to get away from Hillary for a while," Cheryl said. "From everything you've told us, that woman is bad news."

The last few weeks of school kept my mind off of what I was getting myself into—especially as I took in the fact that kids came up to me and asked me to sign their yearbooks while writing things in mine like "Have a great summer—hope to get to know you better next year" and "U have killer style!" But now that school was over and I was about to move in with my brother, I was getting more and more nervous, to the point where my appetite was almost nonexistent.

"What if it's really dirty?" I asked Nicola as we got out of my car on D-day ("Will you *please* stop with the negative attitude?!" Nicola said every time I referred to moving day as that). We hauled my stuff to the front door. Originally, my dad was going to come with me—sort of as a quality-time/bon-voyage-type thing—but then Hillary reminded him that she had made plans for them to have brunch with her best friend Cricket ("Did I mention she's one of the top wedding coordinators in the city?").

At least he felt so bad that when Hillary wasn't looking, he slipped me two hundred dollars and told me to do something nice for myself. Which, if I continued to stay this anxious, might possibly include a return to my snack-cake hobby.

I took a look at my new home for the summer. Like a lot of the houses in the neighborhood, it was a Craftsman. But unlike the other ones on the street, with nice landscaping and flowers, this one had a gnome family in positions that wouldn't exactly earn it a G rating if they starred in a movie.

"These are college boys. I'm sure they're very neat," Nicola replied. "Max wouldn't live with a bunch of slobs. He smells too good to do something like that." She smoothed the ends of her hair, which that day, due to an unfortunate run-in with a bottle of red dye that looked more orange once it was applied, was covered with a bandanna that had been worn by an actress who was an extra in *Bridesmaids*. "Do I look okay?"

"He's not here. He's working today."

"Oh bloody hell. I put on mascara and everything." She yanked off her bandanna. "Probably better off, seeing that I look like Ronald McDonald." She took in my baby-blue dress with the sailor collar that I had gotten off eBay for twenty-five bucks, after a frenzied bidding war with some user named VintageVixen. "You, on the other hand, look like you should be boarding a ship for Paris. Nice get."

"Thanks," I said. "I just wish it weren't polyester." I gave a quick sniff at my left armpit, relieved to determine I was okay. Polyester and sweat did not mix well.

When we got to the door, I rang the doorbell, but from the thumping electronica that was coming from inside, we would have been standing out there until tomorrow. As soon as we walked in the door, we both covered our noses.

"Ewwww," I said. I didn't even know how to describe the smell. It was like a combination of rotting pineapple and yogurt that was about three weeks past its expiration date.

"Okay, so maybe you're going to want to buy a can of air freshener," Nicola said.

"A can? Try a case," I replied. I looked around at the pizza-stained paper plates and dented cans of Red Bull that littered the coffee table. "And I should probably get a Dumpster while I'm at it, too."

As we stood there taking in the disaster zone that I was going to call home for the next month, a dust bunny danced its way across the floor. "That thing has better rhythm than I do," I said. "It's moving in time to the music." It wasn't like I was a neat freak or anything, but this was ridiculous. "This is like my worst-case scenario times ten."

Nicola walked over to the plaid couch and yanked out a red-and-white-striped tube sock that was peeking out from between the cushions and held it up. "Were dirty socks included in your worst-case scenario?"

I shook my head. "No. I was trying to stay positive."

She reached in between the other cushions and pulled out a pair of navy-blue boxer shorts with little white whales on them.

"Ewwww!" we screeched in unison.

Boxer shorts were *definitely* not part of the worst-case scenario.

As she threw them toward me, a sleepy-looking short guy with a serious case of blond bedhead and a soul patch walked out of one of the rooms scratching his stomach and the boxers landed smack on top of his head.

He pulled them off and squinted at them. "Oh cool. I've been looking for these. These are Tuesday's."

Nicola pointed to the pair he was wearing—yellow with little green frogs. "So I'm guessing those are Saturday's," she said.

He looked down. "Yes. No. Wait. Saturday's are red with little monkeys. These are . . . Thursday's."

"You haven't changed your underwear since Thursday?" I asked nervously. What had I gotten myself into? Dust bunnies could be taken care of with a broom, but guys who didn't change their underwear?

He thought about it for a second. "Nope. I did. I change them every morning. I was just really tired when I grabbed these out of the drawer yesterday. I swear." He yawned. "Oh, man. I need coffee."

"Are you just getting up now?" Nicola asked.

"Yeah."

"At two o'clock?"

"It's only two? Cool. It's still early," he replied while scratching his stomach. "So who are you guys?"

"I'm Simone," I said.

Nothing. Well, except for another yawn.

"Max's sister?" I added.

"Cool. I didn't know he had a sister."

Nicola and I looked at each other nervously. Because he was so busy looking at the bright side of things, my brother could be a little spacey at times, but it's not like he would've forgotten to tell his roommates I was moving in for a month.

"He did tell you that I'm going to be staying here for a while . . . didn't he?" I asked nervously.

The guy yawned again and thought about it. "Nope."

Apparently, not only *could* he space on it, but he had. This was just great.

"But it's all good. Welcome. I'm totally digging your specs."

"Thanks."

"I'm Chris, by the way," he said. "But feel free to call me Narc. Everyone else does."

"Are you a cop?" I asked nervously. It wasn't like I did drugs or shoplifted or any of that kind of stuff, but just being around cops made me feel guilty. Even mall cops.

"Oooh, can I see your gun?" Nicola asked excitedly.

"Not that kind of narc. Narc as in narcolepsy," he explained. "Where you fall asleep all the time." He pointed to a room where I could make out a messy unmade bed. "That's my room. Well, mine and Noob's."

"What's a noob?" Nicola asked.

"It's not some sort of reptile, is it?" I demanded. My brother did not say *anything* about reptiles. Ever since he had put a salamander in my bed when I was eight and it almost crawled into my open mouth while I was sleeping, I had a huge phobia of them.

"I think you're thinking of a newt." He turned to Nicola. "Hey, are you living here, too?"

She shook her head.

"Too bad," he said with a smile. This Narc guy was pretty cute—especially if you went for the sleepy-eyes/bedhead look, which, from the way I watched Nicola turn red, it seemed that she did. Plus, having her crush on someone who was related to me only by living situation rather than blood would be a lot less awkward for me.

"You could've taught me how to speak with an English accent to impress girls."

So much for that idea. And from the way that Nicola stopped arching her back in an attempt to make it look like she had boobs behind her REALITY IS FOR PEOPLE WITH NO IMAGINATION T-shirt, she felt the same way.

"Anyway, it's not a what—it's a who," he explained. "Noob's real name is . . ." He thought about it. "You know, I don't *know* what it is. Ever since I've met him, he's just always been Noob."

"But how come?" I asked. "What does it mean?"

"It comes from the gaming world. It means someone who's new to a game and really, really stupid," he explained. "As opposed to a 'newb'—spelled n-e-w-b. That's someone who's new to a game but who you can tell will eventually get it. But noobs?" He shook his head. "They're just perpetually clueless. Like low-brain-cell-count stupid."

I nodded. "Got it." Glad to see my brother had left this part out.

Narc yawned again. "I think I'm gonna go crash for a while."

"I thought you said you were going to get coffee," I said.

"I was. But I changed my mind. I'm beat." He padded toward his room. "See you later. Make yourself comfortable. We're pretty laid back around here."

"Yeah, I can see that," I said, as I looked around at the chaise lounges—the kind you saw on outdoor patios—that served as furniture in this place.

Narcs, noobs, pizza crusts, boxer shorts . . . what had I just signed up for?

I turned to Nicola. "Toto, I have a feeling we're not north of Montana anymore."

six

Between the glass-half-fullism and the fact that he liked to put maple syrup on cornflakes, I had always thought of my brother as a little weird. But after I met the rest of his roommates? He looked as normal as someone in a J.Crew catalog.

"Okay, guys," Max said a few hours later, after everyone living in the house had been called together via text for a house meeting. After Narc went back to sleep, Nicola and I bolted out of there. We spent the rest of the day on Abbot Kinney hanging out with Brad and brainstorming about how to tell her mom I was going to have to move in for the month until I got Max's text. "Remember how the last few days I've been saying that I feel like there's something I've been forgetting to do?"

The five guys sprawled around the room stopped chomping on chips and chugging Red Bulls long enough to nod. Until one of the guys—who looked to be a little younger than me and was wearing a HARRY POTTER IS ALIVE AND LIVING IN NEW JERSEY T-shirt—raised his hand. "Wait. I don't remember that."

"How can you not remember that?" Max asked. "I specifically remember saying it during the massacre in the shower as we were watching *Sorority Girl Slaughterhouse* the other night."

Nicola and I looked at each other. The idea of my brother somehow thinking of me while watching a horror movie was a little weird.

"And then I said it again when we watching the original *Halloween* on channel eleven and the commercial came on for the My Pretty Pony doll."

Okay, that made more sense. Back when I was six, Max and I had put My Pretty Pony in the microwave to thaw her out after I had put her in the freezer so she could cool off with some air-conditioning. Needless to say, from the funeral we had to have in the backyard afterward, it didn't go over well.

"And then—" Suddenly, he stopped and peered at the kid. "Wait a minute. Who *are* you?"

The kid reached for some more chips. "I'm Herbert. I live across the street. I came over to give him some pointers on Death Watch Seven." He pointed to a guy with short dreads and a soul patch sitting on the stairs trying to get his arm out from between the slats in the banister.

"Are you Noob?" I asked.

The guy looked up and nodded. "Yeah!" His forehead got all wrinkly. "Wait a minute—how'd you know that?"

"I—"

He gasped. "Are you . . . *psychic*?"

"No. I just figured it out from what Narc had told me."

"Oh," he said, disappointed. He shrugged. "Well, that's okay. I'm not psychic, either."

My brother looked at Herbert. "Herbert, it's very nice to meet you, but this is a house meeting. Meaning for people who live in *this* house—not the one across the street."

"I love that dude House," Noob announced to no one in particular as he tried to wiggle his arm out of the banister, "You know who I'm talking about? The doctor with his own TV show? The one who walks funny?"

"Okay," Herbert said. "I get it. I know when I'm not wanted." He stood up to leave.

"It's okay. You can stay," Max sighed. Max was a sucker for the less fortunate. Which was very time-consuming when you had to walk past people soliciting money for that creepy Children International thing at the mall, because he always stopped and not only donated but then made the mistake of asking the people how they got involved in the organization.

"Cool," Herbert said, plopping back down and grabbing another handful of chips.

"Now. Back to what I was saying," Max continued. "Thanks to my sister, Simone, here," he said, motioning to me as I stood next to him yanking at the hem of my dress because it suddenly felt very short, even though it came to my knees, "I remembered what it was. I forgot to tell you guys that she's going to be staying here for a little bit."

"What about the other girl? Is she staying, too?" Herbert asked hopefully.

"No. Nicola isn't staying here," Max replied. He glanced at her. "You're not, are you?"

I could tell from the way that Nicola's blue eyes bugged out so wide that they were in danger of turning inside out that the fact that my brother had spoken directly to her was going to appear in the next installment of the "Monumental Moments in Recent History" section of her Tumblr. In, of course, some cryptic form so that it wouldn't be clear that she was talking about him in case he happened to Google her and came across it (which, although I didn't say this to her because I didn't want to hurt her feelings, probably wasn't going to happen). After she opened her mouth to speak but nothing came out, she cleared her throat. "Well, I wasn't planning on it, but I mean, if you *wanted* me to, I guess I could ask my parents."

Max looked nervous.

"Or, you know, *not*," she continued. "I could just come visit. A lot. Luckily, I didn't get that job I applied for at the mall—it was to work at one of those carts, for this Dead Sea bath salt thing, which, to be honest, I found to be a little sketchy, because even though it said 'Authentically from the Dead Sea in Israel' on the package, it also said 'Made in Taiwan' in little letters on the back," she babbled, "so as of now, I'm totally free."

As my brother looked at me, confused, I shrugged. So much for Nicola clamming up whenever she was around my brother. It was like someone had given her mouth a laxative.

A guy with red hair and a smattering of freckles across his cheekbones looked up from what seemed to be a very big textbook. "Max, could you better define 'little bit' for us?" he asked. "I think I speak for the group when I say that would be helpful." He looked at the group. "Right, guys?"

The group looked at each other and shrugged.

The guy sighed. "Precision is such an underrated virtue. I'm Ethan, by the way,"

"But we all call him Doc," Max said. "He's pre-med at UCLA. We found him off Craigslist when my roommate Peter backed out when he got that gig as Ryan Reynolds' stand-in in his new movie."

If there was a Ryan Reynolds look-alike living here, I wouldn't care how messy it was. I nodded. "Got it." With his green polo shirt and brown khakis, Doc was the most normal looking of the bunch.

"I like your glasses, by the way," Ethan/Doc said.

"Thanks," I said. I couldn't believe how much mileage I was getting out of them. Even some homeless woman on the street had complimented me on them.

Doc turned to Max. "So. As you were saying. A 'little bit' would mean . . . ?"

"Kind of around . . . a month?"

I waited for a chorus of annoyed "Dude, are you *kidding*?!'s, but all that happened was that Noob let out a loud "Phew!" as he finally managed to free his arm.

For good or for bad, these guys seemed very laid back.

Over by Narc, an Asian guy wearing a Boston Celtics hat sneezed.

"God bless you," I said.

"Thanks," he said as he took out a tissue. "Please tell me that you don't wear perfume," he said after he was done blowing his nose.

I shook my head. "I don't." Now that I was dressing like a girl, it was probably something to look into, but I found it gross.

He sneezed again.

"God bless you again."

"Than—" he managed to get out before another sneeze ripped through him. This one was sort of a sneeze/cough hybrid.

I waited for it to happen again, but other than a donkey-sounding throat-clearing sound, he was quiet. He smiled. "Thanks." He turned to Max. "You didn't mention how polite your sister is."

"That's because he didn't mention he *had* a sister," Narc said.

"Yeah, well, still—none of you guys bless me."

"Don't you have to be, like, a priest to do that?" came Noob's voice from over in the corner. I looked over to see him trying, unsuccessfully, to get up into a headstand.

"It looks like he's trying to do a headstand," I whispered to Max.

"I *am* trying to do a headstand!" Noob called out happily as I made a mental note to remember that what the guy lacked for brains he made up in superhero-level hearing. "You know those little video screens in elevators? Last week when I was making a delivery at this ad agency—I'm doing this bike messenger gig for the summer 'cause it's hard to get a sculpting gig around here—I saw something that said that doing a headstand for forty-five minutes a day, three times a week, was good for your heart."

"Are you sure it didn't say forty-five minutes of *cardio* three times a week?" Max asked.

Noob flopped over again. "Huh. I don't know. Maybe." He looked at me. "I never did very well on the reading-comprehension parts of standardized tests."

The Celtics fan sniffled. "Okay, so you don't wear perfume, but do you by any chance wear scented body lotion?"

I shook my head.

"Huh. I wonder what's causing this allergy attack then."

Narc shook his head. "Dude, what *aren't* you allergic to?" He turned to me. "That's Wheezer."

"You know, Wheezer, I keep meaning to tell you, I think it's rad that you're named after a band," Noob said. "Especially an old-time one. You know that sweater song they sing? It's, like, actually *called* 'The Sweater Song'—"

"I'm not. There's an *h* in there," Wheezer said, "'cause of, you know"—before he could finish, he sneezed again—"the fact that sometimes, when the attack is really bad, I start to wheeze," he wheezed.

Nicola and I looked at each other. Allergy attacks, arms stuck in banisters—what was I getting myself into?

Nicola let out a scream.

"What?!" I cried.

She pointed to the couch. "There's something moving underneath that blanket to the side of the couch!" she cried. In what was an excellent move on her part (albeit a very nonfeminist one) she reached out for my brother's arm. However, in her nervousness, she overshot the mark and ended up grabbing his chest instead. Which, from the look on his face, freaked him out.

"Sorry," she mumbled as she uprighted herself. "I was just . . . see, I . . . you know what? Forget it," she said, staring at the floor.

He smiled at her. "That's okay." Uh-oh. I knew I'd be spending my afternoon listening to Nicola dissect the twenty possible meanings of my brother's smile.

He turned to the blanket. "Hey Blush, what're you doing? Stop hiding and say hi to my sister."

Very slowly, the blob on the floor stood up and the blanket fell to reveal a very tall, very large, very hot African American guy. "Nice to meet you," he said softly, with his eyes to the ground.

How a person that large had a voice that soft was hard to imagine. Also hard to imagine was how he managed to stay hidden under a blanket for that long and not suffocate.

"It's nice to meet you, too," I said shyly. He looked so uncomfortable that it was making *me* uncomfortable.

"He's a little on the shy side," Max whispered, "which is why we call him Blush, but don't worry—he'll warm up."

I nodded. I knew what it was like to be shy. Maybe we could just hang out and be shy together and not talk.

Before I could ask if everyone in the house had a nickname and would I have to get one, too, the door opened and a guy with a shaved head and wearing an ANARCHY RULES T-shirt under a leather jacket and black skinny jeans came striding in. "Reason three thousand eight hundred seventy-six why I hate this dumb city—the traffic!" he fumed as he began to pace. "You'd think that at some point the brain trust here could get it together and get a decent public-transportation system up and running, but no! That would mean giving up their yoga and spin classes and fancy fresh-squeezed juices chock-full of antioxidants that make you live to a hundred and twenty, even though with the way things are going now with the government and the economy and the environment, who really *wants* to live to a hundred and twenty?!"

Scared, I looked over at my brother, but he didn't look too concerned.

The guy stopped pacing. "Huh. I think I just broke through my creative block and came up with my next spoken-word piece." He looked at me. "Who are you?"

"Thor, this is Simone, my sister," Max said happily. "She's going to be living here with us for a while. She's awesome. You're gonna love her. And this is her friend Nicola—"

"Who won't be living here, but will be visiting a lot." She looked at Max. "But not, you know, to the point where it looks like I'm a stalker or anything, because I'm totally not." She looked at Thor. "Cool name."

"His real name is Larry," Narc said.

"Yeah, but what looks better scrawled in the lower right-hand side of a canvas?" Thor asked. "Larry or Thor?" He shook his head. "I still can't believe my parents would give me such a conventional name. There's a lot of passive aggressiveness in that kind of a move." He turned to me. "Thor was the god of thunder."

That made sense. "So you're a painter?" I asked.

"Painting is one of my mediums, yes," he replied. "But I don't like to limit myself. I also do a lot of spoken-word and performance art."

"*And* he plays the ukelele," Noob said. "Isn't that rad?"

The idea of someone so angry strumming a little happy-sounding ukelele was a little . . .

"I know that probably seems ironic to you," Thor said, as if reading my mind. "But it's supposed to be. I'm very into irony. It's part of my personal artistic credo. So *what* if it's a happy instrument? With all the war, and poverty, and corruption in this world, don't you think we could use a little happiness? I mean, this government of ours—"

"Okay, so now you've met everyone," Max interrupted. Leave it to my brother to keep things from getting heavy. "So like I said, Simone's going to be with us for the next month. And just to get a few rules out of the way, I know she's beautiful, but (a) she's only sixteen," he went on, "and more importantly, (b) she's my little sister."

And leave it to him to embarrass me. "What are you doing?!" I hissed.

"What?"

"I keep telling you to stop with the beautiful thing."

"Why?"

"Because it's not true," I hissed louder.

"It so is."

"Omigod—I keep telling her the same exact thing!" cried Nicola. "I had no idea we had so much in common!"

I cringed. I didn't know who I was more embarrassed for—myself or Nicola.

Max looked out at the group. "Guys, is my sister not beautiful?"

Okay, question answered. I was definitely more embarrassed for myself. As my shoulders scrunched up to my ears, I wondered if Blush would mind if I borrowed his blanket.

"Hold on—is that totally wrong for me to say because I'm her brother?" he asked. "I don't want to come off as all creepy—"

"No, man, it's cool," Thor said. "You're expressing yourself. That's key. Our government might not like it, but—"

"I think your sister is totally hot," Noob said. "She could totally be an avatar."

Narc nodded. "For sure." He turned to me. "Just so you know, that's like the highest compliment he could ever give you." Then he yawned.

How did girls who were actually pretty deal with this? Maybe that's why supermodels always looked so pissed off, because they found the compliments so embarrassing. That, or because they were hungry.

"I think you guys need to stop," came Blush's soft voice. "You're embarrassing her."

"Thanks," I mumbled.

"Okay. Well, anyway, like I said, just be cool with her, okay?" Max said. "Just make her feel at home." He turned to me. "I think this is going really well so far, don't you?"

Sure. If you were comparing it to getting a cavity filled without Novocaine.

Originally, I was going to sleep on the couch ("We didn't get it off the street or anything, so it's clean," Max explained. "Wheezer's mom lent it to us after she saw the first one we had. Which we *had* gotten off the street."). But because Max said that as cool as his roommates were, he had woken up that day realizing he couldn't bear the idea of walking out some morning to discover one of them staring at me while I was sleeping, he decided I should sleep in the attic.

Which, if it were all done up or something—like you see on those design shows on HGTV or something—would've been cool. But this was like an *attic* attic. Complete with dusty bikes and cardboard boxes full of old clothes and board games missing either boards or pieces or—in the case of Life—both.

"It's got a lot of potential, don't you think?" Max asked later that night as we positioned the air mattress in the area with the most amount of light.

Before I could answer, a rake fell down from a hook above me, missing me by *thismuch*. "Whoops," he said, quickly picking it up and shoving it to the side. "I guess we should take down anything on the walls that could fall down in the middle of the night and possibly kill you." He started inspecting the corners of the room.

"What are you doing?" I asked.

"Just checking for mouse droppings."

I paled.

"And I don't see any, which is a great thing," he said. "So I guess I'll leave you to get settled."

"Okay," I said.

"See you in the morning," he said, giving me a hug.

"Okay."

After he left, I plopped down on the air mattress, cringing at the fart sound it made. I could tell from the way I was fantasizing about how great a sheet cake from Ralph's would taste that going from spending so much time alone to all this . . . *boyness* . . . was really screwing with my system. Kind of like being thrown into AP English when you had just emigrated from Cuba or somewhere and only gotten a C plus in your English as a Second Language course.

Maybe this was a mistake. Maybe I should have gone with my dad and Hillary and sat in the shade all day as I listened to Hillary talk about herself. And then talk about herself some more. And some more. As I thought about whether it would hurt Max's feelings if I told him that I had changed my mind and was going to go stay at Nicola's, I heard footsteps.

"You decent?" Max's voice called out. "'Cause I wouldn't want to walk in on you if you weren't. We're all about respecting boundaries here."

"I'm decent."

He poked his head in. "Okay, good. Listen—I just wanted to tell you one more thing."

"Try not to breathe too much up here because there's asbestos in the wall?"

"No. I just wanted to tell you I'm really looking forward to this next month," he said. "Getting to hang with you again. And so are the guys. They really like you. Usually, there's no talking when *Sorority Girls Slashers Part Two* is on, but they're all down there talking about how awesome and chill you are. Not, you know, like most girls."

I smiled. "Thanks. That's really sweet," I replied. "It means a lot to me."

"Well, good night."

"Good night."

I guessed I was staying.

For the most part I liked to think of myself as pretty laid back. Which is why, after I almost fell into the toilet the first time I went to pee because I didn't check to see if the seat was up, I didn't freak out. I just made a mental note to look before I sat down, which was a good thing because every time, no matter which of the two bathrooms I went to, it was up. And when I came out of one of them and smacked straight into Thor—who was wearing nothing but a towel—I kept cool and listened to him give me his take on how the world would be a much better place if people would get over their hang-ups about nudity, while praying silently that his towel didn't fall down. And when I discovered that their idea of "leftovers" included hamburgers that had turned green and fruit with mold on it, I only gagged rather than actually threw up.

However, when I came downstairs the first morning for breakfast and came face-to-face with a mouse gnawing at a three-times-removed-from-fresh slice of pizza, I lost it. As much as I knew I'd probably get grief for it, I couldn't stop the high-pitched girly-girl scream that flew out of my mouth. Possibly falling into a toilet was one thing, but rodents as roommates? No way.

"What's the matter?!" Narc asked after he, Noob, and Doc came rushing into the kitchen.

"I . . . it . . . *ewwww*!!" I cried from my perch on the counter (I had had no idea that I possessed the coordination to leap into the air and scramble onto a countertop in one fluid motion until that moment) as I watched the mouse chomp away. Although, I had to say, from the disappointed expression on the mouse's face, he looked pretty underwhelmed by the taste.

"Oh man. Tell me I didn't forget . . ." Noob said as he looked down at his sweats. "Phew," he said, relieved. "For a second I thought I had forgotten to put pants on this morning."

I cringed. The idea of Noob walking around without pants was almost as disturbing as the mouse. "Does that . . . happen a lot?" I asked.

"Not, you know, *a lot* a lot," he replied. "Just like, I don't know . . . every other day?"

The mouse stopped eating. As it made its way closer to the counter, I screamed again. Having never been in the same room as a mouse, I had had no idea I was such a wimp.

"Awww . . . look at that," Noob said. "He wants to be friends with you!"

As the mouse began to chortle, Noob leaned his head in. "What do you think he's trying to say?"

"I think he's saying that he finds it really annoying when humans try to give animals all these humanlike qualities," Narc said. He yawned. "I'm going back to bed. Right after I have some cereal." He walked to the freezer and took out a box of Corn Pops.

"Why do you keep the cereal in the freezer?" I asked. Out of the corner of my eye I kept glancing at the mouse, in case he got any big ideas and decided to try and join me on the counter.

He shrugged. "Why not?" he replied with his mouth full. "It's as good of a place as any, right?" He yawned again. "Well, good night," he said as he padded back to his room.

I shook my head and sighed. Being laid back was one thing. Living in complete and utter chaos and filth was something else. "Not to be one of those people who gets all up in people's business, but I really think you guys need—"

"Some order? Organization? A to-do list that's updated twice weekly and a whiteboard with a chart of everyone's responsibilities?!" Doc cried.

I shrank back. Whoa. Someone was a bit on the Type A side. "Well, maybe not all of that, but something—"

"Finally! A voice of sanity in this place!" he said. "I'll be right back," he said, before he ran out of the room.

"Wait! What about the mouse?" I called after him.

Without missing a beat, Noob walked up to him and scooped him up in his palm. "Hey, little guy. How ya doing? We may be a lot bigger than you, but we come in peace."

Noob may have been lacking in the brain cells department, but apparently he was a mouse whisperer, because the thing didn't squirm or squeak or do any other sort of frightened mouse-like things. Instead, he scurried up Noob's arm onto his shoulder. "Want to say hi?" he asked me as he walked over and turned his shoulder toward me.

In what was probably not the most friendly gesture, I screamed again. Which made the mouse attempt to hide under Noob's armpit.

"He's not going to hurt you," Noob said. "He just wants to be friends," he said as he moved closer to me.

I moved farther away. "I don't have a lot of rodent friends," I said. "In fact, I don't have any."

He shook his head sadly. "You know, I totally get that we still have a long ways to go before we're a color-blind nation. And I think the fact that women aren't paid as much as men for the same work or the fact that we only allow gay people to get married in some states but not all of them is total BS. But it really hurts my heart when I think about how little respect we give to our four-legged brothers and sisters. It's like the Native American issue all over again."

I sat there, speechless.

Doc walked back in the room holding a pad of paper and a pen. "Noob, take the mouse outside, please," he said. "Simone and I are going to have a meeting."

We were?

"Fine. I don't do meetings anyway," Noob sniffed. "Too much pressure." He looked down at his armpit. "Come on, *hermano*."

After they were gone, I jumped off the counter, barely missing a dented pizza box on the floor.

"Okay, so this is what I was thinking," Doc said, flipping to a page filled with a very long list written in very neat handwriting. He handed it to me. "I'd love to hear your thoughts."

"Okay, but I need to get my glasses."

He whipped his off and handed them to me. "Here. Try mine. I'm working on trying to overcome my poor eyesight."

I put them on and blinked. "Hey! We have an almost identical prescription!"

He smiled. "Really? Wow. I *knew* there was a reason I liked you right off the bat!"

I smiled. So far, out of all of the guys, Doc seemed to have the most brain cells.

"Okay. Let's see . . . '*Oh seven hundred hours—morning meeting to go over each housemate's tasks and responsibilities for the day. Said meeting will occur at oh eight hundred on Sundays, in order to give everyone an extra hour's sleep,*" I read aloud. "*Twenty-two hundred hours—evening meeting to go over aforementioned tasks and make sure all have been completed. For those who are unable to attend meeting at that time due to prior commitment such as job/surfing/etc., there will be an alternative one at nineteen hundred hours. For those unable to attend that one, please e-mail Doc with the subject line reading—*" I looked up from the notebook and pushed the glasses up the bridge of my nose. While our prescriptions were the same, the size of our heads definitely was not. "Um, Doc, I totally get the fact that this place would really benefit from a little more organization—"

"I know you do," he said. "That's why I knew you'd be the right person to ask for help—"

"But I think that all this"—I flipped through the pages that were covered with writing—"might be a little too much."

"You do?" he asked, disappointed.

I nodded.

"Even the part where we hire a shrink for a day to

oversee a group therapy session in an attempt to facilitate better communication between group members?"

"Especially that part."

"Oh." His face turned red as he looked down at the ground. "Yeah. I guess when you think about it, it's kind of a dumb idea." He sighed as he reached out for the notebook. Which, because he wasn't wearing his glasses, he missed completely.

I took off his glasses and placed them back on his face. "It's not a dumb idea at all," I said gently. "It's more like, when you're dealing with people who don't have the same values as you, you just need to . . . *adjust your expectations* a little." I had overheard my dad use that term once when he was talking to my grandmother, who had called him to complain about how she found the way that Hillary had offered to get her in for an appointment with her dermatologist to do something about all her wrinkles incredibly rude. That was definitely how I had dealt with Hillary. To the point where I now had zero expectations.

He took his pen from out behind his ear and began to write. *"Rules for dealing with people,"* he said, *"adjust expectations."*

"I would also add 'Try to remember that sometimes you just have to stay in the moment and just read the room in order to get a take on people rather than look at a list for directions' to that particular list," I said.

He nodded. "Okay. I like that," he said as he kept writing. "*Stay in the room and* . . . what came after that?"

"Look, Doc, here's the deal," I said. "You and I know that these guys are a little on the . . . messy side."

"A little?!"

"Okay fine. If they sent someone from the Department of Health to this kitchen to give it a letter rating like they do with restaurants, it would probably be a letter near the end of the alphabet," I admitted. "But what I'm thinking is that instead of setting ourselves up for failure, we just work on the basics. Like, you know, telling everyone that from now on, all food must be disposed of in an actual garbage can rather than just left out on tables and counters in hopes that someone else will do something about it."

He nodded. "Okay. I can get behind that," he said as he wrote it down. "What else?"

"And . . . that each day it will be a different person's responsibility to make sure the sink is clear of dishes," I said. "And not by throwing the dishes in the garbage, but by washing them."

"Another good one," he said as he scribbled away. The thing was, Doc's scribbling was still neater than most people's best handwriting. Which, for a doctor, was pretty rare. "Oh! Oh! I know— How about we all take turns sweeping, vaccuming, and mopping?" he asked. "Because there're eight of us, we'll only each have to do it less than once a week!"

"Sweeping and mopping? These guys?"

"Yeah. You're probably right," he sighed. "That's more like an inflated expectation."

I nodded in agreement. "How about this, though? What if you and I take turns doing that every three days?" I asked. "Actually, because the sweeping and vaccuming will take care of dust, I bet we could even rope Wheezer into helping out with it."

"You'd do that? Really?"

I shrugged. "I don't mind cleaning." I didn't love it, but I loved living in total chaos even less.

"Wow. I'm really touched, Simone." His brow furrowed. "That being said, I'm afraid of the flack we might get—you know, adding fuel to the stereotype of the idea that it's a woman's role to clean."

"I think I'd rather be a stereotype than walk around with sticky feet that are covered with I don't even want to know what. Plus, you'll be cleaning, too, and you're not a woman."

"Good point."

"Now. In terms of groceries," I went on, "what if we start a fund where everyone chips in thirty dollars a week and—" Just as I was about to go into detail about how, if you shopped at Ralph's instead of Whole Foods, 240 bucks went a long way, Blush walked into the room. Actually, because of his height, it was more like he . . . lumbered. In a surprisingly graceful way.

"Oh, hey, Blush," Doc said.

"Hi, Blush," I said.

"Hey," Blush said, blushing a little.

"Simone and I were just coming up with a game plan for how to make this place less of a health hazard," Doc explained. "She's got some great ideas."

Now it was my turn to blush. My inability to take compliments wasn't just limited to stuff about my looks.

"Oh yeah? Like what?" Blush asked.

"Nothing that special." I shrugged. "Just stuff like making sure food ends up in the garbage rather than on the floor. And then I thought that once a week someone could go to the supermarket and do a big shop so we had food for the week. You know, maybe stuff other than chips. Or Mallomars." For some reason, when I looked in the kitchen cabinets the night before for some sugar, I had found six packages of unopened Mallomars. I was really glad I did not like Mallomars, because the stash could have been quite tempting.

"The Mallomars are Noob's," Blush explained. "He plays this game where he tries to get the chocolate part off the marshmallow using nothing but his two front teeth."

You had to give the guy points for creativity. Of all the things a person could spend their time doing, never in a million years would I have thought of that. "That sounds . . ."

"Very Noob-like?" Blush suggested.

"That's a good way of putting it," I agreed.

"So far he hasn't been successful."

"I love the supermarket idea," Doc said. "We should really go soon, though, since we don't have anything here. I'd go, but I have to study."

"But I thought you had the summer off?" I asked, confused.

"I do, but I'm trying to get a jump on second semester of next year."

Wow. Talk about an overachiever.

I looked at Blush. "I don't have any plans today."

He shrugged. "Neither do I."

I guessed we were going together.

Later that afternoon, after collecting money from our roommates, Blush and I set off for the market. In a very non-L.A. move, Blush suggested we walk there, since he had one of those metal carts little old ladies used to carry groceries home.

Which, I decided as I unsuccessfully wracked my brain for a good conversation starter, was probably a very bad idea. Because of the fact that everyone drove everywhere in L.A., it was tough to predict how long it took to walk places, but by my estimation, we were in for a long one.

I quickly discovered that Blush was very comfortable in silence. Like to the point where I wasn't sure he remembered I was with him. I was comfortable in silence, too, but more like when I was alone. When I was with another person, it just felt awkward.

"So, uh, do you have any pets?" I yelled over the *whoosh* of the cars as they zoomed passed us on Lincoln Boulevard. Not only was it going to be a long walk, it was going to be a loud one. And—because of the new black ballet flats I was wearing with a pair of black pedal pushers and a sleeveless red shirt—one probably full of blisters.

He looked at me and smiled. "Nope."

I waited for something more—like, say, ". . . but if I did, I would have a dog." Or a cat. Even a ferret, although I had no idea why someone would want one of those. But nothing came other than more silence between us and more *whoosh*ing from the traffic.

"I don't, either," I replied. I wracked my brain some more. "Hot, today, huh?" Great. I had just uttered the most clichéd thing possible.

"Sure is," he said.

And . . . nothing. Not a "Too bad we don't have a pool" or a "At least, because it's L.A., it's not humid." Just more silence. Punctuated by some obnoxious honking by a kid in a Prius driving behind a very old woman in a silver Buick who was barely visible over the steering wheel.

I stopped walking and put my hands on my hips. "Um, Blush?"

He stopped and turned. "Yeah?"

"Look, this isn't a judgment or anything, but I get the sense you don't spend a lot of time with other people."

Not surprisingly, he blushed. "You're right."

"And the reason I can say that is because if you spot it, you got it," I said. "Meaning, I'm the same way. That being said, you gotta work with me here."

"Huh?"

"Well, two people, when they're walking down a street together, usually have a *conversation*. You know, with both people talking instead of just one."

More blushing. "Sorry. So what do you want to talk about?" he asked as we started walking again.

I shrugged. "I don't know."

It was quiet for a while. Well, other than the pounding bass coming from the tricked-out Chevy waiting at the light. Trying to talk was proving to be more uncomfortable than the silence. I turned to him. "You know what? It's okay, forget it. We don't have to talk."

Maybe it was because it took the pressure off us, but after I said that Blush relaxed and *did* start talking. And talking. And talking. In fact, by the time we got to Ralph's, I was pretty sure Blush may have said more in a half hour than he had in his entire life.

Not like I was complaining. Unlike some people who yakked away because they literally loved the sound of their own voice ("I think my voice has a real honey quality to it, don't you think so?" Hillary had asked me as we had driven home from Kmart that day) or felt like what they had to say was incredibly important ("Obviously, having just been voted one of the most powerful Thirty Under Thirty by the *Hollywood Reporter,* I barely have a minute to myself, but still, I feel like I owe it to the world to start a blog" she said one morning as she tried to get me to eat French toast), Blush *was* interesting.

He grew up in Watts, which was in South Central L.A., with four sisters and his mom, who supported the family by working two jobs. ("When you're surrounded by all those women, you learn to carry Kleenex with you because chances are someone's gonna start crying at some point.") When he got into junior high, the fact that he was the kind of kid who liked staying inside drawing and painting rather then playing outside literally saved his life, as that was when a lot of his friends joined gangs. Because of his size, and his ability to dunk, he got a scholarship to a private high school in the Valley, but when it came time to apply to college, instead of taking a basketball scholarship at USC or UCLA or any of the other schools that wanted him, he applied to CalArts.

"Wow. That's cool," I said as we pushed the cart through the produce section. I was both pleased and impressed to learn that Blush really knew his way around fruits and vegetables when it came to ripeness. Every melon and mango he handed me was just right. "To follow your dream instead of doing something that could earn you millions of dollars and let you date supermodels. Most guys wouldn't do that."

Blush blushed as he effortlessly picked up an entire watermelon with one hand as if it were an apple and placed it gently in the cart. That was something else you didn't see often—people handling fruit with the respect it deserved so it didn't get bruised.

"So you're studying painting?" I asked as we made our way through the snack aisle. Obviously, with the crowd we were living with, I knew there was only so far I could push the whole healthy-eating thing before the group staged a mutiny and voted me off the island. But I was pleased to see that when Blush reached for some potato chips, they were the baked kind.

He shook his head. "Nope. Puppetry."

I looked at him. As did the gum-snapping woman deliberating over Hawaiian- versus Asian-flavored tortilla chips. (Even pre-weight loss, I would've passed on both because they sounded equally disgusting.) "Puppetry as in . . . puppets?" I asked, confused.

He nodded.

"As in . . . *puppets* puppets?" I asked, more confused.

"Yeah. The Cotsen Center for Puppetry and the Arts is one of the best in the country."

"Wow, that's, um . . ."

". . . *weird*," the woman offered, snapping her gum.

I turned to her. Obviously, the memo regarding

supermarket etiquette and the importance of not only not invading someone's personal space but also not offering any sort of feedback unless asked for it had gone to her spam folder. "No, it's not," I said defensively.

"No, she's right," Blush said. "It is weird." He shrugged. "But I'm okay with that." He shrugged again. "Not only do I like it, but I'm good at it. My dream is to open up a puppet theater in Watts and put on shows that deal with stuff the kids in that neighborhood see on a regular basis. You know, gang violence, drugs. So there's a safe place for them to process all of it."

The woman rolled her eyes. "*Tons* of money in that," she said sarcastically as she grabbed a package of French onion-flavored biscuits. I'm sure her husband liked kissing her after *that*.

Blush shrugged. "No. Probably not. But I'm cool with that."

I gave her a dirty look. "I think that's awesome," I said to him. "Like . . . maybe the most awesome thing I've ever heard."

We pushed the cart down the aisle. Never in a million years would I have pegged Blush for a puppeteer. But the fact that that's what he was made the whole thing—and him—that much cooler. Who knew—maybe living here wasn't going to be so bad?

One of the first secrets I learned about guys was that as much as they may have rolled their eyes in front of their friends in order to seem all cool and save face, they actually *liked* to be told what to do. Especially if the order came with the threat that if they didn't do it, the house Xbox/DVD/Roku player/insert other high-end-electronic device here would be placed for sale on Craigslist. According to Doc—who had taken a few psychology classes at UCLA in case he decided to become a shrink instead of a plastic surgeon ("There are just as many crazy people as shallow and vain ones in this city," he explained)—much like children, guys liked structure and boundaries. They *said* they didn't, but it made them feel safe.

On Monday, at the first official meeting of what Noob officially dubbed *Castillo de chicos y una chica*—Spanish for the "Castle of guys and one girl" ("That Google translator thing *rocks*!" he cried, before then going on to spend the next half hour translating stuff like "Dude, the Wi-Fi connection in this country blows!" into Latvian), when Doc first unveiled the combination graph/pie chart he had put together detailing everyone's chores there were a bunch of groans and moans. Once I gave them the sales pitch Doc and I had rehearsed about how much happier they would be living with order and organization rather than swimming in chaos, they began to relax. By Wednesday, although I was still triple-checking the lock on the bathroom door before I took a shower, I had gotten to the point where I was starting to relax and not feel so nervous around the guys. And also I wasn't getting random bruises on my body from tripping over stuff that wasn't put away.

Very quickly, I got into a nice routine. Thanks to a mention in the new hot blog "Pink Is the New Lavender, Which Is Now the New Black" (which had just been optioned as the basis for a TV show by ABC Family a few months earlier), One Person's Garbage had gotten really busy, which meant that Brad needed help at the store. Which meant part-time jobs for Nicola and me. (I knew Hillary had been pushing Dad's agent to try to get him the gig executive producing the show because she thought it would be good for his career to be more involved with the Millennials, but because he had been pegged as "the talking-animal guy," the network passed.) So ever since school ended, for a few hours a day I pasted on a smile and told customers that oh yeah, of *course* that dress made them look like Sandra Bullock's best friend in that movie she did toward the beginning of her career. And I was able to monitor my robin's-egg blue dress and make sure no one bought it.

My 30 percent employee discount was going a long way in helping me assemble a wardrobe that, according to Brad, if I were walking around the Marais in Paris (apparently, the hippest neighborhood) would get me approving nods from French women instead of pained looks. Still, I didn't forget my roots. Hence, the addition of a few vintage tees, but in mediums instead of extra larges. It took some getting used to wearing shirts that actually advertised my boobage (not to mention the stares from guys—

some cute, some just plain gross—that went along with it), but I did my best.

But then on Thursday afternoon, as I waited for a woman named Marge from Pasadena to try on a Halston-esque one-armed silver lamé evening dress that had been owned and "gently worn" (actually, from the faint stains that even the dry cleaner couldn't get out, *not* so gently worn) by her favorite soap actress, I realized that my why-do-today-what-you-can-keep-putting-off-for-tomorrow? attitude had to change. Because as I half listened to Marge yammer on proudly about how she had every single episode of the soap *Nights of Our Existences* either DVR'd, on DVD, or—going back to the eighties—on VHS, I discovered that my dress—the dress that I kind-of-sort-of-maybe thought I was ready to try on—was gone. It wasn't on the Smashing Sixties rack, or the Sizzling Seventies one. And not on the Egregious Eighties one, either. ("Bradley, it's really great that you know a lot of fifty-cent SAT words," Nicola kept saying, "but you might want to try using words that your customers don't have to look up on dictionary.com in order to see how witty you are.") When I couldn't find it on the Nostalgic Nineties, either, I freaked.

"My dress! It's not here!" I cried.

Nicola looked up from lacing on a pair of thigh-high red suede boots that had just come in. According to Brad, they had belonged to some old-school disco diva who had been forced to sell them in order to pay for her most recent rehab stay. "How is it *your* dress if you refuse to even try it on?" she asked. "I think the proper way of saying that is, '*The* dress! It's not here.'" She looked over at Brad, who was skimming the photos of guys on some new dating Web site called Every Pot Has A Lid. "Don't you think, Bradley?"

"I do believe you're right, Nicola."

"Thank you, Mr. and Ms. Grammatically Correct," I said. "But that's not the point! The point is the blue dress is gone! Brad, when did you sell it?"

"Let's see . . . I think it was . . ." He squinted at the computer screen. "*Someone* could benefit from an appointment with a bottle of Nair." He sighed. "I love the tall, dark, and handsome look, but does 'hairy' always have to be part of it?"

"Brad. Focus," I said. "The dress. Who bought it?"

He put his fingers to his temples like one of those cheesy psychics. "Let me see if I can remember."

Even with the blog mention, it wasn't like this was H&M or Urban Outfitters, with tons of customers. (Although thanks to Brad's ability to get hold of size 24 Tall evening dresses, Lady GaGantuan from the hair salon came by on a pretty regular basis.)

"Oh right. It was Tuesday," Brad said. "Or maybe it was Monday." He cocked his head. "No, I distinctly remember it was Tuesday, because it was the same day

I got the e-mail from the guy on eHarmony who used to be a priest before becoming a trapeze artist. Did I tell you about him?"

"Off point, Brad," I said.

"Sorry. It was Tuesday, and it was bought by . . . some girl."

I waited for him to go on.

He shrugged. "That's all I remember—that it was a girl."

I sighed. That part wasn't surprising. Brad didn't have any male customers other than Lady GaGantuan. "Well, I guess it's my own fault, right?" I asked. I glanced over at Nicola. "That was a rhetorical question, by the way." I don't know why I was so upset. It was so . . . *girly* of me. It was only a dress. That probably would've looked stupid on me anyway.

But I was.

I tried to let the dress thing go. I really did. But I just couldn't shake it. Which, when you're living with people who don't spend all their time typing on their iPhones or gazing at themselves in mirrors, is a problem, because apparently, moping makes people uncomfortable. Especially if those people happen to be guys.

I very quickly learned that guys like to fix things. Even guys like Noob, who, in the process of fixing things, ends up breaking other things. (I didn't know a lot about tools, but breaking a wrench seemed like a very difficult thing to do.)

"Simone? Is everything okay?" Wheezer asked nervously as I stood at the kitchen counter stir-frying veggies and tofu for our Friday night family dinner (the "family" thing was Max's idea).

I sighed. "Yeah. Why?"

"Because you're staring into space and about to burn the vegetables," he said, pointing at the wok.

I looked down to see that he was right. "Thanks," I sighed as I shook the veggies around a bit before going back to staring into space.

"You *sure* you're okay?"

"Not really," I shrugged. "But it's okay. I'm sure it'll pass. Eventually. Hopefully."

From the look on Wheezer's face, guys also didn't like such open-ended statements. In fact, it made Wheezer so uncomfortable, he sneezed.

"God bless you," I said.

"Thanks," he said, honking into a tissue. He held out a clean one. "Would a tissue make you feel better?"

I shook my head. "I don't think so."

"Well, can you at least try to tell me what's wrong?"

"I'm not really sure," I admitted. "It's just . . . I don't know how to explain it."

"But how can we try and fix it if you can't explain it?"

I shrugged. "Maybe it's just one of those things that

have to clear up by themselves. You know, like how antibiotics don't kill viruses, and you just have to wait for it to go away by itself."

He looked even more alarmed. "They don't? That's horrible." He sneezed and honked again. "Maybe Doc can devote his medical career to trying to come up with one that works. I mean, the idea of not being able to fix something is just . . . *wrong*."

It was? I guess when you become so used to living with something—like, say, the lack of a social life, or being ignored by a parent, or being invisible—you just get used to it after a while.

"Well, listen, if you figure out what it is that's bothering you and you want to talk about it, I'd be more than happy to listen."

I smiled. "Wow. Thanks, Wheezer. That's really sweet of you."

He turned red. "Just so you know, my last girlfriend—okay, my *only* girlfriend—accused me of being a really bad communicator, so I'm not sure how much help I'd actually be, but I'm a really good listener."

"I'll definitely keep that in mind. Thanks." I followed his eyeline toward the den, where I could see him gazing at *Bikini Bloodbath*, the group's second favorite horror movie after the Sorority Girl Slasher series. "Wheezer," I said, waving my hand in front of his face.

"Huh? Sorry. What were you saying?"

I laughed. "I said thanks."

He dug some crumpled tissues out of his back pocket and handed them to me. "I know you said they won't help, but why don't you take them anyway? They're a little linty, but they're clean. I promise. Some people are multiple blowers, but I'm not. It's unsanitary."

I smiled as I took them, touched. That may have been one of the nicest things a guy had ever done for me.

People usually think it's girls who are all gossipy, but it's not, as I found out the next day. When Doc sent out an e-mail to the Google user group *Castillo de chicos y una chica,* calling an official house meeting (Noob complained that the name was too long until Narc reminded him it had been his idea), I knew I was in trouble.

"Okay, having the Queen of Mean living in your house has rubbed off on you because someone has become a little self-centered and is making this all about her," Nicola sniffed as we walked the aisles of Barbarella's Beauty Supplies for a Bodacious You. Now that I had kind-of-sort-of gotten the wardrobe thing down, Nicola had insisted we tackle hair and makeup, which, from the pile of stuff in my basket, seemed to include things like bobby pins with little rhinestone palm trees on the ends ("For the days and nights you're feeling tropical," it said on the package) and a giant roll-on tube of glittery bronze highlighter. ("Yes, on most paler-than-pale people like you, it might look kind of dumb, but that's because they don't have the attitude to pull it off like you do!" Nicola exclaimed.)

I plucked a package of false eyelashes out of her hands and put them back on the shelf before turning to her. "Nicola, the subject line said, 'To figure out how to get Simone to stop moping and make her happy again.'"

"Oh. Huh. Then I guess it is about you," she agreed. "But look at how *nice* that is! They're such sensitive guys." She sighed. "Your brother has such great taste in friends. I can't wait until he and I are dating. I bet he'll be a total prince when I'm PMS-ing."

Not like he'd be able to get a word in. Every time Nicola was near him, it was as if all the words she had stored up *not* talking to him were released. It would have been one thing if what came out were her typically witty observations on life (also available in the "Witty Observations on Life" part of her blog), but it wasn't. It was just chatter. Like the kind that gives girls a bad name.

"Yeah, it is nice," I agreed. "But still. It's embarrassing."

"How come?"

"Because I feel *stupid*."

She shrugged. "Well, that's the thing about friends. Sometimes you just have to feel stupid in front of them. So you can see that they're not going to ditch you for being less than perfect. And after a while you get used to it, and it's not so hard anymore."

I sighed. Sure, I could do that with Nicola, but a group of guys was a whole other story.

Later on, after Noob had gathered everyone into the living room by blowing the bugle he had gotten earlier at the Salvation Army Thrift Store ("I asked them if they had one of those shofar things—you know, the ram's horn thing they blow on Rosh Hashanah? But they said they were all out."), he stood in front of the group—which, per a group vote via e-mail, also included Nicola and Herbert, even though they didn't technically live in the house.

"Here ye, here ye!" he bellowed. "And now begins the official house meeting!" He gave a loud, long toot on the bugle.

"Will you stop with that thing already?" Narc cried, covering his ears.

"I'm just trying to make it official," Noob said defensively. "And now, I'm going to . . ." He reached into the back pocket of his jeans and pulled out a crumpled piece of paper. "Hold on—I need to check my notes." After what seemed like an awful long time to unfold a piece of paper that was only folded into quarters, he squinted. "Man, I hate when I can't read my own writing. Oh right—and now, I'm going to turn the meeting over to Thor! So please help me give him a very warm welcome."

As Thor strode up to the front of the room, he looked at us. "You heard the man. A warm welcome!"

At that, a smattering of applause could be heard. While I had quickly learned that Thor's bark was a lot worse than his bite, and that he, too, got misty-eyed at ASPCA commercials, you also didn't want to risk making him mad. ("I'm an *artist*—if we can't express our dissatisfaction about things, who can?")

"I really like the way you clap," I heard Nicola whisper to my brother. "It's very rhythmic." Most people, if they had received the kind of strange look my brother shot her, would've shut right up. But not Nicola. "Some people, when they clap, it's all out of sync," she babbled. "But yours isn't. Plus, it's got a very *happy* feel to it."

"Uh, thanks," he whispered back. "But I think we should pay attention."

"Okay, so here's the deal," Thor said. "We have a friend in need, people. And what do we do when we have a friend in need?"

"We make a donation via PayPal and receive a packet every month with an update on their progress?" Noob suggested before Narc flicked him in the head. "What? That's the way they do it on that infomercial about the kids in Tanzania."

"No! We don't make a donation—we *help* them!"

"A donation is help," Noob retorted.

Wheezer shoved some tissues toward him. "Noob, why don't you stick these in your mouth and shut up for a while?"

Noob stood up. "You know what? I'm sick of being kicked around by you guys. I'm leaving. But you can forget about me telling you where I'm going." He began to stomp off. "I'll be in the kitchen if anyone needs me."

Because I went to such a competitive high school, the teachers there had a way of making you feel that if you didn't have a 3.99 average, you weren't going to get into a decent college. But if Noob could get accepted to a school, I was pretty certain that there was a place for anyone.

"You have to give the guy credit for expressing his feelings and taking a stand," Thor said. The sound of some pans crashing to the floor could be heard. "Even if it's done in an uncoordinated fashion." He turned to me. "So getting back to the subject at hand. Simone, we've been talking, and we've noticed that you haven't been your usual sunny self the last few days—"

I looked at Nicola. "I have a sunny self?"

"*Anyone* has a sunny self compared to Thor," Doc said.

He had a point.

"You know, if I wanted to, I could probably take that as some kind of insult," Thor said, "but because I'm really working on not getting bent out of shape when some-one slights me because they're not able to see that my somewhat rough exterior is merely an armor to keep my sensitive interior from becoming wounded, I'm gonna let that one go." He stomped over and stood by Doc. "But I wouldn't try it again."

"Okay," Doc mumbled as he shrank back in his chair.

"Good." Thor turned to me again. "So Simone, what's going on?"

Even if it's with what looks like genuine concern, having eight guys and Nicola stare at you as they wait for an answer (although he wouldn't come back into the room, I could see Noob peeking through the crack of the kitchen door) is pretty painful.

"Oh man, I am so glad I'm not you right now," I heard Nicola murmur.

"I . . . you know . . . I really . . ." I stammered.

"Guys, I think we should table this," Blush said softly from his perch over on the window seat. Because he was so tall, he kind of had to scrunch his limbs up to fit in there, but he made it look like it wasn't too uncomfortable. Maybe it came from handling the marionettes. "If she wants to talk about it, she knows that we're more than happy to listen. Right?"

I nodded.

"But I thought girls loved to talk about their problems," Wheezer said, confused.

"Yeah, like, *to death*," Narc grumbled.

"Even I know that," Herbert added. "And I'm only in junior high."

Max turned to me. "You *sure* you don't want to talk about it?"

"If you don't want to talk about it in this big group,

maybe just the three of us could talk about it," Nicola blurted out. "You know—me, you, and Max. Or maybe Max and I could just talk about it alone."

Maybe Doc could devote his medical career to coming up with a cure for DIBD—Disclosure of Inappropriate Blurting Disease. "Thanks. But, yes, I'm sure."

Max nodded. "Okay." He turned to the group. "She doesn't want to talk about it."

"Can we just stop talking about the fact that I don't want to talk about it?" I pleaded.

"Next order of business, then," Thor announced. "Wait—scratch that. We don't have any other orders of business. Meeting adjorned."

As everyone got up to leave, Noob's muffled voice could be heard from the crack of the kitchen door. "Wait—I have another order of business. *Ow*. You just hit me in the face!" he cried as Narc pushed the door open.

I looked over at Blush, still hanging out on the window seat, and gave him a grateful smile. It was nice to be friends with someone who knew that sometimes the best way of communicating was done without talking.

Not talking was something that Blush and I did a lot. Although it was very clear on the color-coded Excel chart that Doc had made that all housemates were supposed to take turns doing the grocery shopping ("It's an excellent way for everyone to deepen their knowledge of food additives," he explained to the group), whenever it was time to go (which, when you're living with a bunch of guys, turns out to be pretty much every other day), the job seemed to fall on my shoulders ("You're just so good at it," Narc said. "Probably some sort of female intuition thing"). And Blush—because he was a nice guy and could carry at least three grocery bags in each hand in addition to his cart—always offered to accompany me.

The day after the official house meeting, which was a Sunday, we decided we'd go to the farmers market in Santa Monica on Main Street. I was still feeling kind of blue and would have rather stayed holed up in my room in the attic all day watching *The 400 Blows* on Netflix. But because I knew that Blush wouldn't ask me what was wrong every five seconds, when he knocked on my door and asked me if I wanted to go, I said yes.

"So are you feeling better?" he asked as we walked down Main Street with bags full of peaches, plums, blueberries, and cotton candy (a special request via text from Noob).

Why couldn't these guys just be *guys* and be totally clueless? How come I got stuck with some who were actually thoughtful? I opened my mouth, ready to give my stock "Me? Oh yeah—I'm fine. Everything's great" answer; the one I used with my dad on the rare occasions when he looked up from his iPhone.

But that's not what happened. Maybe because it's hard to be intimidated by a six-foot-two basketball player who has admitted to you that his dream is to work with puppets, but instead of lying, what came out during our walk back to the house was my life story. About never knowing my mom. About how, up until recently, my main hobby was eating. About Zumba. About how, up until Operation Blackbird, or whatever it was called, I hadn't worn a dress since I was eight and I was still very much getting used to this whole . . . *girly* thing.

"Really?" he asked. "That's hard to believe. I mean, you're so . . . I don't know . . . put together."

"Nicola pretty much picks out my outfits," I admitted. While I had done well on my own at Kmart that one day, Nicola still did most of it for me.

"That's not what I mean," he said. "I mean you seem so sure of yourself."

I looked at him. *"Me?"*

He nodded in his slow way, which, had someone else done it, would've driven me crazy, but because it was Blush it didn't bother me.

"Yeah, well, I don't feel that way," I admitted. "I feel . . . I don't know . . . *uncooked.* Kind of like instead of being medium well, I'm medium raw, and I'm scared that I'm going to get salmonella or one of those other food poisoning thingies now." As a truck rumbled by, I held down the skirt part of my red-and-blue-striped sundress so it wouldn't fly up. "And I don't know if I'll ever get used to these things."

He laughed. "I get you. When I got my scholarship and left South Central and started going to high school with all these rich kids, I kept feeling like they could literally see through me."

I turned to him. "You mean, like you were invisible?" That would be too weird.

He laughed. "No. When you're this tall and this black at a rich private school, that doesn't happen. It was more like they could see inside me, and that when they did, they could see that everything inside me was different than their stuff. Like it was the cheap generic version of what they had. And that it was only a matter of time before someone told on me and I got kicked out."

I sighed. "I know that feeling." Maybe that's part of why losing the weight had freaked me out so much. Because I no longer had something covering the fact that, at the end of the day, I wasn't like them. I looked at him again. "Can I tell you something really stupid and you'll promise not to laugh?"

"Sure."

I could tell that Blush was the kind of guy who kept his word. "Okay. Well, see, the reason I've been so bummed actually has to do with a dress . . ." God, could I sound any more, I don't know . . . *Hillaryish*? I glanced over expecting to see an eyebrow shoot up, but there was none of that. Instead, he was just waiting patiently for me to go on. "It was this dress that I had been stalking for months. And I was afraid to try it on. First, because I was afraid I'd rip it or something when I was zipping it up because it would be too tight. But then, even after I was sure it would fit, I still wouldn't do it. Because I felt like . . . I don't know . . . I didn't deserve something so . . . *nice*."

Someone else may have rolled his eyes or looked at me as if he had no idea what I was talking about, but not Blush. He nodded. "That sounds like me with the Nike Zoom Kobe Fours." Okay, so maybe Blush was a little more guylike than I had originally thought. Still, the important thing was that not only did he understand what I meant, but he made me feel as if I wasn't completely stupid for feeling like that. "So have you changed your mind? Are you going to get the dress?"

"That's the thing," I said. "The other day, when I thought that maybe I was finally ready to try it on, it turned out it was gone. Someone else bought it. But when I realized that, I was less upset that the dress was gone and more upset with myself, you know? That I had let being scared get in the way of something I wanted." What was I doing vomiting my deepest darkest secrets to this guy I barely knew? I was barely able to talk like this with Nicola.

"I get it. My grandmother used to say, 'Miles, there are only three things you need to remember in life. And if you remember these things, I promise you you'll be happy—' "

"Your name is Miles?" I asked, surprised.

He nodded. "Yeah. After Miles Davis, he's—"

"—like, the best jazz musician ever," I finished. "*Kind of Blue*—"

"—is, like, the best album ever," he said with a smile.

I smiled back. "So what are the three things?"

"Number one is to always bet on yourself. Number two is to constantly ask yourself, 'What would I do if I weren't afraid?' and number three is that when you're making corn bread, use real butter instead of margarine or else it'll crumble."

My stomach started to rumble. I *loved* corn bread. I thought about it. The asking myself what I'd do if I weren't afraid—that seemed doable. And smart. "If I hadn't been afraid, I would've bought that dress even back when it didn't fit and bet on myself that one day I'd fit into it." I looked at him. "So did you ever end up getting the sneakers?"

He nodded. "Yeah. On eBay. Brand new and for half price."

I smiled. Sometimes life really had a way of working out.

"And you know what else his grandmother said?" I told the Zumba Brigade at the Coffee Bean the following Tuesday afternoon post-class. A class where, I was proud to report, I had been singled out by Jorge and asked to demonstrate a particularly difficult move that, after I did it perfectly, earned me a "Who says white girls don't have rhythm?!" "She said to always use butter instead of margarine when making corn bread."

"Ahhhh," the group said in stereo as they bobbed their heads. "Hold on—let me write that down," Cookie said, taking out her little notebook. "Oh wait—what am I doing? I don't eat corn bread." She looked at the group. "Gluten makes me bloat."

Rona cleared her throat. "Forgive me for being so bold," she said, "but when might you think you and this Blush gentleman might finally go out on a date?"

"A what?" I asked, confused.

"A *date*," she said. "You know, those outings where you don't feel bad for ordering dessert because it's a special occasion?"

My iced coffee almost shot out of my nose. "I can't *date* Blush."

"How come?" Cookie asked.

"Because, well, he's . . . *Blush*. We're just friends."

"You do realize that your face lights up whenever you talk about him, right?" Marcia asked. She turned to the group. "As a therapist, we learn that the nonverbal reactions are often just as important if not more important than what the patient is saying."

I suddenly had a lot of compassion for Sophie Greene, this girl in my grade whose mom was a shrink. Granted, she was a little weird with her obsession with these romance novels about some woman named Devon

Devareaux, but still, to grow up under a microscope like that and have to train yourself to keep a straight face all the time must have been exhausting.

"And friendship is the most important building block for a relationship," Cheryl said. She sighed. "I keep trying to teach my son that, but I'm not sure he's listening."

I felt myself turn even redder. As if things weren't bad enough, she had to bring up Jason? "I've only known him a week. For all I know, he has a girlfriend," I said.

Cheryl shook her head. "I don't think so. At least not that I can tell from his Facebook page."

"I meant Blush," I said. Or did I? Jason at least wasn't a *friend* friend.

"Has Blush ever mentioned a girl?" Gwen asked.

"Well, no, but you know, he's really cute. And you know, nice," I replied. "Not to mention he's a puppeteer."

As had happened whenever I had brought up that fact in the past, some grimacing went on. But because (a) everyone in the Zumba Brigade was so nice, and (b) there was a substantial amount of Botox in their faces, you'd miss it if you blinked. Personally, I thought the idea that Blush was going for a career in puppetry was awesome. When someone said he was a lawyer, or a doctor, or—in this town—an actor, that was boring. But a puppeteer? That was definitely worth at least a few minutes of conversation, if only to discuss what actually went into puppeteering (I had learned during one of our walks that there was a lot—like set design, costumes, script writing . . .).

"Yes, but is there a 401(k) in puppetry?" Cheryl asked.

"Um—" I wasn't even sure what a 401(k) *was*. "Or insurance?" Cookie asked.

"I don't—"

Marcia sighed. "With our economy in the toilet, you do *not* want to be without insurance at this time in history."

Okay, fine, so maybe puppeteers weren't raking in the big bucks, but he was committed to his art.

"Well, if you're not going to date Blush, then you should be dating someone," Rona said.

"Exactly," Gwen agreed. "Can't let your new look go to waste."

Why was everyone on my case about dating someone? Not to mention these were *adults*. Shouldn't they have been all worried I was going to go out and get myself on *Teen Mom* or something? "Can we talk about something else?" I pleaded.

"Sure," Cheryl said. "So have you heard from your father and Hillary?"

I cringed. That was only a slightly better topic than the dating one. "Yeah. We Skyped last night," I replied.

"Was it a good conversation?" Cookie asked.

"Sure," I replied. "I mean, the parts where my dad was listening rather than writing revisions on a script as I told him about the guys at the house and Hillary wasn't jumping in front of the camera asking whether, now that she had a tan, her lips were as red as mine."

This time, the collective cringe wasn't as fleeting. This time it stayed on their faces, which, because it was filled with compassion and pity and all those other things that made me feel uncomfortable, made me look away and start picking at my cuticles. "But Hillary did send me a gift," I added.

"She did? Really?" said Gwen.

I nodded. "Yeah. Some apple-flavored Italian candy."

"But you're allergic to apples," Cheryl said.

I loved how these women knew more about me than the woman who lived in my house. "I know, but she keeps forgetting that."

"Not to be a bee-itch or anything, but I get the sense that if something doesn't have to do with her directly, she forgets it," Cookie said.

"It's bee-atch," I said.

"That's it, Simone!" Marcia cried. "Let it out! Let that anger out that's been bottled up inside of you because we live in a society where the unconscious message we're given is that it's not ladylike for women to do that!"

"Actually, I was correcting Cookie," I said. "It's bee-atch, not bee-itch."

Cookie rummaged in her bag (her yellow leather one with tassels and studs, as opposed to her orange or fuchsia one) for her notebook. "I *knew* that didn't sound right. I always get that one wrong!"

Gwen shook her head. "You know, I didn't say anything about this earlier, but I have to say, I really don't like the sound of this."

"Of what?" I asked.

"Remember when you told us about that time in the parking lot at Kmart? When she almost 'accidentally' ran into you with the car?"

I nodded.

"And now the apple candy?"

I shrugged. "I don't know . . . she's always offering me apple things." I hadn't told them about the boxes of Hostess apple pies.

"Right. Even though you've told her you're highly allergic to them. To the point where *it could cause death.*"

The group gasped.

"What are you saying? That Hillary is trying to *kill* me?"

"Maybe not *kill* you," Gwen replied. "Maybe just seriously hurt you and prevent you from breathing, which would result in your heart stopping and/or the flow of oxygen to your brain, which would ultimately result in you dying."

"Oh my God," Cookie moaned. "That's beyond insane to the noggin."

"Insane to the brain," I corrected.

She nodded. "Insane to the brain. Got it."

"Or," Gwen—who, pre-twins, had been a criminal attorney in a big Century Century law firm—continued, "if she managed to hit you with the car, shatter your spinal cord, resulting in the loss of your legs and your inability to walk. Perhaps, with enough force, making you into a *quadra*palegic rather than just a parapelegic."

"In other words, you're saying she's trying to kill me."

She shrugged. "Well, if you want to get more specific, then yes, that's pretty much what I'm saying."

"Look, I agree that it's obvious Hillary doesn't like me, but the only thing she's killing are the dreams of novelists when she takes their books and changes the endings of them to make them more 'happily ever after'-like," I said. "She's not, you know . . . *dangerous*."

Marcia shook her head. "I don't know about that, Simone. Did you *see* last's week's episode of *CSI: Miami*?" She clucked. "That killer, she was just as pretty as Hillary."

Cheryl nodded. "There is no place for discrimination when taking crime suspects into consideration."

I shook my head. "I appreciate the concern, you guys, but Hillary could never do that. She wouldn't be able to survive having to wear one of those ugly jumpsuits in jail."

That being said—it was a little weird.

The Zumba ladies weren't the only ones who were up in my grill about dating.

"They're right, you know. I've been on you to date for months," Nicola said that next night as we sat on the floor in the corner while we all watched a horror movie called *Sorority Girl Slasher Part 7*. Well, while the guys watched it. Seeing that this was the third time that week that they had put it on, I didn't need to watch it again. They, however, were mesmerized by it. To the point where a big glob of pizza fell out of Narc's mouth because his jaw wouldn't close during the shower scenes. She grimaced. "Do these guys ever actually chew their food, or do they just swallow it whole like that all the time?"

"They just swallow it whole," I said. "You should've been here the other night when they grilled steaks and sausages. It was like watching one of those documentaries on the Discovery Channel about wild dogs."

She shook her head. "I'm so glad your brother isn't like that. He's got manners. 'Cause I would never date a guy without manners."

Right then my brother let out a huge burp. Right before he scratched his stomach.

She shrugged. "On the other hand, I think it's great that he feels so comfortable around me that he can just relax like that. From the conversation we had in the kitchen earlier, I can tell that our relationship is really moving to the next level."

I turned to her, surprised. "Like a *conversation* conversation? Not just you talking and talking so he can't get a word in edgewise?"

She nodded. "Uh-huh."

"How could you not mention that?!"

She shrugged. "Because it was somewhat personal."

Exactly how personal was personal? I wanted to know, but the combination of the words "personal" and "my brother" made me feel a little queasy.

"Okay, so this is what happened," she gushed, "While you and Blush were trying to help Noob get off from the top of the slide in the backyard—by the way, first of all, why would someone with a fear of heights get up on top of a slide to begin with, and (b) it's not even high, so why was he freaking out so much?"

"Um, I think if we've learned anything the last few weeks, it's that when it comes to Noob, logic kinda-sorta doesn't apply," I replied.

"Good point," she agreed. "Anyways, so I was in the kitchen getting some water—by the way, the water in the Brita thing is green, so whoever's chore it is on Doc's computerized chore list to change the filter better get on that. *Anyway*, so I was in the kitchen and Max came in and said hey and then I said hey back and then he said would you mind passing me a paper towel and I said no problem and when I did he said I know it's weird but I've always liked using paper towels instead of napkins I think because they're sturdier and it makes me feel like I'm really getting my mouth clean when I wipe it and I said Omigod—I feel the *same* way!"

I waited for her to go on, but she didn't. "So then what happened?" I finally asked.

She shrugged. "Nothing. That was it."

"*That* was the personal conversation you had with my brother. About the fact that you both like paper towels rather than napkins."

She nodded.

And here she was giving *me* advice about boys? Before I could tell her that, Narc stood up and dinged his Red Bull can with a pencil. (With the number of them he drank, he should've had complete insomnia, but obviously they did nothing for him.)

"Attention, roommates!" he bellowed. He turned to Nicola. "Oh, and nonroommates, too!"

Because it was a particularly gory-slash-every-girl-in-a-skimpy-bikini scene, everyone ignored him. Luckily, Noob's bugle was right there. After he had gotten everyone's attention by blowing (not that we could hear anymore), he yawned. "Man, that was exhausting."

"So what's the announcement?" Max asked.

"Omigod—I was *just* about to ask the same exact thing," Nicola gasped.

I shook my head.

"The announcement is this. I was thinking that it's been a while since we've had a party."

"We actually haven't had any parties," Doc corrected.

"That's what I mean," Narc said. "It's been a really long time. And because of that, I think we should have one."

"But what's the occasion?" Wheezer asked right before he sneezed.

"I know what it can be!" Noob exclaimed. "In can be in honor of Video Games Day!"

"There's an entire day that honors video games?" Nicola asked.

Noob nodded. "Well, *yeah*. There's actually two—there's also *National* Video Games Day in September."

Narc shook his head. "I don't know. That might be kind of a turnoff to chicks."

"I know something it can be in honor of," Max said. "It can be in honor of Simone moving in! She's been here a whole week and a half!"

Okay, I was incredibly lucky to have such a sweet brother, but because I was still getting used to the visibility thing, that was not an idea I was interested in.

However, from the nods and "I like that"s, everyone else in the room thought it was a great idea.

"Excellent. It's official then. Party for Simone on Friday," Narc announced. "I'm going to have to get some serious nappage in before then." He yawned. "In fact, I think I'll start now."

"I have an idea," Nicola said a little later as we walked toward Abbot Kinney. I could take the Frito-like odor that permeated the house—no matter how much Doc and I cleaned—for only so long before I needed fresh air. "One of my more brilliant ones, if I don't say so myself."

I braced myself. Nicola + brilliant ideas = dangerous.

"I think you should invite Jason Frank to the party."

I stopped walking. That wasn't just dangerous—that was *ridiculous*. "Okay, I think that Frito smell is messing with your brain."

"I'm serious. I think it would be a great opportunity for you to serve humankind by helping to foster better relationships between the popular and the nonpopular," she said. "You could be a *role model*."

I shook my head and started walking again. "No way."

"I hate to point out the obvious, but you're being a little selfish here," she replied.

I started to make a left, toward Ciao Venice, the gelato place we liked to go to. For a while I had stayed away from sweets all together. But the other day, Doc explained how, if you stayed at a certain calorie level, your body got used to it and then freaked out if you started to let yourself eat normally. So I had decided to let myself have sweets a few times a week. Not like crazy Tastykake binges, but like a normal level of sweets. I was a little scared that I would end up right back where I had been before, but so far I wasn't anywhere near there. It was weird, maybe because I was busier—and happier—but I could have some gelato, or a cupcake, or a cookie, and then just stop and go on with my life instead of it escalating into a bingefest.

"Let's go to Licks instead," Nicola said.

Licks was an ice-cream place down on the other end of Abbot Kinney. "But you hate that place," I said. "You always say they stiff you on the amount of ice cream they give you."

"Well, yeah, they do. I mean, who do they think they are charging five bucks for what essentially ends up being two spoonfuls of ice cream?! And that's without any toppings!" she grumbled. "In fact, when I get home tonight, I'm going to blog about it. They'll be sorry when those lines around the corner are gone."

"Good idea," I agreed, following her the other way but leaving out the part that, because she only had four followers—me, Brad, her grandmother in England, and this barista in Starbucks with a tribal tattoo across his face who had a crush on her—I didn't think it would really put a dent in their business.

"I know you're sick of me bringing up the boy thing, but I just think you're missing out on taking advantage of this once-in-a-lifetime situation of having all these guys around to coach you," she said. "Do you realize how lucky you are? It's like being on a reality show without having to go through the hassle of auditioning!"

"I really hope you reconsider the whole pre-law thing when we get to college, because you'd be awesome at it," I said.

As usual, there was a huge line at Licks. Which included—I soon saw as I felt the blood leave my face—Jason Frank and his fellow Testosterone Twit Brock Fleckman. And from the way the blonde surfer chick Brock was trying to hit on kept rolling her eyes at her dreadlocked friend and trying to edge him out with her back, he was striking out big-time.

"Oh wow. Look at that. Jason's here. How weird," Nicola said all innocent-like.

My eyes narrowed. "Oh really? Because the way you say it doesn't make it seem like it's weird *at all*. Spill it—how'd you manage this?"

"Foursquare?" she squeaked.

I shook my head. "It's bad enough you stalk your ex-boyfriend with that thing, but now you're stalking someone for *me*?! That's just wrong." I grabbed her hand. "C'mon. We're getting out of here before they see us."

We were *thisclose* to the door when I heard it.

"Simone!"

"Great," I sighed. I turned around to see Jason walking toward us. Actually, it was more like he loped. Which, I had to admit, was kind of cute.

"Hey," he said.

"Hey," I said to my navy-blue patent leather pump. I had never thought I'd ever be a heel girl, but I had discovered that once you got the hang of them, they were pretty easy to walk in. As long as they weren't ridiculously high and skinny. Brad had gone to this estate sale at the house of some old Hollywood starlet from the 1940s the weekend before and had come back with an entire SUV filled with dresses and shoes and hats and purses. With my discount, they were pretty affordable, even if I had to stuff them with tissues near the toe because they were a little too big.

"Hey, Nicola," he said, continuing to look at me.

"You know my name?" she asked, surprised. She turned to me. "He knows my name. Huh."

Apparently, Nicola's lack of a filter between her brain and her mouth didn't rear its head just around the guys she liked, but also around guys she thought *I* should like.

"So what's up?" he asked.

"Not much," I replied.

"Actually, you know what's up?" Nicola said. "What's up is that—"

"So how's your mom?" I quickly interrupted before she could tell him about the party.

"She's good. You know, she thinks you're pretty awesome," he replied. "The other night she mentioned you're really coordinated."

"Which is really funny 'cause she didn't used to be," Nicola said. She turned to me. "Remember that time in seventh grade in gym when we had to dismount from the balance beam and—"

Okay, next lifetime? Best friend will have filter. I glared

at her. "Yes, I remember, and we're not going to talk about that now, okay?" The rest of that story had to do with the fact that when I did my dismount, I slipped and landed *on* the beam. As in right between my legs. Just thinking about it made me wince and start worrying again about whether I had ruined my chances of ever having a baby.

"My mom told me you're crashing at your brother's place for a while," Jason said.

"Funny you should mention that because—" Nicola began to say.

"—because we have to get back there," I said, yanking at her arm. "I . . . forgot to turn off the stove, and I don't want them all to die of carbon monoxide poisoning." Right after the words came out of my mouth, I flashed back to the time in February when I had walked into the kitchen to find that Hillary had left the burners going. When I had pointed it out to her, she said it was because she was so busy and just forgot. But after my conversation with the Zumba Brigade, now it all seemed kind of strange.

"Oh. Okay. Well, I guess I'll see you around then—"

"Actually, you know where you can see her?" Nicola asked. "At the party they're having at the house on Friday night."

The one that Nicola wouldn't be going to because she'd be dead by then because I was going to kill her as soon as we got outside.

"That's so nice of you to invite Jason to my brother's

party without first running it by me," I said through gritted teeth, "but I'm sure he already has plans and can't come." Like . . . cleaning out his junk drawer. Or cutting his toenails.

"Nope. I don't have anything going on," he replied.

Of course that had to be the one night that one of the most popular guys in the entire grade didn't have plans.

"Fab," Nicola said. "Simone will send you a friend request and message you the address." She winked at me. "Solved *that* problem, huh?"

Yeah. And now onto the one of what to do now that I no longer had a best friend.

Jason nodded. "Sounds cool. See you Friday then."

I wondered if anyone would notice my absence if I just ignored the party and stayed up in the attic watching *Weird Addictions* all night.

As I lay in bed later that night I was so ampped up from my run-in with Jason that I couldn't sleep. Well, that and the fact that because of Narc, I had developed a bit of a Red Bull habit. After spending an hour looking at the photos and wall posts on Jason's Facebook page now that we were officially friends, I got out of bed and padded downstairs, where I found Narc sprawled on the couch in front of the TV watching *Puppy Bowl* on Animal Planet while chomping away on the leftover roasted garlic and cinnamon brussels sprouts I had made earlier.

"Hey," I said.

He jumped. "Ahh!"

Guilt clouded his face. "Please don't tell the guys you saw me doing this," he said as he quickly tried to change the channel. "It'll totally screw up my reputation." He pointed to the veggies. "The food, too. But by the way? They're awesome."

I sat down and took the bowl from him and started to pick straight from it. Living with a houseful of guys had rubbed off on me. "Your secret is safe with me. But if you ever got caught, I bet you could get away with a sleep-walking defense."

He nodded. "Huh. That's a good idea. I like that." He looked at me. "Why are you up so late?"

I shrugged. "Can't sleep. Stuff on my mind."

He sighed. "Yeah. Trying to rank Beatles songs keeps me up at night, too."

I gave him a look, which he missed because he was engrossed again with the Puppy Bowlers. "'Dear Prudence.'"

"Huh?"

"That's my favorite Beatles song."

I nodded. When I first moved in, I had tried to track the guys' thought processes but had quickly given up after I realized that there was no rhyme or reason to them.

He clicked off the TV and turned to me. "So you excited for the party on Friday?"

I felt myself turn red. I hadn't expected to have a *conversation* when I came downstairs at two o'clock in the morning. Especially with dots of Clearasil all over my face. "I, uh . . . actually . . . no." I sighed.

His face fell. "But it's in your honor! Since you're underage and can't drink, I was going to organize a special Red Bull pong game and everything!"

Way to make a girl feel guilty.

"Why aren't you excited?"

I shook my head. "I don't really want to talk about it. It's late and—"

He shrugged. "Okay," he said, as he reached for the remote.

"Okay, I'll talk about it." I decided.

He put the remote down and turned to me.

"But I don't know . . . it just feels so embarrassing."

He started to reach again. "So . . . you *want* to talk about it, or you *don't* want to talk about it?" he asked, his hand hovering in midair.

"I'll talk about it." I sighed. "See, there'sthisguyinmy gradeandforsomeweirdreasonNicolathinkshemightsort oflikemeeventhoughhe'ssuperpopularndthere'snowaythat wouldeverhappenandeventhoughITOLDhernottoshewent aheadandinvitedhimtotheparty."

He looked confused. "Was that even in English?"

I should have just stayed up in my room and continued possibly getting asbestos poisoning. "There's a guy coming to the party on Friday."

"Well, yeah, there are lots of guys coming," he said. "For some reason it's easier to get them than the girls—"

"No. I mean there's a guy coming who I'm going to have to, you know, *talk* to."

"Ohhhh . . . I get it," Narc said. He shrugged. "Well, that's easy."

"How so?"

He yawned. "You just, I don't know, talk to him. Like you would to any other guy. Like me. Or Noob." He thought about it. "Actually, scratch that—not like Noob. Because with Noob, you kind of have to talk to him like you would a five-year-old. Or someone from a foreign country."

"But he's not just any other guy," I said. "He's . . . popular. And on the cute side." Okay, fine, maybe he was on the *cute* cute side, but Narc didn't need to know that.

"And you're on the cute side, too," he said. He cocked his head. "More on the . . . beautiful side." He got all embarrassed. "I hope that wasn't inappropriate for me to say that. It's just that girls fall into three categories: cute, beautiful, or interesting looking. And you're definitely in the beautiful one."

"Interesting sounds good, though," I said. "Why can't I be interesting?"

He grimaced. "No. You don't want to be interesting. That's kind of code for didn't-hit-the-jackpot-in-the-looks department."

Maybe Nicola was right. Maybe I could write a book with everything I was learning.

Narc yawned and stood up. "All this talking is exhausting. I don't know how you girls spend so much time doing it. I'm going to sleep. Good night."

"Good night," I said as he walked away.

It couldn't be that easy . . . could it?

The morning of the party, I woke up out of a dream where I was wearing a dress made out of butterscotch krimpets and eating them one by one so that my maxi dress was soon a mini. I didn't have to be a shrink like Marcia to know it was anxiety about the fact that in approximately fifteen hours, if he showed up, I would be struggling to find things to talk about with Jason Frank. Although I had been trying not to think too much about that, that was hard to do when I kept getting texts from Nicola that said things like *omg r u so freaked out about the fact that ur crush is coming to a party JUST 2 C U?!!!*

As I lay there wondering if the 7-Eleven down the street carried Tastykakes and whether if I had one that would lead to twenty, my phone rang.

"Can we just talk about the fact that in about fifteen hours you'll be standing next to Jason Frank?" Nicola said. "Or maybe you'll be sitting. Actually, I vote for sitting. I think everyone looks hotter when they're sitting versus standing, don't you? And if you do sit, make sure—"

"Nicola, will you stop?! We don't even know if he's coming."

"He said he was."

"Yeah, but he could, I don't know, get hit by a bus," I said. "Or . . . that clown in a tutu statue on Main Street could fall on him and crush his spine and he could never walk again."

"What a chipper thought," she said. "A bit of advice? You might want to keep that super-attractive Eeyore part of your personality on ice until you've won him over and he's totally in love with you. In the meantime, Operation Simone's First Sort-of Date starts at noon at One Person's Garbage. See you there."

When I got to the store, Brad had four dresses set aside for me to try on, including this red halter maxidress I had been eyeing for weeks. Because it had belonged to some sitcom star from the seventies who, according to the tag, had been on the cover of *TV Guide* thirteen times, it was priced pretty high.

"My wardrobe has quadrupled in the last few months," I said to Nicola as she held up a leather bustier that had belonged to the wife of some action-adventure star from the eighties. "I can't buy anything else. Especially not for a party."

Brad rolled his eyes. "I'm not sure what they do for special occasions on *your* planet, but here on Earth, a first date—especially a first date ever—is a bit of a big deal. Especially if said date is taking place within the context of a party."

"It's not a date," I corrected. "It's a . . . gathering . . . that he may or may not show up at."

He looked at Nicola. "I don't envy you."

She sighed. "Tell me about it."

"Just try it on," he ordered. "It would be a loaner."

Not only did it fit great, but every shopkeeper on Abbot Kinney signed off on its hotness factor when Nicola insisted on parading me around and taking a poll. Which, when you were talking about a group of gay men, carried a lot of weight.

"So. Any last-minute advice for her?" Nicola asked Brad as I paid for the red dress. There was no way I was going to let Brad loan this to me—I'd pay for it fair and square, with my discount. In Nicola's ongoing attempt to make me look more normal and less like I was being electrocuted with my new look, she was forcing me to wear the dress for the rest of the day rather than put it on right before the party.

He thought about it. "Yes. Try and keep your arms down as much as you can. I'm not saying you're a big sweater or anything, but this kind of poly blend material tends to be very unforgiving when it comes to that stuff."

That was just as important as stuff about boys, I decided.

"Whatever you do, *don't* let him know you're interested," Kimmy said as she finished blow-drying my bob a little later. Although I had gotten pretty good at blow-drying my hair, Nicola had insisted I get it professionally done for the party. "Guys don't like girls who are interested in them. It's the whole hunting-and-gathering thing."

"So . . . I should pretend I can't stand him?" I asked.

"Right."

"However, there's one loophole to that," said Lady GaGantuan as he got a manicure next to us.

"What?"

"If he either (a) is very insecure and/or neurotic, or (b) has ended a relationship between six and eight weeks earlier, then it's better to give him the full court press and let him know you're very available and interested."

I turned to Nicola. "Are you taking notes? Because there's no way I can keep this all straight."

"But if it's only been four or five weeks, definitely act like you're not interested," Kimmy added.

"Oh, and if you're thinking of trying to gauge what's going on with him from his Facebook status updates, don't," Lady GaGantuan said. "Because people are always fudging those to try and make people think they're doing better than they are."

"Or worse," Kimmy added.

Nicola and I looked at each other. Now I was even more confused than before. "Okay, so maybe asking these guys for advice wasn't the best idea," she whispered. "We need to go to people with more life experience."

Which is how, a few hours later—after a stop at a few makeup counters at the Nordstrom in the Westside Pavilion, done in such a way that it didn't seem like I was totally trying to get an entire free makeover out of the deal even though that was exactly what I *was* trying to do—we ended up at the Coffee Bean, post-three P.M. Zumba class.

"So you're finally ready to admit your crush on Blush," Cookie said. "You get, lady!"

"I think you mean 'you go, girl,'" I corrected.

"Ah," she said, taking out her notebook.

"But actually, this isn't about Blush. It's about another boy," I said. Lucky for me, Cheryl wasn't there, because having to lie to her and not let on that the boy I was asking for advice about just happened to be her son would have been impossible.

"I know you young people go in for that Rules nonsense," Marcia said, "but as a therapist and a feminist, I'm a big believer in honest, forthright communication. So if you like this boy, tell him!"

Gwen shook her head. "Sorry, but it's all about the negotiation. I learned that in law school. You don't want to show your hand too quickly. So act interested, but not too interested."

Cookie leaned in. "Sweetie, before you move forward on this, are you sure you're even attracted to boys?" she asked. "Or do you think you might end up realizing you like girls? The reason I ask is because my granddaughter just came out, and she's very happy, but before that she went through a lot of heartbreak and aggravation," she explained. "All I'm suggesting is that you give it a think."

So much for clarity and experience. I was more confused than ever.

I got home to find the guys in the same position they could usually be found—lounging around watching yet another *Sorority House Slasher* movie. Except for Blush, who was sketching, and Doc, who was reading.

"So what time is the party actually at?" I asked as I grabbed a napkin and picked up something peeking out from under the couch that at one point might have been the top of a hamburger bun before it dried into something that now resembled a fossil.

"I don't know. Nine?" Max asked, without looking away from the TV.

Doc looked up from his book. "Oh. I told people eight."

"These girls I met over on the boardwalk might come

by at seven thirty," Noob said. "I hope I told him them it was tonight and not tomorrow."

I was like Martha Stewart-level organized compared to these guys. Yesterday, I had presented them with a list I had put together for the party—things like "straighten up," "make a party mix iPod playlist," "buy hors d'oeuvres"—but everyone other than Doc had looked at me like I was suggesting we all run a marathon before building a house in Haiti through Habitat for Humanity. The only part they got excited about was the hors d'oeuvres part, but even then, they were more interested in Noob's idea of peanut M&M's rather than mine about the baby shrimp wrapped with prosciutto that I had seen on the Food Network. (Max—who believed that people could easily survive solely on pizza and sushi—said that he remembered our dad once saying that our mom had been a real foodie, so my newfound interest in food must have come from her.) Because of the lack of enthusiasm about the list, I didn't even bother bringing up "go to farmers market for flowers."

I turned to my brother. "Max, did you go buy the hors d'ouevres?" I asked.

"You mean the peanut M&M's and the chips and salsa?"

"Yes. Those," I replied. So much for pretending to act as if this was nothing more than a college rager.

"Um, no," he said. "I was going to, because, you know, you had assigned me that job on the little graph that you and Doc are always updating. But I forgot." He cringed. "Actually, that's a lie. I didn't forget. What happened was on my way to the mini-mart to get the stuff, I came across this old rusted bathtub in the street? You know, those old-fashioned clawfoot ones? And it was just so cool looking, I stopped and took a bunch of pictures of it with my Hipstamatic and I got so into it that by the time I was done, I had totally forgotten that I was on my way to the store."

This wasn't the first time that my brother had been sidetracked by some impromptu photo shoot. But usually they involved pretty girls whom he then ended up asking out rather than old bathtubs.

"I *love* when the artistic impulse overtakes you to the point where you lose track of all space and time!" Thor bellowed. "That's what it's about, man—that's true Art-with-a-capital-A. When you don't know where the creative process ends and you begin. Plus, it's a good excuse if you're the kind of person who tends to be late to things."

"Wow. You can actually *see* the creative process?" Noob asked. "I wonder if I can." He squinted and stared into space. "Nope. Nothing."

I sighed. "I guess I'll go do it then."

"I'll go with you if you want," Blush offered.

"Okay," I said nervously. But why was I nervous? Blush and I always went to the store together. So what if this time I was all dressed up and my hair was straight and I had makeup on? That didn't matter.

With the twenty-five dollars and sixty-eight cents that I collected in my brother's UCLA Bruins hat—most of it in crumpled-up dollar bills, dimes, and nickels—along with the fifty I had taken from the Emergency House Fund (if snacks for a party wasn't an emergency, what was?), we set off for the market.

Because I was dressed up, this time we drove in my Saab. "So you excited for the party?" he asked as we loaded up on all sorts of non-Food-Network-approved hors d'oeuvres like candy and chips at Ralph's.

"Oh yeah. Sure. Can't wait," I said, in what I hoped was a very chipper-sounding voice. The problem was, because I did chipper about as much as I did giggling (which was to say, nearly never), instead I sounded like I was exhaling helium.

He glanced away from the M&M's and over at me. "You sure?"

That was one of the things I liked best about Blush. Instead of saying something like, "Okay, it's completely obvious you're lying," therefore making you feel even more stupid, he was gentle about that stuff. He didn't judge; he didn't tell you how you were feeling—he just put things out there . . . like a question you might want to ponder at some point while lying on a hammock on a perfect spring day as a light breeze went by.

I picked up a bag of peanut M&M's and stared at it intently. "Yes," I said, as all the letters of the ingredients blended together so it looked like one long chemistry compound.

"Okay," he shrugged as he began to push the cart.

That was another thing I liked about him. He didn't push. And because he didn't push, it made me want to be honest. "Fine. No. I'm not excited," I admitted. "In fact, if there was an earthquake right about now and we couldn't have the party, it wouldn't suck."

"How come?"

"Because Nicola invited this guy from our school." The minute the words came out of my mouth, I regretted them. It was one thing to feel comfortable talking to a guy, but it was a whole other thing to bring up another guy—and your complete lack of social skills about the matter—to him. My only hope was that because Blush was so tall, the words had disintegrated during their climb up to his ears and he hadn't heard them. Even though his ears were sort of big and stuck out a little.

He nodded slowly. "So you got a guy coming to the party, huh?"

I shrugged. "Well, he's not really a *guy* guy," I said. "He's just . . . okay, fine. He's a *guy* guy." My face felt like it did the time that Nicola convinced me to put Crisco on because it would make me tan faster. Which, when you're as pale as I am, is like throwing a lit match on dried leaves. "But I don't want to talk about it anymore."

He nodded. "Okay."

We pushed the cart toward the check-out lanes. "But just so you know, I didn't invite him. Nicola did. Without even discussing it with me first."

"Got it."

We started unloading the stuff on the belt. "Okay, fine. We can talk about it. But just a little bit." It was a good thing that, unlike girls, guys didn't spend their time gossiping. Because if they did, and Blush and Narc compared notes, I'd get a reputation for being one of those people who said "I don't want to talk about it," only to then talk about it.

I took a deep breath and told him about Jason. I explained how he was a twit ("Not a tweeting twit," I clarified, "but a Testosterone Twit") but that, based on the few times we had actually spoken, he actually wasn't twittish at all. And how I wasn't saying I liked him or anything, because how could you like someone you had only spoken to a few times—especially someone who sat on the Ramp in the cafeteria when you sat in the way corner—but that if he ended up coming to the party that night, which, even though he said he would, probably wasn't going to happen, especially if the ballerina clown fell on him and severed his spinal cord—I wasn't completely opposed to maybe getting to know him a little better.

"Even though, ultimately, that would be a total waste of time," I said, "because it's not like he and I could ever *really* be friends let alone, you know . . ."

"What?"

"What what?"

"You couldn't really be friends or what?"

I turned red again. "Okay, now I *really* don't want to talk about this anymore," I said, practically throwing the money at the cashier so I could get out of there.

He shrugged and started to follow me into the parking lot. "Okay, so we won't talk about it," he said over his shoulder. Because of his long legs, within a few strides he had already passed me.

"Well, maybe we can talk about it a little bit longer," I said. I had asked all these people for advice, but they were all middle-aged women, drag queens, or gay men. Or Narc, who was his own category. "Like, say, as long as it takes for you to explain what it is a girl should do when talking to a guy who she's not saying she likes, but definitely does not *dis*like."

He shrugged. "I don't know. You just . . . be yourself."

I rolled my eyes. "Narc pretty much said the same thing. But what else?"

He shrugged again. "I have no idea. That's the only way I've ever done it."

"Yeah, but in your case, being yourself works. I mean, you're *interesting*. You deal with *puppets*. But what if yourself . . . just isn't good enough?" I asked softly. "I mean, you know, for someone like this guy."

He looked confused. "What if yourself isn't good enough for a twit?"

"Like I said, he's a twit, but not a *twit* twit. He's just . . . you know what? Forget it."

"But yourself has to be enough," he said. "It's not like you have another choice as to who to be."

Maybe in a world made up of puppets that was true, but we were talking *high school*. In *Lost Angeles*. You couldn't get more cutthroat than that.

"Let's try this another way," Blush said as we got into the car. "Why don't you start with 'hi' and then go from there?"

I glanced at him. "Just 'hi'?"

He nodded. "Yeah."

"But what do I do after that? If, you know, he says hi back?"

"Just start with hi. And then see what happens."

I nodded. "Okay. I can do that," I agreed as I started the ignition. "I think."

Not only was it only one word, but it was just one syllable.

But there was one more thing I couldn't shake: Why did it feel weird talking to Blush about another boy?

seven

"So *this* is what we've been missing all these years?" yelled Nicola later over the thump of reggae music as she munched away on tortilla chips while spilling salsa on her I'M NOT BARBIE—I JUST LOOK LIKE HER T-shirt. In honor of the party, she was wearing her best Doc Marten boots with her shortest denim mini.

I yawned as I popped open another Red Bull (Did people end up going to rehab for this stuff? Because I had a feeling I was seriously on my way) and looked out at the crowd. The guys were on one side of the room, either playing video games or talking about surfing or skateboarding or photography or video installations, while the girls—a mostly artsy, beachy, boho-looking group (except for one scowling girl with a Mohawk, invited by Thor)—were on the other, chatting about lip gloss and comparing tattoos on their lower backs ("You should have Cookie add 'tramp stamp' to her dictionary," Nicola said). "I guess so," I yelled back. "It's just like Staci Kenner's boy-girl party in sixth grade, but everyone's taller and has bigger boobs." Because it was a college party, I wasn't quite sure what to expect. Guys drinking beer while upside down in a headstand? Girls having smackdowns like on *Jersey Shore*? Definitely something more interesting than this. It was a good thing the music was so loud or else I might have fallen asleep.

As I looked around the room, I saw Blush sitting alone on the stairs, doing what I was doing—taking in the crowd and not really talking to anyone. Almost as if he knew I was staring at him, he looked up and smiled.

I waved and motioned him over. Because of the crowd, it took him a while to get there. As I scooted over on the couch to make room for him, there was a tap on my shoulder and I turned to see Jason.

"Hey," he said.

"Hey," I said back.

There was a tap on my other shoulder. I turned to see Blush. "Hey."

"Hey," I replied. For someone who planned on majoring in English, I really hoped my vocabulary improved by the time I got to college.

Now what? "Um, Jason, this is Blush."

"Hey," Jason nodded. Okay, his vocabulary wasn't any better than mine. That made me feel a little better.

"What's up?" Blush replied with a nod.

Nicola stood up. "And now that everyone knows each other, I'm going to go try to find something to eat other than chips!" She turned to Blush. "Blush, will you come with me? I think I saw some Mallomars on the top shelf in the kitchen, and I can't reach them."

As she dragged him away, Jason pointed at the couch. "Do you mind if I sit down?"

I shrugged. "Sure." I left out the second half of my answer, which was ". . . but you're going to have to excuse me because I have this sudden urge to take that bowl of peanut M&M's away from Noob and go lock myself in the attic and eat myself into a sugar coma because I have no idea how I'm going to get through this conversation."

As he settled himself in the couch, which, because it was so old and lumpy and lived in a house with seven guys, had this bad habit of making everything on it kind of fall in toward the middle, the two of us were soon sitting way too close together. Every time I tried to scooch away, I slid back.

Finally, I grasped onto the cushions as if they were life preservers. "So you should try the chips," I said. Leave it to me to talk about food. "And the salsa. They're really good."

He nodded but didn't reach for them. Now what? Usually, the idea of having Nicola around made me nervous because of the no-filter thing, but at least she never ran out of things to talk about. Unfortunately, Mallomars now in hand, she had her back to me as she yakked Blush's ear off. He, however, saw me, and mouthed, *What's wrong?*

While Jason leaned over the chips, I motioned to my mouth as if trying to pull something out of it and shrugged. To most people, it probably would've looked like I was saying I was going to throw up, but Blush somehow understood me and pointed to the iPod that was docked in some speakers.

I nodded and turned to Jason. "So, uh, do you like iPods?"

He looked at me, confused.

Shoot. I had already screwed it up. "What I meant to say was do you like *music*." I cringed. Uh-oh. We had already covered this subject in 7-Eleven. And the outcome was not good.

"Oh yeah." He started bobbing his head. "Like her," he said as Adele sang "Rolling in the Deep." "I love her."

"*You* like Adele?" I asked.

He nodded, starting to sway back and forth a little bit. I looked around to see if anyone was watching. Thankfully, they weren't. "Don't you?"

"Well, yeah, but—"

"But what?"

But Adele was so . . . *not* varsity-team high school boyish. Teenage girl, yes. Gay man, totally. But Testosterone Twit? I think not. Luckily, the song ended and morphed into Jay-Z's "Empire State of Mind." "—but unfortunately it's over," I continued. "But hey, now it's Jay-Z. This is a good song. Don't you like this song?"

He stopped swaying. "Not really. I'm not really into 50 Cent."

Had he really pronounced it "fifty" instead of "fiddy"? Even Cookie had gotten that right a few weeks ago. "Um, this is Jay-Z," I replied.

"Oh. I'm not into him, either," he replied, without the slightest bit of embarrassment.

It wasn't like I had actually spent any of my hard-earned money downloading Jay-Z and 50 Cent songs, or even downloading them for free on Spotify, but even I knew the difference between the two. That being said, something told me that he probably knew all the words to more than a few Beyonce and Rihanna songs. Before we could discover we had even less in common, Noob walked over. "Hey, Simone. You having fun?"

"Oh yeah," I said. "A blast."

"You know what I was just thinking?" he asked.

This was going to be good. "No, Noob. What were you thinking?"

"I was thinking that that movie *Son-in-Law* with Pauly Shore that they play all the time on that cable channel CMT? It doesn't get nearly as many props as it deserves. 'Cause it's *really* good. We're talking classic."

I turned to Jason, who, like most people the first time they encountered Noob, had a confused look on his face.

"He does that sometimes," I explained. "Just goes off on weird tangents like that."

"Hey, did I ever tell you the story about why I had to get the tip of my finger amputated?" Noob asked.

"He's also big on lack of segues," I said. I turned to Noob. "Nope. Don't think you did." This was good. This could possibly eat up approximately ten minutes, during which I wouldn't have to worry about making conversation.

"Okay, so this is the deal," he said as he settled in on the arm of the couch and went on to tell some long story about how, when he was seven, he got his arm caught in the window of the backseat of his mom's car (obviously, he had been shoving his limbs into small spaces from a very early age). But because the radio was on so loud, she didn't hear him yelling and she wasn't a great driver, which was why, when she parked, she brushed against a rosebush, and a few of the thorns cut his pointer finger really deep, and that's why they had to amputate the very tip of it. What was great was that every time he screwed up one of the facts (which, because Noob was Noob, happened a lot) he'd start the entire story over from the beginning. By the time he was done, the party was breaking up, and all I wanted was for everyone to leave so I could change into sweats, roast myself some sweet potatoes, and analyze my entire conversation with Jason word by word with Nicola.

"Well, I guess I'm gonna go," Jason said as everyone began to shuffle out and Nicola stood behind him pretending to be very, very interested in the leftover guacamole when what she was really doing was eavesdropping.

"Simone will walk you out," Nicola said, pushing me toward him.

I gave her a look.

"You're the hostess. And you know how confusing it can be to find the front door in this place."

I led him to the door, and we stood on the front porch. I examined a crumpled red plastic cup as if I were on an archeological dig in Egypt. "So I was wondering . . . do you want to hang out?" he asked suddenly.

"Now?" I thought I saw something in my peripheral vision, and suddenly I jumped. Because when I turned my head, I saw that Nicola and the guys were all standing in the shadows behind the door watching us.

"No. Sometime next week."

"Okay," I shrugged.

I could see Nicola shake her head back and forth in frustration.

"Hey, Nicola, are you okay?" I heard Noob ask with concern. "You look like you have water in your ear."

I needed to get Jason out of here before all eight of them ended up seriously embarrassing me. "That would be nice," I said, quickly pushing him toward the stairs so fast he almost went flying. "See you!" I called over my shoulder as I turned and ran toward the door.

When I got inside they were all staring at me.

"What?" I asked, nonchalantly.

"What do you mean, 'what'?" Nicola cried. "You've got a date! With Jason Frank."

I found myself glancing over in Blush's direction, but he was busy picking up empty soda and Red Bull cans from the floor. "It's not a date. It's . . . a hangout session," I said uncomfortably. "It's a whole different thing."

"It is? How so?" Noob asked.

"I don't know. It just is," I replied.

Regardless, the idea of either of them made my stomach hurt.

"You're judging again," Nicola warned the next day as we helped Brad set up for his Fifty Percent Off Just Because Sale. (He had originally wanted to call it Fifty Percent Off So I Can Surprise Luca with a Cruise to Mexico in an Attempt to Save Our Relationship, but we had talked him out of it because it felt a little TMIish.)

"Oh please. *Adele*?" I demanded.

Brad looked up from his computer, where he was checking out the cruise ship instead of helping us unpack. "Ooh, I love Adele."

I looked at Nicola. "I rest my case." But she was right. I *was* judging him. So he had horrible taste in music, or at the least, atypical taste in music. I could live with that. (Could I? Really? I wasn't sure.) The truth was I was just scared. Maybe "scared" wasn't the right word. It was more like . . . terrified. Not so much about the date part of the date, where you talked (even though from our time together on the couch, that was going to be tough, especially without Blush across the room to give me cues that I then misunderstood and screwed up). But what about at the *end* of the date? If he tried to kiss me?

It was embarrassing to admit, but at almost seventeen years old, the closest I had come to kissing a guy was when, in the privacy of my room with the lights out and the door locked, I would take out the dog-eared copy of *People* magazine that I kept shoved under my mattress and open it up to page 72, to the "in-depth, exclusive look of one of Hollywood's rising stars," and hold it up to my face while I practiced. But unlike most girls in my school who, if they did this, would have chosen someone like Robert Pattison or Justin Timberlake, my kissing partner was Jesse Eisenberg, the star of *The Social Network*. Because all my practicing had gotten the page somewhat wet, the picture was pretty smeared (with a hole where one of his eyes should have been because it had ripped), so it was hard to see the cuteness that made me pick him, but it was there.

Like Michael Cera (who could have played his younger brother in a movie), Jesse was more *nerd* cute than *cute* cute. Unlike Jason, who was definitely *cute* cute. And had probably kissed tons of girls and would therefore immediately realize I had not. Kissed guys. Or girls. Or anyone.

"Would it be really wrong if I told Jason that there's a slight chance I have mono?" I asked them.

Before they could answer, the bell on the door jingled and Hillary came floating in, looking as unwrinkled as ever but with a tan. "Hello, hello!" she cried, giving me air kisses on two cheeks. "Your brother said you'd probably be here."

"Hillary. What are you doing here?" I asked. "You guys weren't supposed to be back for another two weeks. Is everything all right? Is my dad okay?" I panicked. What if something had happened to him?

"Oh, he's fine," she said. "A few pounds heavier because of all the pasta, but I already booked some appointments for him with my trainer. Can't have him looking flabby at the wedding." She flashed a smile at Nicola. "Oh, Nicole. How are you? I didn't recognize you under all that eyeliner. How retro of you." She looked around the store and cringed. "Which I guess makes sense in a place like this."

"You weren't kidding," Brad said under his breath.

"What wedding?" I asked.

She smiled. "*My* wedding! I mean, mine and your father's." She held out her left ring finger, which had one of those ponytail holders with a marble wrapped around it. "We're engaged!"

Little dots of light started to flash in front of my eyes,

like the time I fell on the balance beam. I couldn't believe my father had asked Hillary to marry him without discussing it with Max and me first. The lights flashed faster. Actually, who was I kidding? I actually *could* believe that he had done that—which hurt more than the news itself. I rubbed my eyes. "My father gave you a ponytail holder as an engagement ring?" I asked, confused.

"It's a placeholder," she explained, "until I get him to Cartier. But now that it's official, I wanted to get used to the heft. Anyway, we came back early to tell you kids in person. Actually, we came back so I could get started on the planning, because in this town everything books up so far in advance, but we figured since we're back, we'd take you guys to lunch to tell you so you don't read about it on my Facebook page." She whipped out her iPhone. "But hold on—now that you *do* know, I'm just going to type this in."

"You *really* weren't kidding," murmured Brad.

"Okay. All done," she said. "Come on. Your dad and Max are down the street at Lilly's. We should get going." She looked me up and down. "Did you lose even more weight?"

I shrugged. "I don't know. I don't weigh myself."

"What are you talking about? Who doesn't weigh herself?"

Nicola raised her hand. "I don't."

"I don't either," offered Brad. "'Cause once, there was

this doctor on *Oprah*—I can't remember who it was, but it wasn't one of the famous ones—and he was saying that—".

"Fascinating. *Anyway*," Hillary interrupted, "when we get to lunch, you can have a nice big hamburger and fries to get some meat back on your bones." She smiled. "Maybe even a nice slice of apple pie."

Nicola's eyebrow went up. "Interesting," she said as she began to quietly hum the *Law & Order* theme music.

"I'm allergic to apples, remember?" I said.

"Oh yes. That's right. I always forget that." She squinted. "And your arms. They're so . . . defined." She sighed. "Oh, Simone. I don't even know what to say about that." She sounded like she had caught me doing something wrong. Like smoking. Or drinking. Or listening to Justin Bieber. She walked over to the full-length mirror and began to check herself out. "Although it *is* kind of sweet that if you keep up those Mumbai classes—"

"Zumba," I corrected.

"—then soon we'll have matching triceps," she went on. "Well, maybe not matching, because mine have been so sculpted for so long." She turned around and checked out her butt in the mirror. "Huh. Here I was all worried that I had gained a few pounds, but I think I may have lost some."

I didn't tell her that the mirror was known to kind-of-sort-of make you look a little bit thinner than you actually were. ("It's not to mislead people and make them buy things," Brad said when I asked him. "It's more about helping their self-esteem.")

"Simone, come over here," she ordered.

I made my way over and stood next to her. We couldn't be more different. She was tall and blonde and unwrinkled, with perfect pink nails, and I was brunette and pale, with an almost-threadbare New Order T-shirt and a chipped magenta manicure. Plus, she smelled like coconut body lotion, whereas I still had the smell of burned sausage in my hair from when Max had attempted to cook breakfast this morning.

"Wow. That's really amazing," Brad said as he and Nicola gazed at us.

"What? The fact that Simone and I could be sisters?" Hillary asked. "Because I look so young?"

"No," he replied. "How much Simone has changed over the last few months. You're like a completely different person. If they ever did a biopic about Winona Ryder's life—you know, before she got all crazy and started shoplifting—you'd be perfect casting."

"I love Winona Ryder," Nicola said. "I think she's super hot. She even looked good in her mug shot."

Hillary's smile disappeared. "Come on. We're late," she said, as she yanked me toward the exit.

"I'll keep looking for something for you to wear on Thursday night," Nicola called after us.

"What's Thursday night?" Hillary asked.

If she was giving me this much grief about my weight, I could only imagine what she'd have to say about the fact that I had a date. Which was why I wasn't going to tell her. "Nothing."

"She's got a date," Nicola blurted out.

So much for that plan. I shot Nicola a look.

"Look at you—so grown up and . . . *girl*-like!" Hillary exclaimed. "Who's it with? Someone's cousin? I did that once for this girl I knew in high school who wore a brace for scoliosis—fixed her up with my cousin. I felt *so* good for doing such a good deed. Especially since, because he had horrible acne, it was this *double* good deed—"

"Actually, it's with a totally hot guy who's super popular." Nicola smirked.

"Popular?" Hillary asked, surprised. "As in *regular* popular or *captain of the Mathletes* popular?"

"Oh, definitely *regular* popular," Nicola said. "Like *hot* regular popular."

"Actually, you met him," I said. "It's the guy we ran into in the parking lot of Kmart."

"Really? Wow. He *is* hot."

I tried not to throw up the yogurt I had eaten, now that my soon-to-be stepmother had just said that a high school boy was hot.

"Paging Mrs. Robinson," Brad murmured as he pointed at the poster of the movie *The Graduate,* which was hanging on the wall behind him. In the movie, Anne Bancroft (whose scarf was part of Brad's very-special-and-not-really-for-sale-but-might-be-if-you-offered-enough-money collection in the glass case behind the counter) played this older woman who started sleeping with her daughter's boyfriend.

"I think it's great that you've found a boy who judges people on their personality rather than their looks," Hillary said. "That's a very noble quality to have." She dragged me toward the door. "You can tell me all about him on the walk to lunch."

Except I couldn't, because as soon as we stepped outside she got a text from her friend, Claire, saying that she had heard from her assistant Melissa, who had heard from another assistant at a different studio, that Mandi Morrison, another D-girl at a rival studio who was also a "30 Under 30" and constantly trying to outbid Hillary on scripts, had gotten engaged that past weekend as well. I tended to avoid that *Bridezilla* program because I had no interest in weddings. I had already decided that if I ever got married, I was going to elope. But I'd seen enough snippets of the show while channel surfing to know that the way Hillary began to freak out about this news made those Bridezillas look like the Buddhist nuns Thor and I had watched in a YouTube video a few days earlier. (Thor's shrink had suggested he check out Buddhism to help him deal with his anger issues, but after he stomped out of the room after getting frustrated that the video kept freezing up, it didn't look like that was going to work.)

By the time we had made our way to Lilly's on Abbot Kinney, Hillary had called the top florist, caterer, and band (the fact that they were already on speed dial on her cell was a little weird) and booked them before Mandi could.

As we walked into the restaurant and my dad saw me, his face lit up. "Simone, the beach air must agree with you, because you look just beautiful," he said after he hugged me. "But you've being wearing sun block, right?" he asked anxiously. "Because your skin is just a petri dish for melanoma."

I cringed. He made it sound so gross. "Yes. I'm wearing SPF eighty-five."

"Don't you think that's overdoing it a little?" Hillary asked. "I bet you could get away with four. Or, if you wanted to really be careful, eight."

"She'd burn to a crisp if she wore four," Max said. Hillary glared at him.

Okay, I was almost used to Hillary's comments about me. But this was getting to be too much. Could the Zumba-ites and Nicola be right—Hillary had it in for me?

Hillary shrugged. "But think of how nice and sunkissed she'd look before the burn set in."

As Max and I exchanged a look, my father cleared his throat. "Kids, Hillary and I have an announcement—" he said nervously.

"Oh, honey, don't worry about bothering with all that." She flashed a smile. "I already told Simone."

My dad paled. "Hillary, we said that—"

"Told Simone what?" Max asked.

"They're getting married," I said. "Can't you tell from the fake engagement ring on her finger?"

My father turned to me. "Sweetie, I know this seems sudden, but if you let me explain—"

I shrugged. "Fine. Explain." I braced myself for some poetic from-the-moment-I-set-eyes-on-Hillary-my-world-was-forever-changed speech. Or even a very unpoetic what-can-I-say?-Hillary's-hot-and-a-lot-younger-than-me-and-and-a-"30-Under-30."

"Well, in talking to my accountant and business manager, with the extra money I'll be making this year, based on the projections for how they think the *Ruh-Roh* video game is going to sell over Christmas, getting married in this calendar year will save me a lot in taxes."

Taxes? *That* I was not prepared for. Maybe because it was the least romantic thing I had ever heard in my life.

"So you're marrying her because it's going to save you *money*?" I cried.

My dad turned red. "Well, obviously, that's not the *only* reason—" he sputtered.

"We're also getting married because we love each other a great deal!" Hillary said indignantly. She turned to him. "Right?"

"Of course," he agreed. A little tentatively, if you asked me.

Even though I could have moved back home now, I was going to stay in Venice as long as possible. Hillary on a good day was hard to take, but as a Bridezilla? Forget it.

Max shook his head. "This is ridiculous," he muttered. "All I'm gonna say is that if I end up over forty and still single, it'll be completely understandable, given the role model I have."

Obviously, being a grown-up wasn't all that much different than being in high school. Even at my dad's age, people still dated people who they thought they *should* date, for a lot of reasons other than the fact that they really wanted to be with them. Could it be any more unromantic? Personally, I found the whole two-people-from-different-worlds-meet-and-despite-the-odds-end-up-together-because-they're-meant-to-be fairy tale–like thing pretty sappy and unrealistic, but it was a lot more interesting than getting together for tax purposes.

Hillary smiled. "So. Check your in-boxes for updates as to the wedding. And now that that's out of the way, let's move on to something else." She turned to my father. "Like the fact that your daughter has her first real date. With a boy who's *popular* popular rather than *Mathlete* popular!"

"You have a date?" Dad asked nervously. "I don't know if I'm ready for this. Who is he? What do his parents do?"

Why didn't he just come out and ask how much *money* they made? That was the real question. "I actually know his mom," I replied. "From Zumba. She's really nice."

"And his dad's a big-time director," Max added. "The guy's been nominated for six Academy Awards and won five of them."

Hillary looked up from her texting. "An Academy Award-winning director?! You didn't mention *that* part. Who is it?"

"Stan Frank," I replied.

Hillary gasped. "He's not just an Academy Award-winning director. He's . . . *God*. Do you *know* how many movies I've offered him that he's turned down?!"

"Really? He wasn't interested in directing a movie about a talking fish?" Max asked.

"Oh no. I wouldn't offer him that stuff," she scoffed. "I only went to him with my A-list movies. Like the animated musical version of Cleopatra." She turned to me and shook her head. "I can't believe you're going out with the son of someone so important. That's like dating . . . a *prince* or something. Like someone in the royal family."

As Hillary yammered on about how, if I didn't screw things up and Jason actually ended up as my boyfriend, then the Franks could come to the wedding, I reached for a piece of bread and slathered it in butter. Out of the corner of my eye I saw Max's eyebrows raise.

"It's just one piece," I murmured. I knew that one piece

wasn't so bad, if I stopped at one. And I had to have *something* to soften the blow that my father was definitely not acting like a prince of a guy.

"I can't believe she actually got him to make it official," Max said as we walked home. Dad hadn't even asked if I wanted to come home now that they were back from Italy. And I didn't suggest it, either. The less time I spent with bride-to-be Hillary, the better.

"Yeah, well, it sounds like he didn't exactly fight her too hard on it," I replied, feeling nauseous from all the bread I ended up having. I hadn't stopped at one slice. After three slices, I decided to stop counting.

"And what about when she found out who Jason's dad was? She got so jacked up I thought one of her fake boobs was going to deflate." Wow. It seemed that Max's glass had gone from half full to nearly empty in terms of the Hillary thing. I had to admit—I kind of *liked* this side of my brother.

"Maybe they won't end up going through with it. Maybe she'll have a pitch meeting with a writer who's even more successful than Dad, and she'll dump him and move into that guy's house and redo *his* daughter's room," I said hopefully. Who was the one with the glass half full now?

He shook his head. "Could she be any more jealous of you?"

I looked away from the group of skaters who were staring at me as we walked by. I still found this being-noticed thing very uncomfortable.

"You know, the women at Zumba say the same thing, but to be honest, I have no idea why she would be," I replied. "I may have lost some weight, and, yes, I'm dressing better, and now that I'm used to it, I agree that my hair may have been a little too long and rat's nest-y before, but I'm still the same on the inside." I sighed. "Complete with being totally clueless as to what I'm supposed to do on this date thing." If I thought any more about the wedding, I was going to get seriously depressed. I had to move on to a subject that, while still depressing, was not soul crushing.

"What do you mean you don't know what to do," he said. "You just go and act normal. You know, be yourself." His eyes narrowed. "And you keep all your clothes on and his hands off you."

I rolled my eyes. "What's up with you guys and this just-be-normal thing? You make it sound like it's so easy or something." I sighed. "I wish there were some sort of class I could take. Or maybe they have a *Dating for Idiots* book." I always did score high in the reading-comprehension part of standardized tests. "I know—I'll just watch MTV all afternoon. I should be able to get some tips off there, don't you think?"

His eyes bugged out. "From the network that brings you *Teen Mom* and *Jersey Shore*?!" he cried. He shook his head. "No way. If you want to learn about this stuff, better you learn from some real experts."

Other than the one time I had gotten to the locker room late and had to change in front of everyone else for gym class instead of in the bathroom stall because Monica Betrucci was in there disposing of her lunch via her throat, I couldn't really think of anything more embarrassing than pretending to be on a date with a guy who kept yawning while six other guys watched my every move. Except, say, if the date was being filmed with a flip camera by my best friend, because, according to her, it would be helpful for me to study it later on. Like they do in football. Even though I knew that was a total lie and that the truth was *she* could study it later on, in preparation for a date at some point in the future with my brother.

"Okay, let's try this again," Doc announced as Narc and I sat across from each other the next day at the card-slash-dining room table, which Noob had recently found on the street, pretending to have a pretend meal on our pretend date. According to Doc, if his parents hadn't pushed him into being pre-med, he would've been a film major, which is why he was the most qualified in the group to direct this whole thing. "But Simone, this time, try not to pull your hair across your face every time you say something. It makes it very hard to hear you."

I let go of my hair and nodded. "No hair pulling. Got it."

"But maybe the way she fidgets with her hair and uses it as a shield against connecting with other human beings is just part of who she is," Thor said. "I understand that we're trying to help her here, but that doesn't mean molding her into someone whom she's not. See, that's exactly what's wrong with this city—it's like there's no room to be an individual. They just—"

"We got it, Thor. L.A. sucks. Duly noted," Max interrupted.

"Omigod! I feel the *same* way about L.A.!" Nicola gasped. Was it my imagination, or did her pupils get ginormous whenever she was around him? "I can't believe we haven't discussed this. You know, I actually wrote this blog entry with a list of one hundred and one things about the city I don't like. If you go back to last February—"

"Let's just get back to this and get it over with," I interrupted in an attempt to save my brother. I turned to Nicola. "You ready?"

"For what?" she asked, all hazylike, as if she had taken one too many of Wheezer's Benadryls.

I pointed to the camera. "With that."

She turned red. "Oh. Yeah," she mumbled as she turned it on. "Simone's Fake Date, take thirteen!" she yelled—from the way he cringed—right into Max's ear.

Narc looked at me and smiled. "Hey," he said.

"Hey," I murmured as I sat on my hand to stop myself from hiding behind my hair. I glanced over at Blush, who was sitting on the stairs watching the whole thing with a small smile. Like the kind that people watching monkeys at the zoo have on their face, especially when the monkey does something particularly stupid. *Not a word,* I mouthed to him.

He smiled wider. It was too bad his shyness stopped him from doing that too often because it was a really great smile. *I'm not saying anything,* he mouthed back. It was kind of cool when you reached a point in a friendship when you could understand what someone was mouthing across a room. Nicola was pretty much the only person I had been able to do that with. Except when she was chewing gum—then it got all complicated and made it look like she was speaking Chinese.

"You might want to speak up," Noob yelled. "Like I'm doing right now. You know, protect your voice."

"I think you mean 'project,'" Wheezer wheezed.

"Okay, okay," I said. I turned to Narc. "Can we start over?"

"Sure. Let me just get into character again." He cracked his neck a few times and fluttered his lips. "All set."

"And we're rolling!" Nicola yelled. "Wait—scratch that. We never actually stopped rolling."

"Hey," Narc said.

"Hey!" It came out so loud it sounded like I was talking to someone who was very hard of hearing. I turned to Doc. "I hate to do this. But we can start over just one more time? I think I'd like to try it with 'hi' instead of 'hey,' I swear it'll be the last time."

"Take fifteen!" Nicola yelled.

"Actually, it's take fourteen," Wheezer corrected.

I glanced over at Max, who had his head in his hands.

"This *was* your idea, you know," I said defensively.

"I know it was," he sighed. "Just start again."

"Hey," Narc said.

"Hi," I replied.

"That was great!" Wheezer wheezed. "Good volume. And just the right amount of flirt without being all skeezy and easy. Kind of says, 'If you play it right, then—'"

"Okay, dude? I do *not* want to hear this," Max said, covering his ears.

"You can tell all that just from 'hi'?" I asked, amazed.

Wheezer shrugged. "Well, yeah, sure." He looked at the group. "Right?"

They nodded.

Huh. Maybe I had underestimated them and they weren't as clueless as I thought.

"And it also says 'I'm going to have the burger, medium well,'" Noob said.

Well, some of them weren't.

"Okay, we're still rolling, so keep going," Doc ordered.

"So . . . how are you doing?" Narc said.

I shrugged. "Fine. I mean, you know, a little nervous because it's weird having to be on a pretend date in front of a bunch of people, but other than that, I'm good."

"I think he was asking you that in character," Max said. "As part of the date conversation."

I looked at Narc. "Were you?"

He yawned as he nodded.

"Are you yawning because of the narcolepsy thing or because I'm boring you?" I asked.

"The narcolepsy thing," he replied as he yawned again. "At least I think."

Seeing that I still didn't know where the date was going to take place, we jumped ahead to the saying-good-night portion of the evening ("Tell him that kissing before marriage is against your religion," Max said) when the front door opened and Hillary's perfectly unfrizzed head could be seen. I never thought the day would come where I'd actually be happy to see Hillary, but if it got me out of my fake date, I'd take it.

"Hello, hello!" she cried. "Is everyone decent?" she

asked, without waiting for an answer before she *click-clack*ed in holding a garment bag. She looked at the guys and smiled. "Max, you didn't mention how *handsome* your friends were."

My brother and I looked at each other and cringed. Hillary clearly had no problem with the age difference between her and the guys. My father was lucky that none of these guys had made a Mark Zuckerberg–like fortune by inventing some sort of social networking site. Luckily, they all looked pretty freaked out by the cougar-esque look on her face. Except for Noob. He just looked confused.

Hillary took in the messy living room. "Well, this is certainly—"

"I hope you're not planning on saying 'messy,'" said Thor. "Because although it might appear that way to the average person, what we're going for here is actually a well-thought-out artistic decision to mirror the chaos that currently surrounds us on both a national and international scale. Not to mention what we, as young men on the threshold of adulthood, must struggle with—"

"*Anyways,*" Hillary interrupted, "I just swung by because I bought Simone a little something for her date," she said as she held up the garment bag. "It just felt like a sweet soon-to-be-stepmother thing to do." She held up her still-ponytail-holdered hand. "I'm not sure if Simone and Max mentioned it, but I'm now engaged to their father."

Who *didn't* know? Not only did all of Hillary's 756 Facebook friends know, but she had also tweeted about it *and* started a blog called "Countdown to Bliss—How You, Too, Can Lasso the Man of Your Dreams."

"Wow. I've never seen an engagement ring made out of marbles. That's really cool. A lot cooler than diamonds," said Noob.

I stood up. "That's so nice of you. Let's go up to my room." I grabbed Nicola's arm. "You, too."

"Well, look at this," Hillary said after we got to the attic. "This is equally charming." She pointed to the wall. "There's not asbestos in there, I hope," she said.

Nicola and I looked at each other. Was it my imagination, or did she actually sound a little hope*ful*?

"I have no idea."

"Well, I guess we'll find out soon enough." She shrugged. She held out the garment bag. "Here you go."

I unzipped the bag and gasped. Inside was a stunning emerald-green silk 1960-ish sailor's dress.

Hillary smiled sweetly. "I know if your mom was alive, she'd make a big deal about the fact that you're going out on your first date."

"Omigosh—it's beautiful," I gasped.

"Wow. It is," said Nicola. "It's so . . . *Mad Men*."

"It is, isn't it?" agreed Hillary. "You know, I think it's wonderful that there's a show on TV that features full-figured women like that." She walked over to the mirror and turned around to get a glimpse of her butt. "Unlike, you know, thin women like me. I got it at Decades. Bedbug-free, I promise."

Decades was a very upscale resale store over on Melrose, which meant it was expensive. I'd probably be too nervous to wear it. As I looked at the label on the neck, I realized I wouldn't have to worry about that. "Hillary, this is incredibly nice of you . . . but it's a size six."

She looked at it. "Oh, is it?"

"Yeah."

"And the problem with that would be . . . ?"

"I'm a ten."

"Maybe in *regular* clothes you are, but it's different with vintage couture things. They run *bigger*."

"Really? I thought the expensive stuff ran *smaller*." Especially vintage.

She held the dress out to me. "Just try it."

With Nicola standing guard, soon enough I was in the bathroom with the broken lock (a complete nightmare when you were a girl living in a household full of guys) stepping into the softest, silkiest dress I had ever felt. At first it zipped up without a problem. But then . . . not so much. I stepped up onto the ledge of the tub so I could get a glimpse of myself. From my knees to just above my waist I looked just great. But from there on up I looked like a sausage that was about to squeeze out of its casing. I sighed. It was as if in one second, I was reminded that no matter how much weight I lost, how different my hair was, whether I got asked out on a date or not, I could only go so far before I was reminded of my place.

"How's it going in there?" I heard Hillary call out.

"I don't think it's going to work," I called back as I cringed at my back fat. As soon as I got back to my room, I was grabbing a T-shirt and some cargo pants.

"Let's see," she said as she flung open the door.

I was so startled that I slipped and landed butt-first in the tub. "Omigod—are you okay?!" Nicola panicked. "You didn't break your butt, did you?"

"Forget about her butt—you didn't rip the dress, did you?!" asked Hillary.

I stood up. Everything seemed to be in working order. "I think I'm okay."

"Good. Don't take this the wrong way, but you look like you should be on that *Oh No They Did Not* show," said Nicola.

"This is nothing," Hillary said, marching over to me. "It's just a little snug."

"A little?" I gasped as she yanked at the zipper. "If that thing goes up any higher, my intestines are going to shoot out my mouth."

"Oh please. I've wriggled my way into things way tighter than this," she said. "If I can give you one piece of stepmotherly advice, let it be this: learn how to hold your breath for long periods of time. It will come in very handy."

"What an empowering thought," said Nicola.

Hillary yanked the zipper up even farther. "How's that feel?"

If I had any air left in my lungs to talk I would've said, "If you removed five of my ribs, it might be okay," but I couldn't because I didn't. Instead, I just gasped.

"I think she's turning blue," said Nicola.

"Oh, she's fine," replied Hillary. "It's just the bad lighting in here."

"I really think it's too tight," I managed to get out.

"Simone," she laughed as she zipped it up even higher, "I had no idea you were such a drama queen! How cute! You think this is uncomfortable? Just wait until you start getting Brazilian bikini waxes. Now *that,* my friend, is pain."

As she yanked the zipper up a little more, I felt like I was going to pass out. "I really can't breathe," I gasped.

But Hillary just kept zipping.

"Didn't you hear her?" Nicola cried as she pushed her aside and began to unzip me.

Hillary shrugged. "Okay. If you want to give up *that* easily," she said. "But it's called 'slave to fashion' for a reason, you know."

I shook my head. Nicola had gotten the zipper down enough that I could finally draw air back into my lungs. "Yeah, well, that's never going to be me," I said as the oxygen began to return to my brain. "Even if I become a size zero. Which, by the way, I have no interest in being. Plus, how are you supposed to eat if you can't breathe?"

Hillary patted my cheek. "Ohhh . . . how cute. You really *are* that naïve. I thought it was just an act. Women don't actually *eat* on dates, silly. You order a salad and you pick at it and then you pig out when you get home!"

Nicola's eyes narrowed. "You know, I saw something like this on a TV movie once on Oxygen. Where a woman tried to kill another woman by suffocating her with a dress. I think it was called something like *Murder in Milan*."

"Another drama queen! How cute! No wonder why you guys are BFFs." She shrugged. "If you're going to give up so quickly, I guess you should give me the dress back so I can return it. You know, it wasn't cheap." Her iPhone rang. "It's the caterer. I have to take this."

After she *click-clack*ed out, Nicola turned to me as I changed back into my clothes. "If we were characters on one of those detective shows right now, I would be turning to you and taking off my sunglasses and saying, "Let's get her in for questioning *stat*," Nicola said.

"I think they only say 'stat' on the hospital shows," I said as I struggled to get my hair untangled from the hook on the back of the dress.

"Whatever. But don't you think all of this is a little weird?" Nicola asked as she untangled me.

"What?"

"Hmm . . . I don't know . . . trying to suffocate you with a dress, for instance."

"Oh, so this, like the apples and the almost running into me in the parking lot, is yet another attempt to kill me?" I asked.

She shrugged. "If the shoe fits. Or rather, if the dress *doesn't* fit."

"Well, seeing that there's a good chance I might not live through my date, she might not have to worry about that," I sighed.

While I definitely considered myself a feminist and had already decided that if and when I got married, my husband and I would definitely switch off when it came to taking out the garbage, my feeling about dates was that it was up to the date-asker to come up with a plan as to what he or she and the date-askee could do. Because when the date-askee has to call the date-asker at four o'clock on the day of the date to see what time and where said date will be taking place, and the date-askee says, "I don't know. Got any ideas?" it's a little . . . disappointing.

"Well, there's always the movies," I said to Jason as Nicola and the guys crowded around me and leaned in to try to listen. Except for Noob, who had gotten his arm stuck in the stairway railing again. I was all for activities where we wouldn't have to talk all that much.

"Okay. You want to go see that new one about the

FBI agent who goes up against the ex-CIA agent after he takes a group of elementary school kids hostage in a mall?" Jason asked.

"Actually, I heard that was really lame," Narc said in a loud voice.

"Who was that?" Jason asked.

I turned my back to the group. "No one. Just the TV."

"So does that sound okay?" he asked.

According to one of the articles I had read in last month's *Cosmopolitan* (Hillary had a subscription), number five of the ten things on the How-to-Drive-Him-Wild-and-Make-Him-Yours-Forever checklist was "Even when your man suggests a really dumb idea that you have no interest in doing, just say yes!" (Those magazines were very big on the term "your man" and on exclamation points.) "Actually, it sounds . . . kind of dumb," I admitted. So much for following that rule.

Thor ripped out a page from *L.A. Weekly* and thrust it toward me, I brightened. "Hey, they're showing a marathon of Judd Apatow's *Freaks and Geeks* at the New Beverly," I said excitedly. "How about that?"

"What's *Freaks and Geeks*?" Jason asked.

My heart sank. Sure, the series had been canceled after only twelve episodes, but that didn't make it any less brilliant. In fact, *Time* magazine had called it one of the "100 Greatest Shows of All Time." I had watched it so many times the DVDs skipped.

"This TV show on NBC that Judd Apatow did set in a high school?" I said.

"Who's Judd Apatow?"

Did this guy live under a rock? "The director of *Knocked Up*? *Forty-Year-Old Virgin*? Produced *Superbad* and *Bridesmaids*? Our generation's John Hughes?"

"Right. That guy. Now I know who he is. Just took me a second to put the name with the movie. So it's a TV show set in high school?"

"Yeah."

"And you want to watch something about school even though we're on summer vacation?" he asked doubtfully.

"It's really good. I promise."

"Okay. So, uh, should I pick you up?" he asked.

"No, that's okay," I said quickly. "You don't need to pick me up. I'll just meet you there. At, like, seven fifteen, okay?"

"Okay, but I don't mind—"

"No. It's easier this way. Because I have to go pick up some . . . medication at the drugstore first." Oh God. What was I doing?! Not only did I lie, but now he was going to think I had some sort of weird disease. I'm sure the sound of Nicola slapping her forehead could be heard across the phone waves. "Okay. So I'll see you then. Bye," I barely got out of my mouth before clicking the phone off.

Thor shook his head. "Ouch. That was *cold*. Here he

was, taking the risk to show you his courteous, feelings-oriented feminine side, and you shut him down."

"You really should've let him come pick you up," Nicola agreed.

"Yeah. Why didn't you let him come over? Are you, like, embarrassed of us or something?" Noob asked, all hurt.

"No. It's—"

Noob dropped his voice. "I mean, without naming names or anything, I know that some of the people who live here can be a little . . . strange," he said, motioning with his head toward Thor, "but it's not like we'd embarrass you or anything like that." He tried to yank his arm out from the banister but failed. "Uh-oh."

"I'm not embarrassed by you guys," I replied. "It's just that I've never done this date thing before. I'm used to doing things for myself. I'm not used to letting people do things for me. But I'll be more girl-like when I'm on the date. I swear."

In movies, when a girl gets ready for a date, it usually takes so long they have to do a whole montage with little snippets of each part of the getting-ready thing: showering; blow-drying the hair; shaving the legs; putting on makeup; gazing at her very full, very neat closet. According to the movies, it would appear that getting ready takes around an hour, an hour fifteen minutes. As for me, from the time

I got in the shower until I walked downstairs, a whopping seventeen minutes had passed. And that included having to start all over with my eye makeup after I poked myself in the eye with the mascara wand and my eye got all teary and ruined my eyeliner.

When I came downstairs, Blush was on the couch watching a documentary on PBS about the Harlem Renaissance. Even though they were all artists, the only way that the other guys in the house would've known what PBS was, was because of *Sesame Street.* But Blush watched it all the time. Which made him really good at *Jeopardy!*, a fact I had discovered a few nights earlier when we were hanging out and he trounced me in Double Jeopardy.

"You look nice," he said.

I looked down at my READING IS SEXY T-shirt that I had paired with a denim miniskirt and red Worishofer slides. Nicola voted for the black sundress that I had bought that first day of Operation Robin Red Breast, or whatever, but when I greased Noob's arm up with Crisco to free him from the banister, he said that I should go a little more casual. For once I thought he was onto something. Mostly because if I wore the sundress, I would have to wear a strapless bra, which I found very uncomfortable.

"Thanks. It turns out that I'm not very high maintenance when it comes to getting ready."

He laughed. "You're not high maintenance at all."

"Thanks. Wait—that's a good thing, right?"

He laughed again. "Yeah. That's a very good thing."

I plopped down next to him on the couch, and I heard Nicola's voice in my head, saying, "Legs! Legs!" I slammed mine together. I was still getting the hang of this skirt thing.

Blush pointed to my feet. "Cool shoes."

"Thanks. They're actually orthopedic shoes," I said. "Like for old German women. But they're super comfortable. Nicola tried to get me not to buy them, but I did anyway. And then we saw in an article that M.I.A. and Michelle Williams wear them, too. That's the first time I've ever been cool without trying," I babbled. I probably shouldn't have chugged a Red Bull during the getting-ready part. "So can I ask you something?"

"Sure."

"Okay, well, I noticed that during that whole date-tutorial thing, you didn't really say anything."

He shrugged. "I don't know, I just think that whole thing was kind of stupid."

"What part?" I asked. "I mean, personally, I think that *all* of it is stupid, but I'd be interested in knowing what part *you* think is stupid."

"It's just that you throw two people who are both probably nervous together, and instead of one of them or both of them just saying that, which would break the ice, they both sit there trying to play by some rules."

I nodded. "Yeah. I know what you mean." I sighed. "And unfortunately for me, I'm really bad with the rules things. When I was in elementary school I always got 'needs improvement' in following directions."

"So are you excited about going out with this guy?" he asked.

I shrugged. "Sure."

"Huh."

"Huh what?"

He shrugged. "I guess I got the sense from your reaction to his taste in movies and music and stuff that he's not really your type."

I sighed. How could I explain to a guy—let alone a guy like Blush, who really couldn't have cared less about these things—that when you spend your life on the outside of everything, you can't turn down the chance to go out with someone who's on the center of the inside. Jason Frank was like that part of a candy bar commercial when they show the creamy nougat center, and not taking that when offered is just wrong. "Because he's the only guy who's ever asked me out," I blurted. I kind of hated that when it came to Blush I was so comfortable around him that my edit button was constantly broken. Wow. That was even more embarrassing than if I had tried to explain the first thing. I stood up. "And, now, I . . . I have to . . . go be a little more high maintenance," I said as I stomped off.

I had every intention of letting Jason buy the tickets, since he was the asker and I was the askee. But because

I got there early, and because I didn't have anything else to do other than try not to sweat through the armpits of my T-shirt, I just did it myself. And because I was hungry and got some popcorn, I bought him one as well. And a Coke. And an assortment of candy.

"You didn't have to get all this," he said when he got there at seven twenty.

"Oh, it's okay."

He took out his wallet. "Let me give you—"

"No! It's fine," I said quickly. "We should go in. I already got us seats."

He shrugged. When we got to the door, he opened it and stepped aside.

"What?" I asked as I stood there.

"I'm holding the door open for you," he explained as he gave me an odd look.

"Oh. Thanks," I said as I walked in. Only five minutes into the date and I had already screwed it up.

Luckily, for the two hours that followed I didn't have to worry about making conversation. All I had to do was sit back and relax and laugh. And keep an ear open to see if he laughed at the right places. (He did. Well, at least a few times.) By the time we walked out I was a lot more relaxed. Like to the point where I let him open not just one door for me but two.

"So . . . there's that place Milk down the street," Jason said as we got outside as a sea of Seth Rogen-esque guys walked by us. "Their blue velvet cake is awesome."

I waved to Josh Rosen, the guy who had hit me on the head that day in study hall when Jason first talked to me. "Blue velvet cake? I don't know," I said doubtfully. "I'm sort of an expert on the dessert front, and I've never heard of that in my life."

"I'm telling you, not only does it exist, but it's incredible." He smiled. "Trust me."

I cocked my head and smiled back. "Okay." Uh-oh. What was happening to me? What was this . . . *girly* feeling that was coming over me? So he smiled at me. So what? And so what if the smile made him even cuter? I wasn't the kind of girl who could be won over by that. And even if that's what it felt like at the moment, I couldn't go there. I was not going to lose control and let my hormones kick in and get all moony over a boy. Especially when the boy in question listened to *Justin Bieber*. I needed to remember that. If I could, it would all be fine.

A few minutes later we were seated at a table at Milk with a slice of blue velvet cake between us.

"You know, I think you're right," I said as I tried to take a regular-sized forkful of the blue velvet instead of doing what I wanted to do, which was just dive headfirst into the thing. "This might quite possibly be what my friend Cookie would call 'the grenade.'"

"Huh?"

"She means 'the bomb.'"

"Isn't 'the bomb' like so late nineties?"

"She's fifty-five." It was taking everything in me not to suggest we get a slice of the vanilla bean tres leches cake, too. And some oatmeal butterscotch cookies. Apparently, I didn't feel the need to binge on baked goods only when I was sad or anxious, but when I was excited as well. Who knew?

"I told you," he said. "So you trust me now, huh?"

Another smile. Okay, this was not good. Because those smiles—they were kind of dazzling. They had this way of rattling my brain a little so that I felt like I was having these mini-strokes and the world stopped for a second and I couldn't think. And while I was pretty sure those were the reasons that people did drugs, I didn't like that out-of-control feeling. I liked being *in* control. Even when I used to lock myself in my room with sheet cakes, I was *controlling* the out-of-control feeling I got from doing that.

"Yes. I trust you," I replied. Were we talking about the cake, or were we talking about something else?

"Good. I'm glad." Another smile.

I stared at the cake as if it held all the secrets to the universe. Which, not so long ago, I had really thought it had. "Can I ask you something?" I asked quietly.

"Sure."

I looked up at him. "Why'd you ask me out?" Ever since the night of the party, I had been wondering that. Jason Frank could've gone out with any girl. Well, any girl who liked dating boys instead of girls. Although rumor had it that Dakota Fincher, the president of the LGBT chapter, had a crush on him, too. And seeing him smile at me, I understood why.

"What do you mean?" he asked.

"I mean, it's not like we're really in the same orbit. We go to the same high school, but we're in totally different crowds. You're one of the popular crowd. And I, actually, I don't even *have* a crowd."

He shrugged. "I wanted to get to know you better. You always seemed nice. Even, you know, when you were . . ." He motioned to the cake.

"When I was fat?"

"Well, yeah."

At least he was honest.

"And now that you're, you know . . ." He motioned in the air.

"Not fat?"

"Well, yeah."

"And, you know . . ."

"You can see my face because my hair's not hanging in it?" I suggested.

He smiled. "Yeah. And the glasses. The glasses are hot. In fact, when I saw you wearing them, that was the clincher."

I blushed. Who knew that nerdy-looking glasses would prove to be the thing that got me a date?

"Plus, my mom's always going on about how great you are."

Oh God. Did *Cheryl* do this? Was this a mercy date? "So you asked me out because of your mom?" I asked. This was so embarrassing. If this was a mercy date, I was transferring. So what if it was my senior year. It's not like the three that had come before had been fun-filled and I'd miss anyone other than Nicola.

"No. Not at all. I asked you out because I wanted to go out with you, okay?" he said defensively.

"Okay," I said, slumping down. Way to ruin the date. Had I ruined the date? Would it be totally wrong for me to take out my iPhone and Google "signs that you've ruined a date" right in front of him? "Does your mom know we're here?"

He nodded.

Oh great. I was going to get an earful at Zumba for not telling her beforehand. I needed air. Or water. Or a piece of gum in my mouth in case he tried to kiss me later. Which, to my surprise, suddenly didn't seem all that bad. "I'm going to go to the bathroom." I stood up so fast I almost knocked my chair over. "Be right back." Once I got there I found that not only was my face all flushed (which, when you had skin has pale as I did, was more like blotchy) but my teeth—and tongue—were *blue*. No wonder he was smiling at me—it was because he probably wanted to burst out laughing instead, but knew that if he did, I'd tell Cheryl and then he'd get in trouble.

After trying to scrub at them with water, but only

managing to get my T-shirt all wet, I gave up and went back to the table.

"My mouth is all blue," I said.

"Yeah. I noticed."

"But yours isn't," I said.

He shrugged. "Maybe it only happens the first time you eat it?"

"But you didn't say anything."

He shrugged. "It's kind of cute."

I sighed. I so did not understand guys. Not like my brain was in any state to attempt to try at that moment anyway.

The good news about having come in separate cars was that I didn't have to worry about a full-on makeout session in his car where the windows—and my glasses—would get all fogged up. (When you were a glasses-wearing person, did you take them off when you kissed? I had totally forgotten to Google that.) The bad news was that after he walked me to my car, we stood there talking about whether, when you realized a parking meter was broken, you had to put a note on it or else get a ticket. We were talking for a while, when I realized that I had to pee because I had forgotten to do that once I had realized my mouth was blue.

"I guess I should let you get home," he said after we had nothing left to say.

"Yeah. I guess," I said, shifting my weight to my other leg in an attempt to hold my bladder.

"Well, this was fun."

"Yeah. It was," I agreed. Actually, I wasn't sure "fun" was the word I would've used to describe it. "Nervewracking," yes, "okay," at times, but "fun"? Eh.

"We should do it again."

"Yeah. We should." Had that mini-stroke thing taken away my ability to make conversation?

We stood there some more. Finally, when the silence got too uncomfortable, I reached for the door handle. "Okay then. I'm gonna go then I guess." As I opened the door and moved to get in the car, he lunged toward me and put his hands on my shoulders. Which startled me and made me push the door toward him—*hard*—smacking him right in the stomach.

"Uff," he moaned as he doubled over.

"Oh God! I'm so sorry!" I cried. "Are you okay? Here—let me help you," I said as I lunged at him, twisting my ankle in the process and clinging to him as I started to drag him down. Luckily, he yanked me up before we both ended up on the ground, leaving us almost nose to nose. We were so close that I could smell fresh peppermint coming from his mouth (it was nice to know that even though he was popular, he worried about his breath, too).

"Sorry about that," I murmured.

"It's okay."

And then it happened. As he tilted his head to the right and leaned in, I tilted mine. The same way. Until I realized that was wrong and tilted it the *other* way, at the exact second that his nose was coming toward mine, which meant that they collided. *Hard*.

"Ow!" I cried as we ricocheted back from each other.

"What the—?!" He took his hands away from his nose. "Is it bleeding?"

I shook my head and took mine away, too. "No. Is mine?"

"No."

"Sorry about that," I said. "I just—" Did I tell him the truth? That I had never kissed a boy who wasn't literally in a magazine before? "I have this weird neck problem. Where I can't bend it to the left. But the problem is I forget about it a lot. Especially when I'm about to kiss someone." Apparently, no, I did not tell him the truth.

"That's okay." He began to lean in again.

I leaned back. "What are you doing?"

"I was going to try that again," he said, a bit impatiently.

"Oh okay." That time I didn't turn my head. I kept it very, very still. At least until his lips hit mine and started moving around a little, which made me realize that if I didn't do the same, he'd definitely be able to tell that I didn't have a lot of experience with this stuff. Luckily, something took over—like how you never forget how to ride a bike, or, in my case, you forget for a little bit and almost have a panic attack until you remember—and I remembered how to kiss. Even though I had never done it before.

The kiss seemed to go on and on, which was fine with me. I even seemed to know intuitively how to breathe while doing it. And when he slipped his tongue into my mouth, it wasn't slimy or disgusting, like I had feared it would be. It was just a tongue. Finally, after a while he stopped and pulled back.

"Wow. You're an awesome kisser," he said.

Thank you, Jesse Eisenberg. "Thanks," I replied. "So are you." At least he seemed like he was. The mini-stroke thing started up again. I just hoped it didn't happen when I was driving.

We just stood there and grinned at each other.

"Well, I guess I should let you get home," he said again.

"Yeah. I guess."

That time when he leaned in, I tilted my head the opposite way from him so there was no bumping. There was just more kissing, until some car slowed down and someone yelled, "Get a room!" out the window.

"Now I really think I should go," I said breathlessly.

"Okay. I'll text you."

"Bye," I said as I jumped in the car and watched him walk down the street to his.

I knew one thing—spending a Thursday night making out with a guy was a lot more fun than eating snack cakes.

nine

The thing about all those how-to-get-a-guy articles is that once you get them (even if it's just getting them to kiss you), they don't mention the part that comes *after* that. Probably because it's so horrible that if they did, girls would steer clear of guys and become nuns or lesbians. Although I had a feeling that the horrible part happened if you were a lesbian, too.

It was, like, post-kiss, everything changed. But instead of my life turning into one extended music video directed by someone cool like Sofia Coppola, it was more like a horror movie.

"You know, a watched plate never warms," Nicola said at Coffee Bean a few days later as we sat with the Zumba Brigade and I obsessively checked my phone every minute and a half to see if there was a text from Jason.

"I think you mean 'a watched kettle never boils,'" Cookie corrected. She took out her notebook. "But I like that watched plate. It's catchy. Even if it's not particularly hip."

"I know, I know," I moaned, turning off my iPhone and placing it in my bag so I wouldn't be tempted. I had no idea what was wrong with me—while pre-date I had been only mildly intrigued by Jason, post-date and, more importantly, post-kiss, my obsession ballooned like my fingers did when I forgot to use low-sodium soy sauce.

"Who are you waiting to hear from, honey?" Marcia asked.

I glanced at Nicola. Luckily, Cheryl had had to run to a waxing appointment, so she wasn't there, and I didn't have to tell her about how I was freaking out about kissing her son. But even so, I couldn't lie to these women—they were like my family. "I'm waiting to hear from—"

"This boy she went out on a date with the other night," Nicola finished.

At that, all the women stopped what they were doing and leaned in.

"Boy? Who is it?" Gwen demanded. "Is it Blush?"

"What?! No!" I cried. "It's . . ." I sighed. I had to come clean. "Jason."

They all looked blank. "Jason who?" Cookie asked.

Really? They had to make it this hard for me? "Jason Frank."

"That's so funny—Cheryl's son is named Jason, too!" Rona said. "What a small world."

"It's the same Jason," I said, slinking down in my chair.

And reaching into my bag for my iPhone and turning it back on to check to see if there was a text.

I was pretty sure the gasp that went up could be heard over in Japan.

"Tell! Tell!" Cookie cried.

"Everything," Marcia added.

Which I did. Well, other than the hitting-him-with-the-car-door part. "And he said he'd text, but he hasn't." I clicked on Facebook.

"What are you doing?" Nicola asked.

"Checking to see if he wrote some sort of cryptic status update that only he and I would understand," I replied.

Gwen shook her head. "Guys don't do that. That requires way too much thinking."

"Did you check any of your horoscopes online to see if they had some insight?" Marcia asked.

I nodded.

"His sign, too?" Cookie asked.

I nodded. Talk about humiliating. I had stooped as low as astrology.

"It's the oxytocin thing," Gwen explained as I began to pick at Nicola's ginger scone.

"What are you talking about? There weren't any drugs involved!" I said.

"Not *oxycontin*. Oxytocin. From kissing. They call it the 'cuddling hormone,'" she explained. "It's also released when a woman breast-feeds."

"Between the oxytocin and the dopamine, it literally affects your brain as if you're on drugs," Marcia added. "So when it starts to wear off, the reason you get all obsessed is because you want to kiss him again so you can get high again."

"Who says I'm obsessed?" I asked as I reached for my iPhone. Before I could pick it up, Nicola's hand swooped in and grabbed it. "Okay, fine, I'm obsessed." I sighed. "I never would've kissed him if I had known this. You know, there really should be some sort of warning disclaimer or something when it comes to this stuff," I said. "Like those stickers they put on prescription pill bottles that say you shouldn't operate heavy machinery or go out in the sun when you're taking it."

Cookie patted my arm. "It'll be okay. It'll pass."

"When?" I moaned.

"Well, when my Harry and I started dating, it took him three weeks to call me to ask me out for a second date," Cookie said. "About two weeks and three days into it, I gave up and started to forget about him. So see, there's hope."

I sighed. I wasn't sure if I could take another day of this craziness, let alone two weeks. Plus, what was I thinking? He was Jason Frank, Testosterone Twit. Popular Person. Ramp Sitter. And I was . . . not.

Even if he liked to kiss me, it's not like there could ever be a future for us. What would his friends say? What would *my* friends say? Okay, fine—what would my friend, singular, say? Right then I heard Nicola's voice in my head, as clear as could be. And what I heard her say was that I wasn't the Fat Girl anymore. I was no longer allowed to hide out and sit on the sidelines in one of those low-slung webbed lawn chairs that were impossible to get out of and watch the world go by. I had to *participate* in life—not watch it on a TV or movie screen or, better yet, on the screen inside my head. And sure, sometimes it wouldn't work out. But maybe sometimes it would. I mean, if anyone would have told me not even a year earlier that I'd be living with seven guys and would have had my first kiss right now, I never would've believed them.

Sure, maybe things with Jason would prove to be a total and complete mess . . .

But maybe they wouldn't, and I had to let that happen, too.

Still, later that afternoon the obsession was still there. In fact, it had gotten worse, to the point where I was finally forced to do something I had a feeling I might very much regret—confide in my roommates about what was going on. After suffering through being filmed on a mock date in front of them, it's not like I had a lot of dignity left to begin with. What was the harm in losing the rest of my dignity? Plus, maybe they could help.

"I'm a little confused," Doc said, after I stumbled and

mumbled through what I had tried to keep a CliffsNotes-length version of the oxytocin poisoning I had been dealing with post-kiss but had ended up being an unabridged one. "What exactly is it that you're asking?"

Narc shook his head. "Dude. You're being so . . . girl-like. I have to say, I'm a little disappointed," he said sadly.

"I know," I moaned. "I can't help it. I guess what I'm asking is . . . do you think . . . would it be okay . . . if I . . . texted him?"

From the horrified looks on their faces, I was guessing that was very much *not* okay.

"Not, like, a *long* text," I said. "Just like a hey-was-thinking-about-you-and-just-wanted-to-say-hi text."

Wheezer actually started to wheeze at that.

"Okay. Fine. What about just a text that says 'hey'?"

They continued to look mortified.

"Then I guess calling is out of the question, huh?"

Max cringed. "How did I not know I had a crazy stalker chick for a sister? This is so embarrassing."

"What?! I am not a stalker!" I cried. "I didn't even do anything. And I'm *not* going to do anything!" I reached for some Nutter Butter cookies and shoved two in my mouth. "Except eat!"

"Simone, I'm going to let you in on a secret," Thor said. "Even though I'm a huge foe of hypocrisy, double standards, and anything that keeps any group down while giving the white man even more power, when it comes to relations between males and females, at the end of the day, you will be much better served if you follow one simple rule."

"What?"

"Just be the girl and let the guy come after you."

I cringed. "That's completely sexist!"

"I know. But I'm looking at it from a biological point of view. It's programmed into our DNA," he replied. "You have to let him be the hunter and let yourself be hunted."

I cringed. I'm sorry, but that did not sound fun at all. In fact, it sounded very painful.

"Once you're a couple, you don't have to do that," he went on, "but that first communication post-date? It's a good idea. After that, knock yourself out with all the communication you want."

I looked at the guys, who all nodded.

"And when he does finally text you or call you, you need to wait at least twelve hours to respond," Wheezer said.

"Twelve hours?!" I cried.

"But if you could wait twenty-four, that would be even better," Max said.

"Even I know that," Noob added. "And I've never had a real girlfriend in my life."

Just then a text came through.

All it said was "hey," but that was enough to make the jackhammers that had been going nonstop in my chest suddenly stop. "It's from him!"

"What does it say?" Narc asked.

"It says 'hey.'"

"'Hey' is good!" Thor said.

"It's *awesome,*" agreed Noob.

"So what are you going to write back?" asked Max.

I plopped down on the couch. "I don't know. I'll text him back later." Now that I had heard from him, I felt calm again. I still didn't think I'd wait twelve hours before responding—that just seemed crazy. Now I could breathe again. At least until I began to worry about what I would write back, and then have to suffer through waiting for him to write back, and whether he'd ask me out again, and what would happen at the end of that date.

With that, the jackhammers started up again.

No wonder I had avoided this dating stuff for so long. It was as if I knew intuitively all along that it was trouble.

ten

If there was one thing I missed about my Weird Fat Girl days, it was that getting dressed took under five minutes due to my limited wardrobe choices. Now that I was all girly and had a great nose for bargains, I had a lot of options to choose from. Especially when Brad told me that I could borrow anything in the store as long as I dry cleaned it before giving it back.

The problem being, even with all those options, I still couldn't find anything to wear for my second date with Jason.

"Simone, I've given this a lot of thought, and I really think you should go with a Jackie look," Brad said the following Thursday, the morning of my second date with Jason. "I'm not talking her White House days when she was First Lady. I'm talking when she was married to the Greek billionaire." He pulled out a very colorful, very flowy maxi dress. "Can't you just see her wearing this on that giant yacht he owned? Kicking back with a martini? Actually, I think Jackie was more a champagne kind of woman—"

"Uh, that's very nice, Brad, but I kind of think it might make me look like a couch," I said.

"Fine. If you want to be like *that,*" he sniffed, all put out.

I flopped down on a pink velvet chaise lounge. "I'll just grab something out of my closet when I get home. It'll be fine."

"Okay, (a) you don't have a closet," Nicola said, "you live in an attic, remember? And (b) don't take this the wrong way, but you don't have enough experience doing this to just grab something on the fly. If you were the Stuck-Up Popular Girl in a rom-com, who was about to get her comeuppance when the Cool Indie Girl showed her up at the prom, then, yeah, maybe, but you're not."

It was great to have a best friend who had no problem telling it like it was. Sometimes. This, however, did not feel like one of those times. "Fine, but seeing that I've tried on every single dress in this store, I don't really have any other options."

As Nicola and Brad looked at each other, she gave a slight nod.

"Not *every* dress in the store," he said. He walked back to his office-slash-closet and came out holding the robin's-egg-blue dress.

"What?! Where'd that come from? I thought someone bought it!" I cried.

"Someone did buy it," Nicola said. *"Me."*

"Okay, I'm confused."

She took it from Brad and held it out toward me. "I bought it for *you,*" she said. "I was going to hold on to it and give it to you for your birthday, but I think you could use it now."

I looked at her. My multicolored-hair, multipierced, tell-it-like-it-is BFF. Sure, she could be annoying sometimes—like, say, when, because she knew me better than anyone, she called me out on stuff that I thought I was doing a decent job of hiding. But underneath her sarcasm and dry humor was a ginormous heart. One that, if you looked at it up close, was probably striped and polka-dotted. I felt my eyes fill up. "You are—"

"I know, I know," she interrupted, waving her hand. "You don't have to say it. I get it."

A ginormous heart, and a phobia of any sort of mushiness. I was assuming it was the English part of her.

"But if you're not willing to try it on now, I'm going to have to break up with you," she said. "Because I had to fight Lady GaGantuan for this. He wanted to buy it for some drag queen who dresses up like Kim Kardashian." She shuddered. "Which, seeing that Kim Kardashian already looks like a drag queen, must be a very scary sight."

I took it from her. "I'm putting it on. I'm ready," I said with a smile.

Brad clapped. "Omigod—this is just *so* 'movie moment'!"

As I stepped out of my clothes in the dressing room, this time I didn't avert my eyes. Not only that, but I actually *smiled* at myself, which, had there been security cameras in there, would have probably looked pretty stupid. Chances were I was never going to be a size 2 or 4. Maybe not even a size 6. But I didn't care. I'd rather be a healthy size 8 or 10 with a booty and boobs any day of the week than some hungry-looking skinny chick. As I stepped into the dress and began to zip it up, I waited for it to stop but it didn't. There wasn't a lot of wiggle room, but it definitely fit. When it was zipped, I stood back. The blue of the dress against my pale skin and dark bob totally worked. Did I look French? I had no idea. All I knew was that I looked like . . . me.

"There's no reason to be nervous," I whispered to myself as I sat on the couch later, waiting for Max to get ready so we could leave for the gallery. After Jason's "hey" text, I had planned on waiting a decent amount of time before texting him back—about an hour—but broke down after four and a half minutes. After that, I hunkered down with my *The Man Who Loved Women* DVD and a bag of baby carrots (the only thing that was in danger of happening to me with that, if I binged and ate the entire bag, was turning orange—a much better fate than breaking out on my chin from sugar) to wait for him to make the next move.

I was only five minutes into the movie when my phone rang. I was so surprised Jason had gotten back to me so quickly—and not just with a text!—that I forgot to be nervous and ended up having a perfectly natural conversation with him, during which not only did I manage to avoid any sort of awkward silences, but I also made him laugh. Four times. Actually, it was more like four and a half, but the last one was kind of a laugh/cough combination, so I decided not to count it fully. When he finally asked me—fifteen minutes and twenty-three seconds into the call (not like I was paying attention)—if I wanted to do something, I was glad that I was able to at least wait until the entire sentence had left his mouth before saying yes.

"Cool. So any ideas about what you might want to do?" he asked.

"Well, there's an opening at this gallery where my brother works on Thursday night," I said nonchalantly. "This famous photographer named Zooey Woodston. Maybe you know her? Kinda supermodelish? Takes pictures of her own butt? Anyway, it should be pretty good. There's a reception from six to eight," I rambled. "Over in Culver City on Venice Boulevard. There's parking on the side streets." I cringed. "Not that I've done a lot of research about it or anything."

"That sounds cool."

"I thought it could be good 'cause it's . . . *cultural*." Actually, that wasn't true. The reason it had seemed good was because Nicola and my roommates would be there, and then she could watch me with him and give me pointers afterward.

"Pictures of butts are cultural?" Jason asked.

"The way she does them? Oh yeah. Absolutely," I said. "Her photos make very strong sociological and political statements."

"Okay. Sounds good."

Despite the fact that I had discovered that kissing most definitely did not suck, I still wasn't sure I was ready for the PDDH ("Post-Date Drive Home," explained Nicola), where I'd spend the time freaking out about what I'd do if he tried to do more than kiss me—i.e., put his hands in places that no one put their hands other than the woman at Macy's who was fitting me for a bra. I didn't even want to think about what Max would do if he knew about that possibility.

Because I was so late to the game with the kissing, sometimes I felt like I was in the remedial class of Male/Female Stuff. There was a part of me that wanted to make up for lost time now that I had kind of a tutor, and get up to speed on the stuff that most girls my age were doing. If only so that I wouldn't feel like a total idiot when I was eavesdropping on their conversations from various bathroom stalls around school. I didn't want to be AP-level advanced, like Erika Sandler, who, rumor had it, knew in a very close, personal way members of more than a few Castle Heights varsity sports teams. I just wanted to be . . . normal. Whatever that meant. But that being said, I wasn't sure if I was ready for all the stuff that seemed to make up "normal" at my school.

Which is why, when Jason asked me if I wanted him to pick me up—even though him going from Santa Monica to Venice would be out of the way—I told him not to worry about it and that I'd get a ride with my brother. And then I went on about how, in this day and age, I felt it was imperative that we all do our part to conserve oil whenever we could and that if Los Angeles ever got their act together and got a decent public-transportation system up and running, it would be a much better place to live.

Going separately but not bringing my own car was perfect. If the date seemed to be going well, then, when the opening was over, I could tell my friends that I'd just catch a ride home with Jason (although I could already tell that my brother would probably come up with at least five reasons why that wasn't a good idea). And if it wasn't going well, I could go back with Max—having to listen the whole time about how, while he wasn't religious or anything, it was better this way and that I should strongly consider taking an abstinence pledge.

"He's just a guy," I continued whispering as I sat on

the couch. "Two arms. Two legs. A penis." I cringed. "Backspace on that last part. Just make sure not to look at his lips, and you'll be fine—"

"Who are you talking to?" a voice asked from behind me.

I whipped around to see Blush standing in the doorway. "No one," I said quickly. "I was just . . . reciting a poem. It's my form of meditation."

He gave me a look. Without even saying anything, he got right to the heart of it. How did he do that?

"Okay, fine," I admitted as I slunk down. "I was talking to myself."

He nodded. "That's cool. I do that all the time," he said as he walked over and sat in the chair across from me. "What were you talking about?"

"I was telling myself that there's no reason to be nervous. You know, on my date."

He shrugged. "That's good. 'Cause there's not. But like we talked about, just stay away from the what-are-you-thinking-about-right-now? question."

I nodded. Blush had turned into my go-to guy in terms of all the everything-you-wanted-to-know-about-guys-but-were-afraid-to-ask-for-fear-of-sounding-stupid questions I had. "Right, right." I wished I had a notebook like Cookie.

Through him I had learned that asking a guy, "What are you thinking about right now?" was like holding a stake in front of a vampire; that the reason they left the toilet seat up is because of their short attention spans; and that being able to sit in one position on the couch and play the same video game for five hours had to do with that same cavemanlike save-the-world-and-win-at-all-costs thing as wanting to be the one to contact the girl. And also through him I had learned that it was possible to be friends with a guy and not freak out and worry that you had committed a crime punishable by death if you mistakenly burped or—on one occasion that I kept trying very hard to push out of my head—farted in front of them (thank you, brussels sprouts).

Although his shyness was still a problem in large groups, when you got Blush one on one and he trusted you, he was *really* funny. The kind of quick wit that you see on the best TV shows—mostly cable. If my dad's show was actually funny, and if they hired writers who were actually talented, I totally would've pushed Blush to write a sample episode to see if he could get a job. And his puppets were *amazing*. Completely lifelike and detailed. When he put on a show for me up in the attic one afternoon, he was so good with the voices that I was fully transported from the house in Venice to South Central L.A. I was so into it, I stopped hearing the shrieks of the sorority girls on the TV in the living room. At least until Noob started shouting, "Amber! No! Don't go in there! The killer is waiting for you!"

I never really saw Blush get all weird and defensive and clam up unless I said things like, "I can't believe you don't have a girlfriend." I understood where he was coming from, though, because I did the same thing when people said that kind of stuff to me. Technically, it was meant to be a compliment (the unsaid part of the sentence being ". . . because you're so awesome"), but I always took it as a criticism and made the unsaid part be ". . . there must be something seriously wrong with you that I can't see at this moment but must come out when you're around a guy."

But with Blush, it was true—I *couldn't* believe he didn't have a girlfriend. Not only was he hot, sweet, and funny, but he was also great at anything electronic-related, like how to fix the volume control on an iPhone which, for some reason, I continually managed to screw up and then forgot how to fix even though he showed me over and over.

Blush deserved an awesome girlfriend. That was a tall order to fill. Not just figuratively, because he was so awesome, but literally as well. Because if he ended up with someone short—like under five-two—it would look very strange.

"You'll be fine," he went on. "But in case you start to freak out, just come find me and I'll talk you down."

"You're going to the opening?" I asked.

He nodded.

"With the guys?"

"No. With . . . Aleka."

I sat up. "Aleka as in that gorgeous Hawaiian girl who works at Coffee Culture on Abbot Kinney? That Aleka?"

He blushed as he nodded.

"The one who's pre-med at UC Berkeley and who plans on devoting her life to discovering a cure for autism? And is a better surfer than Narc?"

He nodded again.

I couldn't believe it. Blush had a *date*. With a *girl*. A very pretty girl. Who he had never mentioned to me before. "Oh. That's nice," I said. "So it's a date."

He blushed deeper. "I didn't say it was a date. We're just . . . going together."

"Are you going in the same car?"

He shrugged.

"Then it's a date."

"Why does that make it a date? You and Jason are going in separate cars, and it's a date. If you and I were going in the same car to the opening, would that make it a date?"

Now I was the one who blushed. "We're not talking about me and you. We're talking about you and Aleka. Your *date*." Okay, why was I getting so upset about this? Had I not just been thinking about the fact that, because he was so cool, Blush didn't just deserve a date, but a girl-friend?

"Why are you getting all upset?"

"I'm not getting upset," I replied. Not only was I

getting upset, I was lying about it. "I'm just being clear. Clarity is very important."

"You're right. It is."

"Plus, why would I be upset? I have no reason to be upset. It's a free country. You can go to a gallery opening with whoever you want," I continued.

He shrugged. "Okay."

"But what's making me upset is the fact that you think I'm upset," I went on. "Because I'm not."

"Yeah. We've established that."

"Good," I said as I stood up and marched out of the room, as fast as my heels would allow me.

"Okay, so let's go over this again," Max shouted as we drove down Venice Boulevard in his Volvo later toward the gallery, making it so the little bit of maintenance I had put into my hair was completely whipped out by the wind coming from his open windows. "What do you do if he offers to get you a soda?"

I turned to him. "Huh?" As much as I was trying to put it out of my head, I couldn't stop thinking about Blush and Aleka. She wasn't even *tall*. She was my height.

"A soda, Simone. What do you do if he offers to get you a soda? We've been over this."

I rolled my eyes. "I thank him and tell him that while that's very generous, I'll get my own, so that way he doesn't have a chance to slip some sort of weird drug into it."

He nodded. "Very good. And what else are you going to drop into the conversation?"

"That I have a black belt in karate and recently completed a forty-hour self-defense course. Even though that's not the truth." Kind of like saying that if you were a guy and you were going with a girl to a gallery opening in the same car but it wasn't a date wasn't the truth, either.

He nodded. "Excellent. And if he—"

"Okay, you know what? You need to stop," I interrupted.

"Okay, okay." We drove in silence for a bit. "Did you bring a whistle by any chance? I meant to stop at CVS and get you one—"

"Max, I'm serious. You need to stop this," I said. "You saw his Facebook page. He's a totally normal high school junior. Not a serial killer."

"Do you know how many serial killers look totally normal?" he demanded. "Two words for you: Patrick Bateman from that movie *American Psycho*."

"That's seven words."

"Whatever." He sighed. "I just don't want to see you get hurt."

"How could I? You're probably not going to let Jason get near me."

"That's not what I mean. It's just that . . . he's, you know, a . . . *guy*."

"And the point that goes along with that would be . . . ?"

"I just don't want him to pressure you into doing anything you're not ready to do. Because it's the ones who look the most normal who are the best at doing that."

I looked at him.

"Not like I have any experience doing that," he added nervously.

"You better not."

"All I'm saying is that if he's a good guy, he'll be okay with going slow."

While I was grateful to have a brother who cared so much about me (and my virginity), this was getting uncomfortable. "Max, I love you, and I totally get what you're saying, but can this please be the end of the Very Special PSA?" I asked. "'Cause you're kind of starting to creep me out."

"Okay. Yes. Probably a good idea we stop here," he said, swiping at his red face with his hand. "But you hear what I'm saying."

"I do."

We went back to being quiet.

"It's just that sometimes guys lose the ability to think with their heads, and they—" he blurted.

"Max!"

"Okay, okay."

Turning on the radio helped stop the conversation. As did the sight of the paparazzi when we arrived at the gallery. ("I guess the fact that Ashton Kutcher tweeted about the fact that he just bought a bunch of her prints gave it a boost," Max said.)

Inside, the place was packed. Each person was hipper and more beautiful than the last. It was like being on the Ramp at school, but with Botox.

"What a *fabulous* dress!" exclaimed a very tall older woman wearing something that, in most places, would probably pass as a beach cover-up but that here in L.A. constituted high fashion. "Very Joan Holloway from *Mad Men*."

Apparently, I was going to have to start watching that show, because she was like the fourth person who had compared me to this Joan chick

"I find it very exciting to see young women embracing their full figuredness."

Unfortunately, because her facial expression remained blank because of the Botox, I was just going to have to take her word about the fact that she was excited. I smiled. "Thanks," I replied, pretty sure it was a compliment.

"And your hair. Just fabulous." She pulled over an equally old, equally blank-faced woman who was examining one of Zooey's photographs with a short bald man wearing a pink-and-white-pinstriped suit and debating what the one-butt-cheek-in-shadow-one-in-light might signify on a psychological level. "Diedre, doesn't this young woman remind you of the model we had on the cover of the March 1968 issue of the magazine?"

Nineteen sixty-eight? My mother hadn't even been born then. Exactly how old were these women?

Diedre squinted. Minus any lines around her eyes or between her eyebrows. "She does. She's like . . . Audrey Hepburn. But with breasts and an appetite."

As I stood there while the two of them examined me from head to toe as if I were a piece of livestock, I learned that Fiona—the beach-cover-up-wearing woman—had been the editor of *Au Courant*, a fashion magazine similar to *Vogue* way back when, and Diedre had been her second-in-command.

"Beautiful bone structure," Diedre went on as she took my face between her hands (even her liver spots were elegant) and moved it from side to side.

"Oh, you're so sweet to say that!" came a voice behind me. "I think she takes after me on that front."

My eyes widened at the same time as Max's, who was walking toward me. I knew that voice . . . but why was it in this gallery at this moment? The gallery where I was meeting my date?

A hand shot out in front of me. "Hillary Stone, senior VP, Production, LOL Films. And you ladies are?"

Diedre and Fiona were so confused, there was actually some lineage on the foreheads.

Max stepped up next to me. "Hillary. How'd you—"

"—manage to get on the list after my stepson-to-be told me that he couldn't get anyone else—not even his *parents*—on the list, even though this is considered *the* social event in town tonight?" she finished. "Easy. I told my assistant to take care of it or she'd be fired."

"Is my dad here?" I asked. Just what I needed—for my date to meet my entire family.

"Yes. He's over there in the corner being antisocial," she replied.

I turned to see his fingers flying along on his phone. From the way that he was breathing through his mouth, I knew that he was probably writing a script.

Hillary took out her own BlackBerry. "I need to add that to the list of things to have this new shrink fix in him—the antisocial thing." When she was done, she slipped it back in her purse and gazed at me. "Did you get that dress from that bedbug place?"

I nodded.

"It looks—"

"Divine? Don't you think?" Diedre asked.

"I love the contrast of the blue against your lips. It gives them such a rich color," Fiona said.

Hillary whipped out her snake compact and a tube of lipstick and quickly put some on. "How about mine? I just got this at Neiman's."

The women looked at her. "There's a somewhat . . . *green* undertone to it," said Fiona.

As Hillary began to wipe it off with a tissue, Jason walked up to the group. "Hey," he said.

I turned to face him. His faded-just-right jeans and

sapphire-blue polo shirt totally matched his eyes. Did guys think about that stuff as they were getting dressed? I made a mental note to put that on my Things-to-Ask-Blush list. Before I remembered that I had gotten all huffy during our last conversation and probably owed him an apology first. I had Blush on the brain so bad that I had almost forgotten that I had a date with Jason. Which was not cool, seeing that (a) Blush was my friend, and (b) any moment would be walking in with *his* date.

Like, say, *that* moment.

With her long black hair rippling down to her butt, and the pink gardenia that was tucked behind her ear, and the purple sundress that wrapped around her curves just right, it was hard not to notice Aleka. Especially with someone as tall and, frankly, cute as Blush next to her. I waited for her to do something annoying, like flip her hair back and giggle, but she didn't. Instead, the two of them looked a little uncomfortable with the way that everyone stopped what they were doing to look at them.

"Simone?" I heard Jason say.

I turned to him and smiled. *Focus, Simone,* I said to myself. *You're on a date with a Testosterone Twit. Tons of girls would kill to be in your position. So what if Blush is with a totally hot girl who will probably win the Nobel Prize one day. It's not like you could ever like him. Plus, you need to pay attention to make sure Hillary doesn't embarrass you.* "Yeah?"

"You look way hot," he said.

Way hot. I knew it was a compliment, but somehow, when I had allowed myself to fantasize about what my hypothetical boyfriend would say to me, "way hot" was not part of the equation. "Way hot" was way not romantic.

"I'm so glad you appreciate my handiwork," Hillary said.

I turned to her. "*Your* handiwork?"

"Well, yes. Remember how I took you shopping that day?" She looked at Jason and smiled. "Hillary Stone, senior VP, Production, LOL Films. We met briefly in the parking lot that day. By the way, I'm a *big* fan of your father's work. *Huge*."

"That's cool. You'll be able to tell him in person, actually." He turned to me. "I didn't know when we talked, but it turns out my parents already had plans to come here." He smiled and lowered his voice. "I told my mom if they embarrass me, I'd kill them."

As Hillary began to yak away to Jason about Italy, I kept stealing glances at Blush and Aleka. Luckily, there was no PDA going on, but the way that she kept putting her hand on his arm so that he'd lean his head down to hear her seemed awfully familiar. Once when he caught me looking at him, he smiled, and I gave him a (fake) smile back before I put my hand on Jason's arm. Or meant to put it on his arm.

"Uh, Simone?" I heard him say.

"Yeah?" I said, fake smiling at Blush.

"You, uh . . . I'm not sure . . ."

I turned and saw that I had overshot his arm and my hand was clutching his chest.

"Whoops. Sorry about that," I said, quickly removing it.

"Hello! Hello!" sang Cheryl as she made her way through the crowd, dressed in a bedazzled Indian shirt over black leggings ("You think with all the Zumba-ing, I'm not going to show off these things?" she said, when Marcia commented one day at coffee that Cheryl never wore anything else). I guess because he had won so many Academy Awards I had thought that Jason's dad would be, I don't know, dressed head to toe in black or something equally... Academy Award–like, but the guy who was trailing behind Cheryl looked more like a balding chemistry teacher.

I squinted. "Your dad has a pocket protector?" I asked.

Jason sighed. "I told him to leave that at home tonight."

"Honey, look at how *gorgeous* you are all dressed up!" Cheryl cried as she smothered me in a hug. She let me go. "G-o-r-g-o-u-s!"

"Cheryl, you forget the 'e,'" said Stan. "There's an 'e' before the 'o.'"

As an excellent speller myself, I already liked Jason's dad a lot.

"Stan, sweetie, this is the girl I've been telling you about—my Zumba friend."

Hillary laughed. "I just think it's *so* cute how Simone is so into irony."

Because she was so tiny, Cheryl made up for her lack of height with a very loud voice. That, even though the gallery was packed, was loud enough to make a few people turn. Including Diedre and Fiona.

"Oh, we Zumba, too," said Diedre.

"I find it to be just divine!" said Fiona.

Diedre turned to her. "You know the magazine has an entire feature devoted to it this month. Apparently, it's become quite the rage. Rumor has it Nicole Kidman was spotted doing it in Nashville."

Hillary whipped out her phone and pressed a button. "The minute you get into the office tomorrow, I want you to sign me up for a Zumba class," she whispered into the receiver. "Do a Google search for 'best Zumba class to run into celebs' and get me into that one. Actually, don't wait until tomorrow. Do it now," she demanded before clicking off. She smiled. "Just leaving a little friendly reminder for my assistant."

The smile that seemed to be permanently etched on Cheryl's face, because she was one of those freaky people, like my brother, who was happy pretty much all the time ("And no antidepressants involved, thankyouverymuch," she said proudly when Gwen commented on it once at the Bean), disappeared. "You weren't kidding," she murmured.

Why did everyone keep saying that? It made it sound like I was a total exaggerator or something.

Cheryl stepped back and looked at Jason and me, and the smile came back. "Oh, you don't know how happy it makes me to see the two of you together!"

"They *do* make a cute couple, don't they?" agreed Hillary. "You know, Jason, my first boyfriend looked a lot like you." She gave him a flirty smile. "Of course, unlike Simone, I was only ten when I started dating."

I rolled my eyes. That was wrong on multiple levels. This was getting more and more uncomfortable by the minute. A waitress walking by with a tray of hors d'oeuvres stopped. For a second I was tempted to hijack the entire tray and lock myself in the bathroom with them. But that would have been really really wrong.

I reached for one. "What are these?" I asked her.

"Apple fritters with a smidge of crème fraiche and a dusting of cinnamon and a pinch of cardamom."

I pulled my hand back and sighed. Just my luck. "Oh. Thanks anyway."

Cheryl turned to the group. "Simone's allergic to apples."

Hillary looked up from her snake compact. "Oh, yeah. I always forget that."

"Mmm-hmmm," Cheryl said, giving me a look.

Hillary turned to Jason's dad, who was busy trying to stop himself from yawning. "Actually, you know what that reminds me of? That scene in the movie you did set in—where was it? India? China?—I can't remember where, but it looked like one of those places that's very overpopulated and smells just awful. The one where the man starts to believe that he may be the reincarnation of Jesus?"

"It was Nepal, and it was Buddha," Mr. Frank said icily.

"Exactly. That's what I meant," Hillary said, reaching for his arm and batting her eyelashes.

I looked over at my dad, who was typing away on his iPhone in the corner.

"And explain to me, if you can, what that has to do with an allergy to apples?" Jason's dad asked.

"It was more like a *segue*," Hillary said, "to start talking about your movies and your incredible talent and the fact that I'd just love to have you come direct something for me."

I spent a lot of time dreaming up worst-case scenarios, in my life. But this took the cake. I don't think I could even have come anywhere near the nightmare this evening was turning into if I'd really tried. It was one thing for Hillary to embarrass me in front of a guy, but in front of the guy's father? Who happened to be an award-winning director?!
"I'm, uh, going to go look at some of the photographs," I announced as I drifted away. The farther away I was from the scene of the crime, the better. Plus, it would give me a chance to spy on Blush and Aleka.

"What do you think that is?" a voice asked a few minutes later as I stared at one of the photographs. Or, rather, pretended to stare at it while what I was really doing was watching Aleka laugh at something Blush had just said. Since when had he become *funny*? I mean, in public. That was one of the things I liked about him. That, unlike most people, he didn't spend all his time making jokes in order to cover up feeling uncomfortable. Like, say, I did.

I turned to see Stan squinting. Oh God. Really? Now *this*? "I think it's . . ." What was the best way to say this to the father of the-boy-whom-I-was-technically-on-a-date-with-but-was-currently-ignoring? ". . . a pair of . . . buttocks," I replied. That sounded more parent-appropriate than "butt."

He nodded. "Ah. I think you're right."

He pointed to another bloblike photo. "And this one?"

I stared at it. "Uh, I'm pretty sure that's another pair. It's kind of what the photographer's known for. You can read about it in her artist's statement up front, if you want."

He sighed. "My wife is always on me about spending all my time in movie theaters, but I'll take a bucket of popcorn and some subtitles over this stuff any day. Even with fake butter."

I nodded. "I know what you mean. *L'Homme qui aimait les femmes* is playing at the Nuart tonight. One night only." I would have suggested it to Jason, but considering how he'd reacted to *Freaks and Geeks*, I didn't think it would have been a good idea.

He looked surprised. "You know who François Truffaut is?"

I nodded. "Well, sure. He's like the most important thing to come out of France other than . . . I don't know . . . *croissants*. He's my favorite, actually."

He smiled. "And you refer to the titles by the French instead of in English."

I shrugged. "It just seems wrong not to."

He shook his head. "Amazing." His face fell. "You do realize that this kind of thing is lost on my son?"

I smiled. "Yeah, I know."

"The other day I walked into his room and he was listening to that Jackson Brewster boy."

"Justin Bieber," I corrected. "Yeah, he mentioned that he liked him."

"But he's a good boy. Despite the fact that he doesn't have an ounce of taste when it comes to music." He smiled.

I smiled back. Before I could ask him what it had been like to work with Catherine Deneuve, one of the greatest French actresses of all time, Zooey Woodson began this spoken-word thing about the beauty of butts while some tattoo-sleeved guy banged a gong at the end of every sentence. (Thor would later tell me he thought it was genius.) As Stan and I both stifled yawns, Hillary came *click-clacking* over.

"I just had a fantastic idea. Why don't we all go to dinner? The six of us!" she exclaimed. "That way we can get to know each other, seeing that, you know, our children are dating. And Stan, I can go over our development slate with you, and we'll see if there're any movies that you might be interested in directing!"

"I don't direct movies," he said. "Only films."

Hillary gave one of her tinklier laughs. "Movies, films—same thing."

His eyes narrowed. "Not in my book they're not."

Hers brightened. "Ooh—you write books as well? How did I not know this! Are any of them available to be optioned? Are they plot-driven, or more character-based? Because the character-based ones end up being *so* slow as movies—"

"No, I do not write books," Stan said. "And even if I did, you can be assured that not only would I not option one to you, but I would sincerely hope that you wouldn't even buy one of them to read, because the idea that my readership was made up of people like you would cause me so much distress I'd have to flee the country and only be published by small independent presses that don't have distribution in chain bookstores—"

"Well. *Someone* takes his work quite seriously," Hillary said.

He glared at her.

"Which is a wonderful, wonderful thing!" she cried.

"Number one, I'd appreciate it if you didn't interrupt me because I'm not finished yet," he snapped, "and, number two, yes, I do take my work seriously. Which is perhaps something you should consider doing at some point, as well. In fact, if you were able to put aside your narcissistic self-obsession for a few minutes, instead of allowing your pathological envy of Simone to manifest itself in a multitude of passive-aggressive gestures toward her that are severely uncomfortable for others to behold, maybe you could learn something from her. Because despite her young age, it's obvious that she has more character in her . . . *femur* . . . than you do in your entire personally-trained-to-the-hilt body!"

My legs *had* gotten super strong from the Zumba-ing. Stan wasn't nearly as loud as his wife, but by this time we had drawn quite the crowd. Even Zooey had stopped her spoken-word rant and drifted over to see what was going on.

For a moment, Hillary remained quiet. "So . . . I guess that means I should hold off on messengering over all the scripts we have in active development for you to read?" she finally asked.

"Actually, what it means is that I think you're everything that's wrong with Hollywood today," he replied. "And that maybe you should follow Simone's lead—both in the kind of films you watch and in the way you treat people." He looked at Cheryl. "I think I'd like to leave now." He turned to Jason. "I hope I didn't embarrass you too much."

Jason's neck had shrunk so much the collar of his shirt was touching his ears, which made it so that when he shrugged, it looked like he was about to hurl.

Hillary turned to my dad. "Jeffrey, are you going to let him talk to me like this?"

My dad looked up from his iPhone. "Sorry—what was that?"

Stan turned to me. "It was a pleasure to meet you, Simone. Good luck with everything. One day you should come by the house. I'll screen *Jules et Jim* for you and tell you about the lunch I had with him in Paris when I was just starting out."

That was my second favorite Truffaut movie. It was about a woman who is torn between two best friends. ("What French movie *isn't*?" Nicola liked to say when I brought it up.) I smiled. "That would be amazing."

I looked over at Jason to see if the idea of his father inviting me over completely mortified him, but he was too busy still looking like a turtle.

Cheryl hugged me. "Good to see you, sweetie. You look beautiful. I'll see you at class on Tuesday." She turned to my dad. "Very nice to meet you. Your daughter is wonderful." Then she turned to Hillary. "Hmmph," was all she said before she pulled herself up to her full height—all five-feet-one of her—and walked out the door.

Hillary turned to me, this time not even trying to hide how much she hated me. "I can't believe you would embarrass me like this in public. After all I've done for you!" she hissed through gritted teeth.

"Me?! I didn't even open my mouth!"

"I . . . I . . . took you shopping!" she cried.

My dad came over and grabbed her arm. "Hillary, I think we should go now."

"Fine." She scanned the crowd. "It's not like there's anyone high level to talk to anyway. They're all gone," she announced as she grabbed his arm and began to lead him toward the door.

"Nice meeting you, Jason," he called over his shoulder. "Have her home by midnight. It's not like I'll be there to check, but her brother will, and he's very protective!"

I covered my face. "Tell me all that didn't just happen," I moaned.

"What part?" Jason asked.

I peeked between two of my fingers. "Any of it."

He pulled my hands down. "It wasn't *that* bad," he said. "Compared to . . . stepping on a land mine and having your leg blown off. Or being in solitary confinement and being driven crazy by the slow dripping of water right next to your ear. Or . . ."

I cringed. "Okay. Duly noted. But still, it was awful."

"You want to get out of here and go get something to eat?"

I nodded.

As we walked toward the door, I looked around for Blush. Seeing that there weren't a lot of tall African American guys in the crowd, he would have been hard to miss, but he seemed to be already gone.

eleven

I wondered if I'd ever get good enough at dating so that I didn't spend the entire date worrying about what would happen at the end. Because to have to go through life saying "Really?" and "Mm" every minute and a half so that the guy thought I was listening to him when, in fact, what I was really doing was thinking about how to position myself in the passenger seat so that if we did end up making out, I wouldn't end up with a gear shift in my stomach would be pretty sad.

The good news about being so preoccupied was that when Jason turned on the ignition of his car and "One Less Lonely Girl" blared out of the speakers, I didn't throw up. And when he took me to In-N-Out for dinner and spent the whole time talking about Lady Gaga, I wasn't bored out of my mind. Instead, I just hmm'd and mm'd and really'd while I wondered whether fries gave you bad breath and how I could have been so dumb as not to remember to buy Altoids.

When we had been done eating for a while and had received more than a few dirty looks from the assistant manager because there were a bunch of people waiting for tables, he smiled at me. "You ready to go?"

"Oh. I guess. But I was just going to get another refill on my Dr Pepper," I said nervously. So what if I had already had three in an attempt to keep my hands busy with the straw so that I didn't do the thing I did when I was nervous, which was scrape at my cuticles? So what if I'd have a full bladder and totally have to pee while we were kissing, and instead of saying, "Hey, Jason? Do you think we could stop kissing for a second and find a bathroom?" because I wouldn't want to break the mood, I'd just hold it for so long that it would turn into a bladder infection.

"Okay," he shrugged.

I stood up and smoothed my dress. What was I so afraid of? So we were going to make out. Well, maybe we were. It was wrong to take these things for granted. It wasn't like I hadn't done it before. I totally had. Well, once. And who cared if that time had been on the street in public under a streetlight while this time would be alone in a dark car? It wasn't so different. I sat back down.

"I thought you were getting more soda."

"I changed my mind." I might as well have gotten it over with. Or gotten to it.

"So you want to go?"

I nodded. "Wait!" I panicked as he started to get up.

"I . . . I changed my mind. I do want more soda. But I'm not going to get a full one. Just . . . a little." But instead of getting more soda, I went to the bathroom where I did a head-to-toe inspection of anything that could be considered offensive if Jason and I found ourselves within a two-inch radius of each other. Nothing in between teeth. No offensive smell coming from armpits. (But I smacked some water and liquid soap on them anyway and used the scratchy brown paper towels to pat them dry anyway.) Decent breath. (Shoving five pieces of Eclipse peppermint and chomping for a while before spitting them out helped.) Makeup still intact. (Most girls probably would've taken the time to touch it up, but most girls didn't have shaky hands, which could result in permanent blindness.) Hair not completely flat nor overly sticky from product (thanks to a little wash and dry with hand dryer). Red lips made kissable with the addition of a little (at first too much) gloss.

Angry customer pounding on the door because I was taking so much time.

"Okay, okay," I said as I did one more spin in front of the mirror for a last look. Which, because the mirror showed me only from my head to my boobs, meant I had to step up on the toilet. Not—I realized as I almost fell in—one of my better ideas.

I unlocked the door to find an angry woman who looked like an extra in *Jersey Shore* covered with ketchup stains holding the hands of two equally messy little kids. "Finally. What'd ya do? Fall in?"

"Almost," I muttered as I tried to make my way past them.

"Ya see what I gotta deal with here?" she asked, pointing at the kids. "Maybe next time you can do the rest of us a favor and practice being a supermodel at home."

"I wasn't. I just—see, the thing is—I'monmysecond dateeverandthisreallycuteboyisabouttodrivemehomeand I'veneverbeeninthatpositionbeforeandI'mnotsurewhatI'm supposedtodo," I blurted out.

Her face softened. "Ohhh. Now *that's* a whole other story." She patted my arm with her sticky fingers. "Don't worry, honey. You look hot. And if he, you know, tries anything you're not comfortable with, you just tell him that your father *knows* people."

"Huh?"

"You know, like Tony Soprano kinda people?" Her left eyebrow arched. *"Capiche?"*

She wanted me to tell him my dad was in the *Mafia*? "Sure. *Capoosh*," I replied. I studied French rather than Italian, but that seemed like the likely past tense.

She looked confused. "Huh?"

"Nothing. Thanks for the advice," I said, as I darted around her and made my way back to Jason.

"You okay?" he asked when I got back to the table.

"Oh yeah. Fine. Long line at the soda thing. Decided to

drink it there." I gave him a smile. "All ready to go if you are!"

The drive back to Venice was filled with more small talk. I tried not to compare Jason to Blush—how Blush, when he asked me a question, let me get my entire answer out and really seemed to think about what I said before he responded. Or how when I was with Blush, we talked about movies and music and TV, like Jason and I did, but then we also talked about other things. Like our families. Or our most embarrassing moments. Or how when I was with Blush, I felt comfortable blurting. Not in an awkward, fueled-by-nerves way, like I sometimes did with Jason, but because I felt relaxed and comfortable and didn't feel the need to rewrite and revise everything in my head before saying it.

But Blush was busy listening to Aleka blurt.

The ride was also filled with more Bieber. Which didn't help.

"Oh, I love this one," Jason said, turning up the volume as we turned onto my street. "It's called 'U Smile.'"

I tried to smile back. The last time Blush and I had hung out, he played this song "In a Sentimental Mood" by Duke Ellington and John Coltrane, which, up until then, I had never heard but quickly decided was my new favorite song.

Suddenly, Jason pulled over to the side of the road.

"Um, my house is farther up the block," I said.

He smiled. As if listening to the Biebs go on about how the girl's lips were his biggest weakness, and how he was all in, with his cards on the table, wasn't bad enough, suddenly, I had to listen to Jason sing it *with* him. In a voice so off-key it would have frightened small children.

How could someone so cute be so tone-deaf? I thought to myself as I nodded along and tapped my hand on the armrest. What was wrong with me? A cute boy was *serenading* me. Not just a cute boy—a cute popular boy who sat on the Ramp. I should have been thrilled. As a girl, I was supposed to love this kind of stuff. At least that's what books and movies said. But all I could think about was whether it was possible for ears to get bruised from certain noises and if so, how long it took for them to heal.

"So what do you think?" he asked when he was done.

"That was *great*," I lied.

He smiled. "Thanks. My mom's always saying it's too bad I'm such a jock because I'd be great in chorus."

That had to be the unconditional-love stuff that you always heard about between mothers and kids, because Cheryl was not that clueless.

"So you still hate the Biebs?" he asked.

"I—uh—"

He laughed. "I saw you getting into it. I think you might just be a Belieber now."

As if.

He looked at his watch. "It's only eleven. Want to take a ride down to the beach?"

"Okay." Maybe the sounds of the waves would wash away the sound of his singing that was still ringing in my ears.

Once we parked, he turned the music down so that it was only slightly rather than completely annoying. In all the times I had thought about my first real makeout session, this was not the sound track I had thought would accompany it. "You're pretty cool, Simone, you know that?" he asked as he moved toward me.

"Thanks. So are you," *Other than your taste in music*, I thought as his face moved in toward mine.

But once his lips hit mine, all thoughts of Justin Bieber, Blush, and Hillary disappeared. Instead, I thought about . . . actually, the longer we kissed (which felt like hours, or maybe seconds, I couldn't decide) the more I was unable to think about anything other than the fact that I was going to be *totally* screwed the next day when the oxytocin/obsession thing took full effect.

And then Jason took his hand and tried to snake it down the neck of my dress. Then I snapped back into thinking.

Despite my lack of experience, I was pretty sure that saying, "What do you think you're doing?" would probably kill the moment, which is why I decided to gently grab his forearm and yank his hand out of there. Which worked . . . for about two minutes, until he tried it again.

Luckily, I cut him off at the pass. As difficult as it was to separate my lips from his, I did. "Look, Jason, I really like kissing you. And I'd really like to keep doing it. But do you think we could just, you know, keep it at that for now?"

"What do you mean?" he asked, just as breathlessly.

Really? He was going to make me spell it out for him? "I mean . . . do you think you could stop putting your hand down my dress?" That wasn't so hard. In fact, it felt really empowering.

"Sure," he said as he pulled me toward him and started kissing me again.

Wow. That was easy.

Or at least I thought so, until he took his hand and, instead of putting it down my dress, decided to attempt to put it *up* it.

"Hey! What do you think you're doing?!" I yelped as I pushed his hand—and him—away. "I just told you I wanted to slow things down!"

"No you didn't. All you said was not to put my hand down your dress!"

I glared at him.

"Oh, Simone, come on," he said as he leaned toward me again. "I *like* you. And it seems like you like me. It's not like I'm going to post about this on Facebook."

My eyes widened. I hadn't even thought about that. "I like you, too," I replied as I pushed him back. "But I want to go slow."

He leaned over again. "But you have such an awesome body. I know a lot of guys like those anorexic types with no boobs, but I think a girl with meat on her is hot."

"Meat"? That was so *not* hot.

I pushed him away again. "I said I don't want to." I

may have felt shaky inside, but my voice was surprisingly strong.

He fell back against his seat. "Whatever."

"We can still kiss."

He didn't even look at me. "Actually, I think I should get you home."

"Okay," I said quietly, pinching my thigh through my dress so I wouldn't cry. This wasn't fair. Why did I feel like the bad guy here?

He drove me home in silence, which was even worse than Justin Bieber. Then, as he pulled up in front of my house, he didn't even put the car in park. He just stared straight ahead.

"Well, thanks for dinner," I said.

"You're welcome."

"Hey, did you know that In-N-Out uses cottonseed oil to make their fries?" I asked. "I read that somewhere. Apparently, it makes them healthier. I meant to bring that up earlier. You know, when we were actually at the restaurant." I know it sounded like more of my nervous babbling, but it really wasn't. I was trying to come up with ways to stay there just a little longer so that Jason would have the opportunity to realize what a complete jerk he was being and apologize. Otherwise, I would be left with the fact that, unless I was willing to do more than kiss, he wasn't interested in hanging out with me.

"Fascinating," he replied, still staring ahead.

I waited. Nothing.

"I guess I should go," I finally said.

He couldn't even be bothered to nod.

I got out of the car. I didn't have a lot of experience with guys, but I knew I'd never hear from Jason again. When school started again, if we passed each other in the hall, I knew he'd conveniently manage to look away. Which was why before I walked away, I needed to take this opportunity to be really honest and tell him what was on my mind, so that I wouldn't turn into one of those girls who filled notebook after notebook with angsty poems and song lyrics about the experience.

"Jason?"

"Yeah?"

"I just need to tell you one thing."

"What?"

I dipped my head into the car so he'd be sure to hear me. "I will never, ever be a Belieber. And to be honest, the fact that you are?" I shrugged. "It's a little creepy."

I didn't even wait to see the look on his face before I started walking toward the door. I didn't need to. Because there was no way it could've matched up to how proud I was of myself for coming up with that comeback in the moment rather than three weeks later.

twelve

Most people, when they're really bummed out—because they didn't get accepted to their top college; or their dog died; or, in my case, the guy they were hanging out with turned out to be a total wiener—might decide to drown their sorrows with a second scoop of ice cream. Perhaps, if they feel really horrible, an entire sundae. But for someone like me, dipping into the junk food is a very slippery slope.

Luckily, I had a great best friend. Not just to listen to me say "I just can't believe Jason Frank turned out to be such a jerk" about every fifteen minutes either by text, phone, or in person, but to pick me up and take me to Whole Foods and point me to the deli section and say, "Get as many pounds of grilled veggies as you want. My treat."

Which is how I ended up pigging out on red peppers and squash and portobello mushrooms and dripping balsamic vinegar and olive oil on my too-big Old Navy khakis and stretched-out Joy Division T-shirt. (Because of my fragile state, Nicola had let up on her "You now have all these nice new clothes and *this* is what you wear? Think of all the girls in third-world countries who are starving for the kind of dresses you now own!" song.) Nicola, on the other hand, was pigging out on Uncle Eddie's vegan chocolate chip cookies (an old favorite of mine, but obviously dangerous to go near at that moment) in a sort of sympathy binge. I felt so crappy that I had even let her convince me to spend the afternoon watching romantic comedies starring Jennifer Aniston and Katherine Heigl—two actresses I couldn't stand—on cable.

"Tell me again why we're doing this?" I asked miserably as Katherine Heigl sparred with Gerard Butler in *The Ugly Truth*.

"Because we need to restore your faith in guys," Nicola replied. "And these movies always get tied up neatly in the last ten minutes with some dumb pop song and a ridiculously happy ending." She reached for another cookie. "Ooh—maybe *He's Just Not That into You* is on somewhere in cable land. That one will definitely help, because it's got, like, seven ridiculously happy endings."

But the veggies and the movies didn't help. Neither did Brad's offer to lend me this cool seventies-style paisley maxi dress I had been coveting that had once been worn by Janeane Garofalo (*Reality Bites* was one of my favorite non-French movies) at an awards show. For two days I just moped around. I didn't even have the energy to wash my hair, which resulted in a little trail of pimples on my hairline because of all the stupid product on it.

There was a part of me that wanted nothing more than to be able to go back to how things used to be. Disappear into my room with a case of Tastykakes and eat until I felt nothing and then put on my baggy clothes and go through life invisible. At least when you were invisible you didn't have to take risks. You didn't have to be seen and connect with people and let yourself get excited about possibilities. When you were invisible, you had a pretty good idea what each day was going to bring—in most cases, exactly the same as the day before. Boring, sure, but it took away any opportunity to get disappointed.

In my head, I knew that I hadn't done anything wrong with Jason, that he was just a jerk and a guy and I probably wasn't the first or the last girl he was going to treat that way. But everything below my head—i.e., my heart—was a different story. Because even though I had gone out with Jason only twice, and even though I had a sense from the Bieber and Adele thing that, at the end of the day, he wasn't going to end up being my guy, I felt dumb. Dumb for getting excited. Dumb for trusting him. And dumb for ever thinking that someone so cute and popular would ever like someone like me.

By Sunday, the second evening of my moping, when not only had the pimples begun to migrate from my hairline over to my chin and nose, but I was actually starting to smell a little funky, my roommates got involved.

"What's going on?" I asked when, after my brother texted me to come downstairs while I was holed up under the covers in my room watching *The Notebook*, I found all of them except for Blush waiting for me in the living room.

"An invention," Noob replied.

"What did you invent now?" I asked suspiciously. The last thing Noob had "invented" was this remote control that, when you aimed it at a garage door, it opened. ("I hate to tell you, Noob, but they already sell those," I told him after he took about a half hour to explain it to me one afternoon. "They're called garage door openers.")

"He means an intervention," corrected Max.

"But I haven't had any sugar," I replied. "Only veggies. I swear." I looked down at my bloated stomach. I really needed to ease up on them.

"We're not talking about food," Doc said.

"We want to know why you've been so bummed out the last two days," said Narc.

Uh-oh. I had been afraid this would happen. Why did I have to live with guys who were so nice and actually noticed my moods and cared about me? Why couldn't they be more clueless? Because I was *not* telling them about what had happened the other night in the car. It was one thing to admit to them I had a crush, but it was a whole other thing to talk about that stuff.

Wheezer coughed. "Is it that hormone thing again?"

"'Cause remember how you were all jacked up that he hadn't gotten in touch and you were all bummed out and then he did and you were all happy?" asked Noob.

I shook my head. "No. It's not the oxytocin thing." I wondered if there was some sort of pill you could take to stop the oxytocin altogether. Like an antibiotic or something. Because I was already way over it. I walked over to the TV and turned on the DVD player. "Hey, you guys want to watch *Sorority Girl Slasher Part Twelve*?" I asked brightly as I held up the case. As gory as it was, the nightmares from that wouldn't be as bad as the ones I'd have if I ended up telling them what had happened.

Max took it away from me and dragged me over to the couch, where he plopped me down between Noob and Narc. "No. We want to talk about *you*."

Noob sniffed. "Is that new perfume? It smells really good."

I looked out at the group of guys, all of whom were focused on me. Including Narc, who was wide awake. In fact, he hadn't yawned once. I may have said I wanted to go back to being invisible, but the truth was, I didn't. The truth was, I felt incredibly lucky to have such awesome friends. And the truth was, I was incredibly lucky Blush wasn't there to witness all of this because, if he had been, I would have been even more mortified than I was at the moment. I sniffled a little. Just as the door opened and Blush walked in.

"Hey. What's going on?" he asked. I'd been avoiding Blush since the opening, to the point where I had gone grocery shopping by myself the day before. Which, while a good workout for my arms, hadn't been much fun.

"Nothing. We were just—" I began to say.

"—waiting for Simone to tell us why she hasn't showered since before her last date with Jason," finished Thor.

"And why she's been so mopey," added Wheezer.

"And why she's been posting links to YouTube videos of depressing Smiths songs on her Facebook page," said my brother.

Obviously, I was very much *not* invisible.

I sighed. I already knew they weren't going to let me out of there without telling them what happened. I took a deep breath. "Okay, well, see the other night, there was sort of an incident," I began.

"Did it involve an illegal firearm?" asked Noob. "'Cause that's what it says in the paper all the time. 'At nine oh-seven P.M., there was an incident with an illegal firearm at—"

"No," I cut him off. "There were no firearms involved. This incident had to do with—"

The door opened again and a mousy-looking woman with frizzy blonde hair, no makeup, and bad skin, wearing sweats and a ratty *Toy Story 3* T-shirt peeked her head in.

Did nobody knock anymore? Venice had a high percentage of homeless people, and I had gotten to know a lot of them very well, but they'd never barge into a house. And I had never seen this woman before.

"Can I help you?" Max asked.

She stepped inside, and I gasped. It wasn't a homeless woman.

"Hillary," I said. "What—"

She smiled sadly. "I apologize that I'm not as put together as I usually am. I've just been so distraught over what happened between us at the gallery the other night that I haven't been able to do anything."

"Ohhh . . . so *that's* the incident you were referring to, Simone," Max said softly. "What went down with Hillary."

"Um, right. Exactly," I whispered back. Okay, so it was a lie. If I wasn't going to eat cake, I was allowed to act out *some* way.

He put his hand on my arm. "I hadn't realized how much that had affected you," he said. "As your older brother, I should have been more sensitive about that."

"Oh, it's okay. No one's perfect."

Hillary held up something round covered in aluminum foil. "All I could do was bake you this cake, as a peace offering. I thought maybe we could eat some as we talked things over. That is, if you could find it in your heart to give me a chance to apologize."

I looked at my brother, who shrugged. "You should

hear her out," he whispered. "Maybe she's had some huge spiritual awakening and become a totally different person. Or Dad got her on meds."

Of course Max would default back to looking on the bright side again. But even though she sounded sincere, something in me didn't trust Hillary. I could just see the Zumba Brigade shaking their heads at me. That being said, there was something to the fact that she would actually go out in public looking the way she did. Maybe Max was right—maybe she had become a totally different person in two days . . . because she had a lobotomy.

"Sure," I sighed. "We can talk."

She came over and hugged me. "Thank you so much. This means a lot to me."

She may have looked horrible, but unlike me, she had definitely showered. And slathered that expensive vanilla body lotion that she liked so much all over her.

"But I don't think it's a good idea for me to have the cake," I said.

Her face fell. "Oh. Okay. I understand. It's fine. I mean, it's just my great-grandmother's recipe for her everything cake, which has been handed down from generation to generation," she said. "It's very complicated and therefore took me four hours and thirty-five minutes to make."

Hillary had made it? She never cooked. Other than that time she turned the stove on and forgot to turn it off. But that wasn't exactly "cooking."

"It's just something that we used to have on special occasions, or would make as a peace offering," she continued. "But it's fine. I thought it could be a nice bonding thing for us, but I completely understand if you don't want any. I know in the past I've been a little aggressive about trying to get you to eat. And I was wrong. I should have been more supportive of your weight loss."

I studied her face. She sure looked sincere. Could it be possible that something had happened where she had had a change of heart? Like, say, maybe my father threatening to call off the wedding or change the pre-nup so that the amount of money she would have gotten in case of a divorce was greatly reduced?

"Okay, I'll have a little piece," I finally caved. "But seriously, just a sliver."

She smiled. "Great."

Max looked at the guys. "Hey, guys, let's head out and give them some privacy."

"But dude, we can't miss this. This is going to be *awesome*!" cried Noob. "I bet it's like a hundred times better than those Real Housewives shows." He turned to us. "Not to say you're all cheesy like they are."

"Out," Max said as he pushed him toward the door and the rest of them followed.

After they were gone, I cut us two slices, and we settled on the couch. "So what did you want to talk about?" I asked.

"Oh, let's eat first," she replied. "It's not exactly the kind of conversation to have on an empty stomach."

I looked at the cake warily. "What's in it?"

"A little bit of everything—that's where the 'everything' name came from. Coconut, raisins, peanut butter, chocolate chips."

Huh. That sounded awesome. I speared a piece with my fork and examined it. "There's not any apple in this, is there?"

"Of course not! You're allergic to apples." she replied. "I would never forget something as important as that."

"Hillary, you always forget that."

"Yes, but that was before." She took my hand. "Simone, I know we haven't had the best relationship in the past. But I really want to change that. I really want to be the mother figure you've never had. Like I keep saying, because I'm so young, I'm really more of an older sister type, but you know what I mean. And part of being in a family is remembering important things like severe allergic reactions that can lead to anaphylactic shock and possibly death."

"Wow. Hillary. I . . . I don't know what to say. I'm really touched."

As I went to hug her, she patted me on the back then pushed me away. "Oh, I'm so glad. Now eat up."

I took a big forkful of cake. It was good . . . until a few seconds later I started to get dizzy. "Whoa."

"Is everything okay?" Hillary asked innocently.

I began to clutch at my throat. "I don't . . . I feel . . ." I wheezed. "My throat . . ."

"Huh. Maybe it went down the wrong pipe." She speared another piece and shoved it toward my mouth. "Here. Why don't you have some more?"

As I pushed it away, I clutched at my throat and began to slump down. "Hillary! Something's happening!" I managed to get out. "You need to call an ambulance!"

She stood up. After fluffing her hair, she took a red lipstick out of her bag and began to put it on. "You know, sweetie, I would *love* to help you out here, but I'm late for a waxing appointment. I'm sure you'll be fine. Or not. *Anyways*, ta!" she trilled as she sailed toward the door.

I coughed and coughed again. I rolled off the couch onto the floor, and saw the chunk of cake lying next to me with a piece of apple in the middle of it.

The Zumba Brigade was right—she had been trying to kill me all along.

A few hours later, I was in the middle of watching yet another episode of *Teen Mom* and thinking of how grateful I was that I had put the kibosh on Jason's hands, because never in a million years would I want to end up like one of those girls, when Blush walked in the door.

"Hi," he said.

"Hey," I said. I hadn't meant it to come out so frosty. The truth was, I couldn't understand why I was so upset that he had brought Aleka to the gallery. It wasn't like I *liked him* liked him.

He walked over. "Why is there cake on the floor?" he asked, confused.

I looked down. "Oh. I thought I had gotten all of it," I said as I got up and went into the kitchen for a broom and dustpan so I could sweep it up. "It was part of my anaphylactic shock performance."

"Your what?"

He sat down, and I explained everything to him. About how after the guys left, I had asked Hillary if there were apples in the cake and she said no. About how I didn't trust her and had pretended to take a bite. About how I pretended to have a severe allergic reaction, and she ditched me for a bikini wax.

"Oh, and there's also the part how when we sat down, before any of that happened, I pushed the voice recorder app on my iPhone, so I've got the whole thing on tape for my dad. And the police," I said.

"But you're okay? You're not hurt?"

"Nope, I'm fine. Never better."

"You sure? I mean, how'd you even think to do all that?" Blush asked.

I shrugged. "I guess I've seen too many *Law & Order* episodes. I need to call my dad and tell him, but I've been putting it off." I sighed. "He's going to be bummed to know he's engaged to an almost-murderer."

"I'm glad you're all right," he said. "And you should really call your dad and the police. She really is a lot to deal with. But Simone, I know that fight with Hillary is not the incident you were talking about earlier."

I began to study the cuticle of my left thumb as if it held the answers to all the secrets in the universe. "Yes, it was."

"No, it wasn't."

I looked up at him. "How do you know?"

"Because you did that thing you do when you're lying, where you flip your right foot back and forth on the floor and pull at the top of your left ear." Blush blushed and looked at his sneaker, as if the secrets of the universe were actually kept there rather than in my cuticle. "Not like I spend all this time studying you or anything like that. It's just something I noticed once. Or maybe a few times."

"You're right. It wasn't. It was something that happened with Jason."

He joined me on the couch. "Do you want to talk about it?"

I shook my head and stared at the TV. "No."

"Okay," he said.

We watched TV for a bit without talking.

"Okay, fine. I'll talk about it. Just for a little bit. Then I have to call my dad." But because it was Blush, a little bit turned into a lot, which turned into the whole story.

As I told him how Jason kept trying to grope me, Blush got progressively madder and madder. Like to the point where he so did not look like the sweet puppeteer I knew and liked a lot, but more like the killer in one of the Sorority Girl slasher films. "Simone. You swear nothing happened?" he asked when I was done.

I nodded.

"He didn't force you to do anything?"

I shook my head.

"Because if he did, that boy is dead."

"Hey, give me some credit," I said. "I've been all proud that I stood up for myself!"

He took my hand. "You should be proud! Big-time. It's just that if I think of anyone hurting you—him, Hillary, whoever—I get so mad I can't see straight. Simone, you know that you can wait as long as you want to do that stuff, right?"

I nodded. "Yeah, I know."

"'Cause any guy worthy of you is going to wait for you." He cleared his throat and said something, but it came out so softly, I couldn't hear him.

"What?"

He cleared his throat again. "I said—"

But his voice dropped so I still couldn't hear him.

"Blush, I'm sorry, but I still can't hear you."

"I said, 'I know I would!" he shouted.

I flinched. Boy did he have a set of lungs when he needed them. "You would what?"

He sighed. "Man, you are *not* making this easy. I would wait for you. Until you're ready. Because . . . well, because you're the most beautiful, coolest, funniest, strongest girl I've ever met."

Wait. What? Was he saying what I thought he was saying? "But what about Aleka?" I blurted.

"Huh?"

"Aleka. From the place on Abbot Kinney. You're seeing her now, right? I mean, you brought her to the gallery."

He shook his head. "No. It was just that one date. She's not my type."

"So what is your type?"

He laughed. "Like I said, you are not making this easy. "*You*, Simone. *You* are my type."

I was someone's type. How about that? I looked at Blush. Sweet, tall, mumbling Blush, who, instead of earning millions of dollars a year playing basketball, wanted to use puppets to help the kids in the neighborhood in which he grew up. Blush, who knew when I was lying by looking at my feet, who listened to what I was saying, who made me feel more me when I was around him than when I was with anyone else. Blush, who would've liked me even back in my Tastykake days.

Blush, who was absolutely-positively-without-a-doubt my type as well.

epilogue

When you live in the capital of the moviemaking business, you get used to everything that goes along with that. The celebrities in the supermarket. Big trailers taking up an entire block of parking spots when they're filming. Kids at your school going to movie premieres because their parents acted/directed/wrote them.

But having a movie made about your life was a whole other thing. Not like a movie made about you when you're like ninety years old and have lived this insane life where you were a president or a country music star or a hostage in some war-torn country. Like a movie made about you about something that happened when you were almost seventeen. Like, say, your almost-stepmother trying to kill you with a slice of everything cake.

It all started when I finally played the tape for my dad later that night after Hillary tried to poison me. He started to cry, which, while sweet, was a little embarrassing. When we got to the police station, the cops were very impressed and grateful that I had been smart enough to tape the whole thing—probably because it meant less work and more doughnuts for them.

Because it was such a juicy story (and because Nicola tweeted/Facebooked/blogged about it incessantly for the next few months) the whole thing ended up going national. And my dad proceeded to apologize profusely at least ten times a day for the next six months (including during our flea market forays, which had begun again when Hillary left) for having allowed himself to fall under the spell of someone like Hillary. I even got flown to New York to be on *The View*, which was incredibly cool and gave me firsthand experience in understanding why people were always saying that that Elisabeth Hasselbeck woman was so annoying.

After that, the TV movie producers started calling. I wasn't interested in a TV movie, especially when, in their pitches to me, more than a few of them were telling me that they wanted to take "some creative license" and make the reason that Hillary tried to kill me was because she and Jason had fallen in love. But then, one afternoon when I was in Watts watching Blush do one of his sold-out puppet shows (I had convinced him to go to the local Y and ask if he could try putting one on. It was a huge success, so he started doing more of them), I got an e-mail from the head of Olympus Studios saying that they were very interested in developing a movie based on my story as a possible vehicle for Stan Frank to direct and how it would be really classy and more like a Greek myth than some sleazy, ripped-from-the-headlines Lifetime movie.

It seemed like it might be a little weird to say yes, after what had happened between Jason and me—as I had predicted, when school started back up in the fall, whenever I'd pass Jason in the hall, he'd conveniently turn his head away so he didn't have to talk to me. But I was still friends with Cheryl, and after Jorge had left Zumba in August to become a contestant on a new reality dance show, the class went downhill, which is why a few of us defected and started going to this new Kuumba Latin Dance Fever class with African drums. And I had really liked that conversation I had had with Stan at the gallery.

So I said yes, and a few months later I was sitting in one of those director chairs with a headset on watching and listening as Emma Stone played me. Obviously, she looked nothing like me, but *Easy A* was one of my favorite non-French films, and I really loved her voice because it was deep and gravelly. I even convinced Stan to let Brad do Emma's wardrobe, and he did a great job. So good that he ended up having to close the store because he became so busy with his new career, which was too bad since Nicola and I lost our after-school jobs. But I did get some great stuff for the low, low price of 100 percent off at the going-out-of-business sale.

Being known as the "BFF-of-the-Girl-Whose-Stepmother-Tried-to-Kill-Her" got Nicola a lot of mileage—so much so that she turned her blog *Confessions of an Overachieving Underachiever* into a book. And, of all people, my dad then optioned it as the basis for a sitcom. He was finally so happy to be working on a show about real people instead of talking animals that he calmed down and didn't take work as seriously. He even let people start fixing him up—with sane women—which is how he met Sarah, this nutritionist-slash-private-chef-to-the-stars. She is beyond awesome and taught me all about eating right for my particular body and blood type and, unlike Hillary, has no interest in trying to make my dad marry her. She always says she's totally content to take things slow, partly because, according to her, she's got some commitment issues to deal with.

As for Hillary, she ended up taking a plea bargain and a shortened sentence, since they couldn't prove premeditated attempted murder (apparently, she was a much better actress than she was a D-girl). She tried to sell her side of the story, too, but apparently, not a lot of people want to do business with a convicted criminal. Even in Hollywood.

The premiere of the movie was amazing. I went with Blush, of course, and the rest of the guys met us there. Noob—once I freed his arm from in between the theater seats—told me he was a little disappointed about the guy who played him in the movie ("Is it just me, or did he seem *really* dumb?" he asked afterward), but overall everyone liked it. Even Thor. At the after-party Nicola and Max ended up getting into a lengthy discussion about egg rolls versus spring rolls, which led to a discussion about their mutual desire to travel to exotic places, which led to him friending her on Facebook the next day, which led to the exchange of phone digits and then texts, which led to his asking her if she wanted to go to the opening of a photographer named Hamish Bullocks who was known for his giant sculptures made out of toilet paper rolls

After the party Blush drove me home and we parked down the street and talked in the car for a while. Well, talked and made out.

But that was it. Strictly kissing. Nothing else.

Because according to him, I'm a girl worth waiting for.

PROM.

The best dress. The best shoes. The best date. Cindy Ella Gold is sick of it all.

Her anti-prom letter in the school newspaper does more to turn Cindy into Queen of the Freaks than close the gap between the popular kids and the rest of the students. Everyone thinks she's committed social suicide, except for her two best friends—the yoga goddess India and John Hughes-worshipping Malcolm—and shockingly, the most popular senior at Castle Heights High and Cindy's crush, Adam Silver. Suddenly Cindy starts to think that maybe her social life could have a happily ever after. But with a little bit of help from an unexpected source—and the perfect pair of shoes—Cindy realizes that she still has a chance at a happily ever after.

"A big heart + an insanely keen sense of humor = exactly the sort of book I love to read!" —Lauren Myracle, *New York Times* bestselling author of *TTYL* and *Thirteen*

PRINCESS, MEET FROG . . .

Dylan Shoenfield is the princess of L.A.'s posh Castle Heights High. She has the coolest boyfriend, the most popular friends, and a brand-new "it" bag that everyone covets. But when she accidentally tosses her bag into a fountain, this princess comes face-to-face with her own personal frog: self-professed film geek Josh Rosen. In return for rescuing Dylan's bag, Josh convinces Dylan to let him film her for his documentary on high school popularity. Reluctantly, Dylan lets F-list Josh into her A-list world. But when Dylan's so-called Prince Charming of a boyfriend dumps her flat, her life—and her social status—comes to a crashing halt. Can Dylan—with Josh's help—pull the pieces together to create her own happily-ever-after?

"The perils of popularity are showcased in a lighthearted contemporary novel filled with snappy dialogue." —*Publishers Weekly*

WHO'S AFRAID OF THE BIG BAD WOLF?

When Sophie Green goes to spend Spring Break at her grandmother's house in Florida, she never dreams she'll end up catching the eye of the hottest guy she's ever seen. As much as Sophie craves excitement, she's a seat belt–wearing, three-square-meals-a-day, good girl at heart. . . . She doesn't even have the guts to wear Dark as Midnight nail polish. But Sophie dreams of being the girl who isn't afraid to live on the edge. So when a motorcycle-riding hottie calls her "Red" and flashes her a wolfish grin that practically screams Danger, what else is a nice girl to do but jump at the chance to walk on the wild side?

"Robin Palmer takes a classic fairy tale and spins it on its head! *Little Miss Red* is funny and full of heart. You won't be able to put it down." —Jen Calonita, bestselling author of the Secrets of My Hollywood Life series and *Sleepaway Girls*

© Nicole Dintaman

After growing up in Massachusetts and New Jersey, **ROBIN PALMER** graduated from Boston University in 1990 and moved to Hollywood, where she worked in television for ten years before regaining her sanity and quitting her job to write. In addition to her modern retellings of fairy tales (the second of which—*Geek Charming*—was recently made into a movie for the Disney Channel), she is also the author of the middle-grade series Yours Truly, Lucy B. Parker, as well as various screenplays, television pilots, and misplaced To Do lists. After four years in New York City, she regained her sanity again and now lives in a big pink barn in the Hudson Valley.

Visit her online:

www.robinpalmeronline.com

www.robinpalmer.blogspot.com

http://robinpalmer.tumblr.com